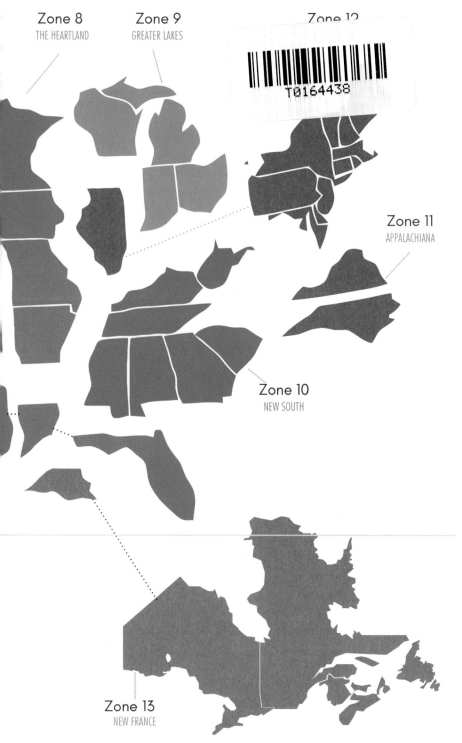

Zone 8
THE HEARTLAND

Zone 9
GREATER LAKES

Zone 12

T0164438

Zone 11
APPALACHIANA

Zone 10
NEW SOUTH

Zone 13
NEW FRANCE

Southern Louisiana & Eastern Canada

Book Two: Be Careful What You Wish For series

TWO ROADS TO PARADISE

A Novel

Gordon Jensen
with
Cara Highsmith

Editing by Cara Highsmith, Highsmith Creative Services, www.highsmithcreative.com
Cover and Interior Design by Mitchell Shea
Interior art by Mitchell Shea

ISBN: 978-1-7351181-3-0
eBook ISBN: 978-1-7351181-4-7
LCCN: 2021925293

Printed in the United States of America
First Edition 14 13 12 11 10 / 10 9 8 7 6 5 4 3 2 1

DEDICATION

For my children, Gordon and Brooke.

CONTENTS

TWO ROADS TO PARADISE

CHAPTER ONE

It had been weeks since their last conversation and the better part of a year since they'd actually been face-to-face. This made Lydia's urgent request for a video call all the more troubling. Sure, the intrigue was alluring, but Hunter knew Lydia was not an alarmist, so it must be something big . . . quite likely earth-shattering, given their history.

And it wasn't as if they could just pick up the phone and chat. Even getting a message to him that they needed to talk was a risky proposition. It had to go through back channels and was encrypted and held no revealing details. If you're a fan of spy stories, this had all the elements of a good one.

Hunter Young had been embedded in the Marshall administration for two years. He had been feeling of late as though this was a pointless exercise. He had yet to discover any useful information that they didn't already know or reasonably suspect. And even with that, there was no evidence, no paper trail, no secret tapes. As far as covert ops go, this one had seemed like a real bust.

His other purpose for infiltration was to be the inside man who could head off any shady deals at the pass, but he'd heard not even the faintest whisper of anything that was worth reporting, let alone disrupting.

The sole focus of the last two years had been overseeing the fertilization of the world's women to rebuild the population and restoring the infrastructure of the devastated areas so everyone could not only move back toward normalcy, but get back on the road toward progress that had long been abandoned. It didn't even appear that this was being accomplished through unscrupulous means or at the expense of the "little guy." For the first time in centuries, possibly ever, the government and its leaders truly seemed to be working in concert to make the world a better place for everyone.

Of course, that is precisely what had Hunter and Lydia and their coalition concerned. When had those with power ever been benevolent in their wielding of it? When, in the history of humanity, had anything related to bureaucracy ever been entirely as it seemed? Something was off. It was too quiet on the political front, too much cooperation.

Hunter, ever the skeptic, had actually been wrestling with himself over why he couldn't just let sleeping dogs lie. He asked himself each morning why he had to go looking for trouble and couldn't just enjoy the peace for a change.

And he always answered himself, "Because you know damn well this is just the calm before the storm. Don't go getting soft. Remember, they aren't giving you this cushy job and rent-free townhouse inside the Beltway out of the kindness of their hearts. It comes at a cost. You just haven't gotten the bill yet."

And so, each day Hunter would psych himself up to grin and bear it as he sat down at tables with his enemies. He armored up for battle before walking out the door, but instead of tactical gear and weapons, he wore a suit and tie and a deep-seated lack of trust for everyone in his daily life. Well, everyone except his assistant, Cady Dorian.

By all accounts, Cady had hardly earned her stripes. She was not even old enough to rent a car on her own, and she was a bit hapless and overly eager to please. But, what wasn't in the accounts, what only a few people knew, was that she was Special Forces trained, a master of spy craft, and fully capable of handling herself in any setting. She spoke three languages fluently and two others conversationally. She also was thirty-five and just passing as a twenty-something entry-level ingénue. She was a plant, an operative for the Resistance, and Hunter's handler. What he had not learned yet, was that this was not Cady's first assignment in the Marshall administration or her first time teaming up with Major Lydia Statham. Cady had been President Marshall's press aide previously and was feeding information to Lydia from the Leader Summit after the Alpha Centauri crew returned. Fortunately, even though Lydia was burned after she conveyed classified information to Hunter, they never made the connection and Cady was able to stay on the inside. The trust she had established with the president led to her being passed off to Hunter to become his assistant. A fortuitous turn of events for the Resistance, to be sure. Whether it was due to dumb luck or a fundamental failure on the part of the administration isn't clear, but the organization seized the opportunity and used it to their full advantage.

Hunter wasn't convinced Cady was her real name, and he didn't know for sure, but was pretty certain she could kick his ass all the way back to the black hole he came through if he gave her any lip, so he was careful not to give her any reason to think she needed to prove him right.

This is why, when he walked through the door of the office suite at 8:02 and was nearly tackled by her small but taut frame, obviously anticipating his arrival with fervor, he knew he would no longer be coasting through this gig.

She stared at him with stern, cold eyes that were far more admonishing than should be possible for someone you could just as easily picture in yoga pants and a ponytail. The paradox would have made Hunter laugh if he had much of a sense of humor. Instead, he followed her into his office and began unpacking his attaché as she closed the door and whispered coarsely.

"You have exactly eight minutes before we have to be on a secure line with Major Statham," she said hastily, not bothering to mask her frustration over his tardiness.

"What? Why?" and with that she had his attention.

"I don't know. I just got a communique on my way in this morning to set it up."

"They didn't say what's up?"

"Do they ever?"

"Well, no, but I haven't heard from her since our last scheduled debriefing, and we don't have another one on the books for at least three weeks." Hunter began pacing, his alarm rising to match hers.

"I know. Clearly something has changed because she also wants video feed."

"Seriously? Now I'm concerned. Are we doing it here?"

"No, you need to get down to parking Level K. Here is a cloaked device with the connection set up," Cady said, handing him a clunky box the size of a transistor radio with a screen and several buttons that looked like something out of a 1960s Sci-Fi B movie. "Just don't activate it until you are at Level K, stall 224."

"Okay."

"Hunter, look at me." He stopped turning the toy over in his hands and met her eyes.

"Cady, I got it."

"Say it back to me."

"Jeez. Level K, stall 224. I'm not a novice."

"It's important. You have the single solitary square footage of that parking spot that is blacked out. Outside of that range the signal can be intercepted."

"Really?"

"Yes, it is a targeted EMF, and we have to keep it laser focused so it won't be detected. Remember where you are."

"Okay, okay. I get it. I'd better go or I won't be there in time. If I have to run, that's only going to draw attention."

"Come straight back."

"Will do."

Hunter left the office, calling back to Cady, saying, "Left my phone in my car. Be right back." There wasn't anyone else in the office suite, but he felt he couldn't assume he wasn't being surveilled.

When Hunter reached the designated spot Cady had reiterated one more time as he was heading out the door, he pushed the sequence of buttons she'd demonstrated for him and the antique actually hummed to life. Within seconds, the snow on the screen coalesced into a figure that eventually looked like a woman, and through the crackle he heard her voice.

"Lydia?"

"Hunter."

"What is this thing? It looks like some kind of relic from the Cold War." Hunter turned it over in his hands, inspecting it. He quickly realized he had flipped the camera away from himself and turned it back to look at Lydia, smiling sheepishly.

"It is," she said flatly once she saw he'd stopped fumbling with the novelty in his hands.

"Ours or theirs?"

"Hunter. That's not important . . . and I can't say anyway."

"God, it's good to see you," he said, straining to make out her features.

"You too. You clean up well." He could almost see a smile creep across her face.

"Considering the last time I saw you we were on the lam, that's not all that high a bar."

"Still. You wear it well."

"Eh. It's not hard when the president sends you to her tailor." He stroked the lapel of his tailored blue jacket and nodded with appreciation.

"For the love of god, Hunter, just take the damn compliment!"

Lydia was both amused and growing impatient. She had forgotten how hard it was to resist his hapless charm, and still wasn't sure how much of it was an act.

"Sorry. I've never been comfortable with that," he said, blushing.

"Well, we don't have time for you to get comfortable. In fact, all of that is about to go away."

"Why? What's going on?" he asked, wondering if she was referring to the suit, the job, or just his comfort in general.

"I don't have long, so listen close. I am in Nevada and I need you out here ASAP."

"Nevada? What are you doing there? The last we talked you were up in Maine."

"Things are developing quickly and I don't have a lot of intel right now. That's why I need you."

"Okay. I'm there. Whatever you need." Hunter visibly shifted gears into his no-nonsense, taking care of business persona that was more familiar and the man she desperately needed.

"We discovered a lab where they are working on a cure."

"Lydia, that's old news. They've been distributing it globally for months."

"No."

"What do you mean? They're not giving people a cure?"

"No . . . I mean, what they have is definitely something, but this is something else.

"That's really cryptic."

If not for what they had been through together since his return to Earth, he would not have tolerated this kind of cagey exchange. But, she had earned his trust and had proved credible and wise over the past two years.

"I don't know much more than that and wouldn't say it over long distance even if I did. I just need you to meet me out here so we can figure out exactly what the hell is going on."

Hunter sighed heavily, scratched his head, and gave her a nod that said he would follow her anywhere, under any circumstances, no matter the mission, no matter the risk. She knew this and was careful never to abuse his loyalty.

"You know I'm there. Just . . . how do I do that without raising suspicion? There are bound to be lots of questions. I definitely can't come straight through the Red Zones without proper documentation and a good reason."

"I know. We are working on that now. You will get a travel kit with everything you need and an itinerary."

They both paused for a moment, taking in the weight of what was about to unfold.

"Lyd . . . I can't wait to see you."

"You, too, but I honestly cannot tell you what we are about to get into other than I know it's going to be dicey."

"I'm ready. I've been sitting behind a desk too long. I need some adventure.

"Be careful what you wish for . . ."

"Yeah, yeah. I know. But, for real . . ."

"I know. I have to go now. See you soon."

"See you soon."

She dissolved into snow and static, and then was gone. Hunter stood there for a minute just absorbing the shock and then made his way back to his office as quickly as possible while trying to look casual and unconcerned.

The look on Cady's face when he walked through the door told him he had not pulled that off as well as he thought. She jumped up from her seat, nearly vaulting her desk to meet him.

"Okay, chief. What's the plan?"

"Cady, what have I said about calling me 'chief'?"

"Just keeping up appearances, *boss.*"

"That doesn't work for me either. But, to answer your question, there isn't a plan . . .
yet."

"So what was with all the subterfuge? You can't tell me something big isn't
happening."

"Oh, it is. I just don't have the Op plan yet."

"Okay, but what's going on?"

Cady handed him a cup of coffee and ushered him in to his office out of earshot of any accidental or intentional eavesdroppers. Hunter continued, lowering his voice and using hand gestures where possible. He had been promised autonomy in this position, which suggested a level of trust. But that trust was not returned. He had dutifully played his part very well, serving as personal counsel to the president. His biggest achievement was turning the tide of the harsh criticisms leveled at President Marshall around her handling of their return from space and managing to get her re-elected for another term against unfathomable odds. It definitely earned him some degree of credibility with her, and his ongoing participation in the dog and pony show helped secure his position as an advisor with the ear of the Commander in Chief. But he still believed he was being watched. Just maybe not bugged.

"She was very cryptic, but what I know is that she is in Nevada and found something that has them concerned. I'm sure you'll be fully read in once they have a plan in place, but the long and short of it is I'm going to meet her out there and see if we can figure out what's going on."

"How are you going to do that and stay off the radar? You're not exactly low profile."

"Yeah, I've been thinking about that. She said they are working on an itinerary and contacts to help with the transport, but I am not sure what route I can take and stay off the radar. With the border crossings between Zones being so restricted, there is no way I can cut straight across the Midwest, and a flight is absolutely out of the question. I would get flagged by facial recognition in any airport, bus terminal, or point of entry."

"And it's not like you can just use your diplomatic credentials to gain free passage."

"No, considering the fact that we are going up against 'the man' on this."

"Do you think Marshall is part of this," she whispered leaning in closer and looking around as if expecting to see someone spying on them.

Hunter sunk into his chair and began to swivel pensively. After a moment, he sighed heavily and leaned forward, but not so much for the privacy that proximity afforded. He was worried.

"I honestly don't know. The longer I'm in this position and the more time I spend with her, I just get the feeling she is not pulling any of the strings in her life."

"Watch yourself! That's how she will draw you into her web. The damsel in distress is the oldest trick in the book!" she said, laughing and wagging a finger at him.

Cady had figured out pretty early how to taunt Hunter right up to the point he would tolerate and not a step beyond. She had never personally experienced his wrath, but she had seen it. It was part of what fueled her admiration of him. Still, she had no desire to be the target of it.

Hunter turned his eyes toward her in a way that made it clear he had considered this possibility on more than one occasion. He was not inexperienced with women by any stretch of the imagination, but between his forty-year absence from our universe and the hyper-focused mission since returning, he wasn't confident about his game. His exposure to feminine wiles had been notably limited to the coy glances of single women in bars seeking free drinks. Still, he felt in his gut, which rarely let him down, that Margaret Marshall was not the evil genius they had feared she might be. She seemed more like a pawn in someone else's game with only marginally more say over her own comings and goings than the rest of the cogs in the machine.

Hunter finally shared what was on his mind, dissipating the ominous cloud of silence hanging in the room.

"Yeah, I don't know. I guess we'll find out soon. Regardless, we have work to do . . . and work to pretend to do . . . so get back to your desk and do something secretary-ish until we receive our marching orders."

"Roger that . . . chief," Cady teased, leaning back in as she was leaving the room.

Hunter rolled his eyes and wadded up the piece of paper he'd been scribbling on during his contemplation, which he threw in her direction as the door closed.

CHAPTER TWO

Two days later, a lunch delivery arrived from a restaurant Hunter had never heard of. As he tipped the courier and closed the office suite door, he asked Cady why she ordered take-out for him when she knew he had a lunch scheduled with one of the Congresswomen from the Heartland.

"Hunter, I didn't order this."

"So, where did it come from?"

"I'm gonna go out on a limb and say, it's probably from . . .," she examined the menu   stapled to the bag, ". . . um, K Street Seaf . . . oh." Cady looked at him, her eyes bulging with intrigue.

"What *oh*?"

"In your office."

She shoved him in the room and closed the door behind them. Hunter didn't like being pushed around, but he got the point that this wasn't just a sandwich.

"Enough, Cady. What's going on?"

"I'm not sure . . . but I've never heard of the K Street Seafarer. Have you?"

"No, but that doesn't mean anything. I haven't memorized every restaurant in DC."

"Yeah, neither have I, but we have a few clues here that let us know there's more to this than meets the eye."

"Pretend I'm dumb."

"Well, that's . . . nah, I'll leave that low-hanging fruit alone."

Hunter made it clear with the cut of his eyes that he did not find her amusing. Cady picked up his cue and quickly shifted back to the menu she was smoothing out on his desk.

"Okay, first, we have the fact that neither of us ordered whatever is in this bag."

"Could have been delivered to the wrong place."

"Could be. But it wasn't. And, anyway, there's the K Street part."

"Yes, it's a real place here."

"Oh, my god, Hunter. I'm not having to pretend at all right now. Where is the skeptic I've come to know and love?"

Cady took a beat realizing she may have gotten a bit too informal. Hunter leaned back in his chair and rubbed the greying scruff on his chin.

"Yeah, I don't know what's wrong with me. I think I'm getting soft in this cushy job. What do you see here?"

"Hunter, why do you think you went to Level K in the parking garage?"

14

"Because it wasn't as easily accessible as Level A or B and not as exposed as the top level."

"Okay. That actually makes sense too. But, no, that's . . . you're being too military tactical-minded. You have to think more subversive and secretive and . . . don't you know who you work for?"

"The resistance?"

"Sure, but you don't know the name of the resistance?"

"No. Lydia and everybody else just called it *resistance.*"

"Wow. I guess you didn't get the orientation."

"Not exactly. I kind of hit the ground running on this."

Cady settled in on the corner of his desk, which Hunter found to be presumptuous and intrusive, but he was bothered more by the realization of just how in the dark he's been.

Cady noticed his discomfort, so she slid off her perch and stood uncomfortably next to his chair. The awkwardness loomed for a few more seconds as she regathered her thoughts and sifted through them to decide what he needed to know and what she could tell him. Finally, she released a heavy sigh and dove in.

"Okay. Here's the deal. You work for The K Group. We get our name from the Greek word *kalokagathia.*"

"What does that mean?"

"I'd tell you if you'd stop interrupting. As you know, the strain of corn that caused the pandemic was called Apollo VI-24. Did anyone ever tell you about the rich irony of that name?"

"No. I know it comes from NASA naming conventions and stuff."

"Yeah, that's how it got the name, but that doesn't get into the symbolism wrapped up in all of it."

"Okay. Educate me. But, really, do it fast. I still have that lunch."

"I'm getting to it. So, Apollo is the Greek god of knowledge, the arts, medicine, and prophecy, AND he was also the god of disease, famine, and plague."

"Are you shitting me?!"

"No. Can't make this stuff up, huh?"

"Not in a million. Did they know this when they chose the name?"

"I don't think so. If they did, that's some next-level evil genius kind of government conspiracy shit."

"Yeah, that's an even deeper dive down the rabbit hole than I'm willing to go."

"Anyway, since the plague that came from this corn began sweeping across the globe, there has been a growing coalition of people who did not like the ways the various governments around the world were taking advantage of the crisis to expand their control over their citizens and pad their pockets in the process. Because of the weakened state of humanity and the collapsing infrastructure, there were multiple factions of the resistance that weren't very coordinated. It wasn't until your return and everything that came after that we had a clarifying purpose and call to action we could unite around."

"You mean putting us on the stud farm?"

"Yes, but the impact of that rippled out into many areas

of body autonomy and government overreach. That's when we came up with the name for our group. It's actually really cool."

"It's Greek to me."

"Hmm?"

"It's a pun . . . I was being . . . never mind. What does it mean?"

"So, using the whole Apollo theme and knowing that he represented this Greek idea . . . oh, I see what you did there!" Cady gave Hunter an approving smile and a playful punch on the shoulder before going on. "Um . . . anyway, so there's this Greek ideal called *kalokagathia* that's basically a code of personal conduct, especially in the context of governing and the military. Apollo was considered to be the ideal, the embodiment of harmony, reason, and moderation. For those joining the resistance, this type of leadership was what we wanted to restore . . . or maybe have for the first time. It's what we decided to fight for. So, that's why we're called the K Group."

Hunter studied the menu in front of him as he absorbed this information. Without lifting his head, he said, "That's pretty deep. I like it."

"Yeah, I do too. So, clearly, we are not dealing with a mis-delivered lunch order."

"Clearly. There's something off about this menu."

"What?"

"I don't know. It just . . . these prices are weird. And it's kind of a strange collection of food, but not really. Something just doesn't quite . . .."

Cady pulled the piece of paper from his hands and scanned it quickly.

the K
Street Seafarer

	PER SERV./PER LBS
ROCKFISH (Blackened/Sauced)	$9.50/$12.00
WALLEYE (Baked/Sauced)	$9.60/$16.15
SMALLMOUTH BASS (Baked/Poached)	$9.60/$4.15
MUSKY (Blackened/Sauced)	$9.60/$13.45
STURGEON (Blackened/Sauced)	$9.60/$22.00
STEELHEAD (Baked/Sauced)	$9.70/$14.30
BLUEGILL (Blackend/Poached)	$9.10/$14.15
CATFISH (Baked/Poached)	$9.11/$14.15
SHRIMP (Baked/Sauced)	$9.21/$18.00
SEA BASS (Blackend/Sauced)	$9.24/$19.00
TROUT (Baked/Sauced)	$9.25/$9.45

*PRICES ARE MARKET PRICES OF THE DAY

"Hunter, this is code."

"How do you know?"

"For all the reasons you just mentioned. I think this may be your itinerary."

"So, how do we crack it?"

"I'll work on it. You go to your lunch. We have to keep things looking as normal as possible right now . . . especially right now."

"Alright. I'll be back in a couple of hours. Call me if you get anywhere with this. I'll be happy for an excuse to leave early anyway.

Hunter slipped on his suit coat, patted his pockets for his wallet and keys, and then reluctantly left the office. Cady was fixated on the page in front of her and shuffled her way back to her desk without taking her eyes off the menu and only half acknowledging Hunter's exit.

*****

At 2:15, Hunter blew back through the door to their office suite, startling Cady, who had her head down, scribbling furiously on a steno pad.

"What do we know?"

"Huh?" Cady mumbled without raising her head.

"Have you deciphered this thing yet?"

"Oh. Yeah. Well, part of it. Still working."

"Okay. What have you figured out so far?" Hunter asked

from his office as he tossed his keys on his desk and slid out of the jacket he found to be so confining.

Getting up from her desk and collecting her work, Cady joined Hunter in his office and laid everything out in front of him.

Pointing to the list of menu items and her notes, she explained, "This is definitely your itinerary. I've been able to pinpoint ports that are connection points. You're definitely doing most of this by water."

"What? Why?"

"Like you said, you can't go the direct route, so we knew it would be a long, circuitous journey."

"Yeah, but water? I hate boats. I get seasick."

"You? You get seasick!" Cady looked at him bemused and struggling to hold in a chuckle.

"Dial it back. I'm just . . . more comfortable in the air."

"But, what about turbulence?"

"It's not the same. If you are in turbulence through an entire flight, you're doing something wrong, but you can't escape that rocking motion on the water. Besides, in outer space, you don't really run into air currents so much." Getting exasperated by feeling the need to explain himself, Hunter quickly changed the subject. "Anyway, that's hardly important right now. How the hell did you figure this out?"

"Well . . ." Cady grinned slyly, "They gave me a big clue on where to start unraveling this in a really sneaky way. See their slogan?"

"Your One-Stop Shop for the Great American Loop Experience?"

"Yeah!"

"I don't get it. What's the Great American Loop?"

"So, you can circumnavigate the eastern portion of the US entirely by boat. Did you know that?"

"No. Remember? Not a fan."

"Oh, right. Well, anyway sailing enthusiasts take this route through the Great Lakes, inland rivers, through the Gulf, and up the Eastern seaboard. It's a whole thing. They take like a year to do it."

"Why? Are they masochists?" Hunter looked a little green just imagining it.

Cady didn't bother responding and just continued, "Anyway, that got me thinking, what if all of these menu items are somehow related to the Great American Loop."

"Very clever. Did it pan out?"

"Oh! It *totally* did!" Cady shouted, as she smoothed the menu out in front of them and started pointing aggressively at each item. "All the details are right here. I think they are embedded in the prices that you noticed were really weird. And I think there are clues in these descriptions."

"Want me to take a look?"

"Yeah, I need a break. I'm getting a little fried . . . no pun intended."

"Funny."

"Okay. Here's what I have so far. I'm going to grab some lunch."

Hunter nodded and went back to the pages that had his attention wrapt, barely noticing Cady had left his office.

An hour later, Cady eased open his office door and poked her head into the room. Hunter looked at his watch, amazed any time had passed.

"Any progress?"

Hunter smiled, quite pleased with himself, and waved her in.

"I think so. I've picked up on patterns here. See how there are two prices for each menu item and how the first one increases incrementally?"

"Yeah, that's good. What do you think it is?

"Well, they start at nine dollars and change, which seems a little low for a whole meal. But . . . we are at the first of September, so I figure these are dates. See, $9.50 for the first one? I think that's 9/5, September 5th, the day I'm supposed to leave. The next thing on the menu is $9.60. That's got to mean I get to the next connection point the following day."

"Yes! That makes total sense!" Cady clapped her hands, impressed with his deductions.

"And, I'm pretty sure this second price . . . it's per pound . . . but it doesn't really correlate with meal price or what I know some of these fish are worth, so I think it's the times I'm supposed to meet my contact, but in military time. Like this one, $16.15 per pound, but if we apply the code that means 16:15, or 4:15 p.m. What do you think?"

"I think you've cracked it. Nice work! And all while I was grabbing a slice."

Hunter's face registered a proud grin for just a moment before turning sullen again.

"What's wrong?" Cady asked, noticing the shift.

"Well, there's all this other stuff and I'm not sure what to make of it. We don't have much time to figure it out. Today is the 2nd, which means I leave in less than three days. That's not much time to get the rest of this decrypted and do any mission prep necessary. Plus, I have to come up with a good excuse for being off the grid for the next two weeks or more."

"Yeah, that's not much time, but you have me, and I'm really good at what I do. Trust me. We'll be fine."

"Okay. Impress me."

With that, Cady collected everything Hunter had written and retreated to her desk to finish unraveling the mystery. She was buzzing with excitement. She too had begun to feel her senses dulling while they were in standby mode. This was just the sort of injection of intrigue and adventure she needed.

CHAPTER THREE

The afternoon yielded to night more quickly than either Cady or Hunter imagined possible. It wasn't until the daylight disappeared and they had to resort to artificial illumination that they took note of the emptiness of their bellies and the sudden need for sustenance.

"Oh, my god, I am starving all of a sudden!" Cady announced loud enough for the entire building to hear.

"Yeah, I was just thinking my tank was about on empty. Is it too late to get something delivered?" Hunter strolled into the outer office, looking a bit drained and peckish.

"Nah. The mess is closed, but we can order in. We'll have to call down to security to let them know it's coming, but that's not a big deal." She reached for the folder of menus she kept close as they spent a lot of mealtimes with a sandwich or container of something at their respective desks.

"Excellent. I want to keep moving on this. We really don't have time to waste. Are you good to stay until we are finished?"

"In for a penny . . .," she said, smiling at her ability to use one of Hunter's old-fashioned phrases.

"Okay. Just order me some pasta I guess."

"On it. After I take care of food, let's go over what we've deciphered. Here's what I've been able to decode." Cady handed him a page with an itinerary neatly charted, Hunter skimmed it, and nodded his approval.

After hanging up the phone, Cady joined Hunter at the conference table in his office where he had the page and the menu laid side-by-side on the table in front of him.

"They said it would be about forty-five minutes."

"Sounds good. Walk me through what I'm looking at here."

She leaned over and began pointing to the various elements.

"See how some of the descriptions on the different fish are blackened while others are baked, and then some say there is a poached option, and only some have a sauce?"

"Yeah, I wasn't sure what to make of that."

"Well, since some of the types of fish wouldn't really be good prepared that way, I was sure this was a part of the code. When I looked at the times attached to each one, it became clear that on some segments you'd be traveling at night and some during the day. I thought of baked as maybe a reference to being baked in the sun and the blackened seemed to be an obvious nod to traveling under the black of night . . .," she explained and paused to gauge his reaction.

"Nice work. That absolutely makes sense, but some of these don't correlate with the times."

Cady beamed with pride and continued, "I thought about that! Since you have travel times, it made me wonder why they would feel the need to tell you that you were traveling during the day or night. Then I thought maybe it is some sort of clue of the type of vessel you'll be on. So, it occurred to me that on some legs it will be safe for you to be out in the open and for others it will be necessary for you to basically be a stowaway. That means the baked/daylight and the blackened/nighttime isn't so much about actual times of day as it is signaling whether you will be up top or below deck."

"You are on a roll. But what about the poached and the sauce part?"

"That was a bit trickier. Since it wasn't on every item, I figured it was some other detail related to your travel. Now, stay with me on this because it may seem a little odd, and I'm really just spit-balling here, but, what if poached means you're kind of on your own, left to your own devices . . .," she searched Hunter's face for a reaction, and he gave her one.

Hunter's incredulousness was obvious. "What the hell are you talking about?"

"I know, I know. I just thought . . . honestly, I don't know what I thought, but it seemed to fit as a contrast to the sauce—being covered. See what I mean? Like your supplies and such are covered . . . probably through a dead drop . . . in some circumstances, but in others you're just going to have to get what you can on the down low. You know, like poaching animals is getting them illegally. Is that too much of a stretch?"

"No, no. It actually does make sense. Boy, they didn't make this easy."

"Well, duh. What good is an encryption if it's easily broken?"

"Fair enough. Okay, so we know when I'm leaving and when I'm supposed to reach each checkpoint. We know where they are and under what circumstances I will be traveling from one point to another. We know how I will get supplies at some points and that I will have to fend for myself in others. This is good, Cady. Really good. But, what about these two spots where there is a grilled option?"

"Yeah, I think that's where you'll have an opportunity to check-in and get any updates necessary. You know, like getting grilled in a debriefing? And the rest of the time you will be incommunicado."

"That tracks. Well, I think that's enough for tonight. After we eat, I think we can call it a day." Hunter checked his watch and reclined in his chair, releasing an exhausted sigh.

"If it's all the same to you, boss, I think I'll stay on and get all of this typed for you and make a list of any prep we need to do."

"As long as you stop calling me boss," Hunter admonished, knowing it was falling on deaf ears. "Cady, I'm not sure what I'd do without you. And I'm going to have to rely on you heavily over the next couple of weeks to hold down the fort and deflect any curiosities that might compromise things. And one other favor . . ."

"Anything. You're the one doing the heavy lifting here. This is not going to be an easy trip!" She looked over the list again and shook her head, considering how grueling the journey would be.

"I need you to help me come up with an excuse for why I'll be gone this long. A vacation just doesn't really fit my M.O. and would rouse suspicion."

"True. And, I've actually been pondering that. When was the last time you talked to your son?" She threw this out hesitantly, knowing this was a touchy subject.

"I don't know . . . I guess maybe six months ago. I've been busy here, and I'm really not sure what to say to him or how to have a relationship. It's a . . . it's complicated."

"Yeah, there aren't too many people who have a biological child almost the same age."

"Cady, I feel fairly confident in saying there is no one else in our situation."

"Okay, you're right. But, I was thinking you could tell the president you have decided to take some time off to try to bond with him, to figure out what kind of relationship you can have, so you're going camping with him for a couple of weeks to spend some one-on-one time together." She gave him a minute to process this.

Hunter seemed to be genuinely considering it. Then he asked, "Do you think that really sounds plausible?"

"More than anything else I came up with. It also explains why you will be off the grid."

"So, do I just say that's what's happening and hope no one checks with him? I'm not sure I want to drag him into all of this subterfuge."

"Well, since he is part of our organization . . .,"

Hunter whipped his head in her direction, shock registering all over his face.

"You mean you didn't know?" Cady made a mental note then and there to talk to Lydia about either making sure he was totally read in on everything or at least giving her a heads up on what landmines to avoid.

"No, I most certainly did not know. I would not have approved of involving him." Hunter was growing angry.

"Hunter, he has been involved with us since you returned and he did his documentary."

"Well, no one told me. This is not what I would have wanted."

"You do realize he is a grown man and was making his own life choices for a couple of decades before you even knew he existed."

"Still, I don't like it."

"Duly noted. Now, I think we tell him just enough so he can stay off everyone's radar while you are supposedly on a trip together and so he can offer other support if necessary."

"Fine. Bring him in for the alibi, but I don't want you getting him tangled up in tactical support or anything else. I still don't know where we stand, and I don't want to have to try to navigate those waters while I'm . . . well, while I'm navigating other literal waters. Got it?"

"Got it."

At that moment, the security desk called to let them know of their food arrival, and they both were grateful for the interruption and for dinner.

*****

Hunter rubbed his hands up and down his face vigorously, trying to get the blood flowing to his head again and looked at Cady to see if she was suffering the lateness of the hour as much as he was. They'd had several late nights in a row finalizing the details of his trip. He figured she would be handling it better with her youth to buoy her, but he hoped he wouldn't have to be the first to cave. He caught a partial yawn and seized the opportunity to shut down for the night.

"Looks like you're fading fast. Let's call it a day," he said with all the nonchalance he could muster.

With a knowing laugh, she said, "Sure. I think we are about done, and you have an early call."

"Don't remind me. I'm gonna have to be up at O-dark-thirty to meet my driver."

"Better get used to it. Clandestine ops aren't usually done in broad daylight."

"No, I guess not," he said, and then paused for an amount of time that was uncomfortable for both of them before continuing, "Listen, Cady, I really appreciate all of your hard work. I don't think I would have cracked this code without you. I'm going to be at loose ends for the foreseeable future, and the only way I can do that with any peace of mind is knowing you are here holding down the fort and running point for me."

"Don't sweat it. I've got your back."

Hunter grabbed his coat and headed for the door, then he paused as if debating his next move. Finally, he turned back to Cady who was tidying up her desk and preparing to leave.

"We do have all of this right, don't we? I mean, what happens if we guessed wrong?"

Cady joined him at the door and nudged him out into the corridor and on his way home, telling him as they made their way to the elevator, "Well, I am confident in our work. This isn't new to me, and I also know how Lydia thinks. But, if we did get something wrong, well . . . I guess you'll wing it."

Hunter looked at her incredulously, almost shouting, "Wing it?! Do you know where I'm going?"

Cady whispered to him, "Shhh, we are out of the safe zone!" After scanning the hallway, she continued a little louder than necessary, "Don't be such a baby! Camping isn't hard. You will be fine. You're an outdoorsy guy. What's the worst that can happen? You've got bear spray, right?"

Once they were in the elevator, she turned to him and said, "Look, Hunter, this isn't going to be like a college road trip. You know that much, already. And I can't promise you nothing will go wrong. But, I also know you are fully capable and our people will be available to help you along the way. If you get in a jam, you can always call me and I will get support to you."

Hunter sighed heavily and confessed, "Yeah, I know. I guess I'm just feeling a bit rusty and it's those prelaunch jitters. But, I'll admit, it's good to know you're a phone call away."

"You know it! But, use it sparingly. I don't want my phone ringing at 2am because you're bored and don't have anyone to talk to."

"Cady, I think you know me well enough to see how ridiculous a notion that is."

"Still, the road does strange things to a man."

Before he had a chance to respond, the elevator doors slid open, revealing a nearly empty parking area. It was probably the already heightened anxiety, but the eerie, cavernous expanse of empty rows spilling out before them didn't help. The flickering fluorescents above them barely provided enough visibility to keep the shadows from dancing like assailants waiting in the wings. So, as they made their way to the spaces where their cars waited, Hunter and Cady found themselves almost tiptoeing, trying not to set off a cacophony of echoing footsteps that unsettled the stillness of the evening.

The pair said good night and got into the safety of their cars, both feeling a bit foolish for being unnerved by an activity they'd repeated every night for weeks with obvious success. They each drove home in silence, keenly aware that their being on high alert was a state they would live with for the foreseeable future.

CHAPTER FOUR

At precisely 0400, Hunter was waiting on his stoop, clad in all black—tactical pants and a long-sleeved pull over, combat boots, and a ball cap, and equipped with nothing more than a small rucksack. You'd think he was heading out for either a jewelry heist or a covert op. He would later discover that both were true in some regard.

A few moments later, a nondescript sedan pulled up and gave no indication of actually parking. Hunter jumped up and opened the front passenger door, saw what he needed to see, and climbed in. Sitting in the driver's seat dressed in a simple black suit and tie was a large man with a familiar face. Hunter recognized him as the body guard who had helped him escape the White House and delivered him to Lydia after he left the Center in Kaikoura, New Zealand two years earlier. Having this touchstone gave him a sense of security he didn't realize he needed so desperately. He finally felt as though he wasn't on his own and the shadowy network actually did have his back. Charlie pulled away without a word uttered between them.

The route they took was circuitous and took longer to reach the city limits than Hunter hoped would be necessary. Even though DC was a neutral zone where citizens of any sector could come and go freely, it was still one of the most surveilled cities in the world, and Hunter was a highly recognizable figure. While the president and those he worked with bought the fishing trip excuse, others outside the administration were more suspicious, so the particulars of his time of departure did not need to be broadcast. He would be on their radar soon enough, once he passed through the Zone 9 checkpoint, but that fit with his cover story and the travel documentation he'd filed. Picking up a tail at this point, before they wanted to be seen, could complicate all future aspects of his journey.

Once they passed Gaithersburg, a slight ease settled over both men, though neither relaxed fully into looking forward. One eye was always trained on the rearview or side mirrors, searching for any signs of a tail. They were two hours in to what became a seven-hour trip thanks to the non-direct route out of town when Charlie finally said, "I think we're clear. Wanna stop for a quick bite?"

Hunter dug in his pack and produced two protein bars, to which Charlie turned up his nose and said, "This may be your last hot meal for weeks, and that will only hold me for about 20 miles. Plus, I need coffee. When the sun rises, my body knows it's time for caffeine, and if it doesn't get it soon after, there are consequences."

"Okay, fine. I just don't want to take too long. I can't risk missing my connections."

Hunter was studying the itinerary Cady had written out for him. She had created her own kind of shorthand in case he was intercepted. They were fairly certain it had not fallen into the wrong hands prior to their receiving it, and they had no indications that any outsiders were aware of the plan, so their paranoia was focused on what might come up on the road.

"We can find something at a gas . . .," he stopped mid-sentence when he caught Hunter's eye and realized that might not be well received. Charlie stammered, "Oh, sorry, man. Maybe that's not . . .,"

Hunter stopped him before he fumbled over an apology for something that wasn't his fault.

"Charlie, relax, it's okay. What happened when the Russians and Africans abducted us was horrible, but I am able to go to gas stations without reliving the trauma. For one thing, it's about the only place to get a bad cup of coffee quickly, and I've never been able to get used to the good stuff."

"Cool. I guess we'll just pull in at the next one I see. And don't worry about making your connection. I know we took a while getting out of DC, but we can make up time now. Your boat leaves the dock at noon."

"Yeah, that's what the itinerary says."

Charlie laughed, picturing the scene, and then reassured Hunter, "We should be there with about an hour to spare."

"Well, I don't want to get there too early. That increases the odds of being noticed . . . and I'm not exactly in a hurry to jump on board with a bunch of strangers. Let's grab that breakfast."

The market where they stopped had premade breakfast sandwiches and coffee that was exactly what Hunter wanted—piping hot and strong enough to run an engine. Once they were settled back in the car and on the road again, Charlie asked him about the itinerary and how they broke the code.

Hunter smiled proudly and began to explain, "It was a tough one to crack . . . at least it was for me, but I'm not a cryptographer or anything. But Cady, man, she was all over it. All I knew was that it was no ordinary restaurant menu. She is the one who figured out that the different fish represented locations. I don't know that I ever would have made that connection. She locked in on this thing on the menu about some loop . . .

Charlie nodded approvingly, "Yeah, the Great American Loop. It's on my bucket list."

"More power to ya. So, with that in mind, Cady noticed there were a couple of types of fish that were so clearly found in very specific places—like the catfish and the sea bass—that stood out to her and she backfilled the rest with a little bit of research."

Hunter noticed Charlie grinning as they talked about Cady and he began to suspect there was something going on there, but he was loath to get into *that* conversation about his assistant with the guy he'd be trapped in a car with for several more hours.

The conversation dropped as he was sorting that out in his head and he quickly realized awkwardness was rising up between them, so he floundered his way into safer waters, picking up where he left off.

"Yeah, but I'm the one who figured out what the prices meant . . . that they were dates and times."

"Nice work," Charlie said, somewhat mockingly, but still extending plenty of legitimate praise.

"I have to admit, I'm still a little nervous that we may have gotten some of this wrong and that I could be walking into a trap."

"Legitimate concern, but you really don't have anything to worry about. Here's how it's gonna work. You will have a contact at each connection point on your itinerary who

will give you any resources you need and brief you on any changes or other pertinent info as you proceed. You will debrief them on anything that came up on the previous leg. They all will keep us updated on your status. I'm gonna get you
to Port Clinton, Ohio, and I'll drop you at the dock there. You have your passport and safe passage forms to enter Zone 9 that indicate you are taking a fishing trip with a companion. For their purposes, that companion is me."

"Aren't they supposed to be under the impression I'm traveling with my son?"

"Yep. That's the story we've been selling."

"Have you seen you? There isn't a chance in hell anyone would believe we are even marginally related . . . beyond being of the same species . . . and no offense, but I'm not sure that's entirely accurate."

"No offense?"

"I just mean . . . look, you are twice my size, and I'm not a small guy. Anyway, I didn't mean it bad, I'm just saying it's gonna be a tough sell."

"It isn't going to matter much. Zone 9 isn't as rigid about border crossings as other Zones. They benefit too much from the surrounding regions to be sticklers on that. But, we'll deal with that when we get there. Back to the briefing. In Port Clinton, you're going to *very* publicly board one of those sport fishing cruises. That is where we part ways, and you will begin your voyage to the west."

Hunter didn't even attempt to veil his annoyance with the prospects of this scenario.

"Also, Cady gave me this to hand off to you when we get to the drop point," Charlie said, fishing a flip phone out of his coat pocket.

He waved it at Hunter, and then slipped it back into his pocket. Hunter had started to reach for it, so he looked confused and a bit annoyed when Charlie tucked it away again, out of his reach.

Charlie grew serious and focused, "This doesn't turn on until we are at the pier and you are safely on your way. It isn't easily traceable, but we can't take any chances. You can use it to check in with Cady if necessary—like, if you miss a connection or something. But, if you get really sideways . . . if you get caught . . ."

Hunter considered what it might mean to miss a connection, but he really didn't want to go down the rabbit hole of other worse possibilities. So, when Charlie paused, Hunter just nodded, hoping he would move on.

"Look, we've got your back. This thing is programmed with one number, and one number only, in the contacts. But it's only to be used in a life-or-death emergency, and for no other reason. You won't know who is on the other end, and they won't answer a second call, so choose wisely."

"Yeah, I get it. We are cloak-and-dagger-ing it. But what's with not even letting me hold it now?" Hunter was feeling a bit wounded by the denial of access.

"Because, if something happens to us before we get there, it's safer this way. There is a biometric key that unlocks it, and it requires your retinal scan. If it's on me, no one will think to link it to you."

"Wow. This is even more critical than I thought."

"Hunter, man, you have no idea what you're getting into, and that's probably for the best at this point. I don't mean to keep you in the dark, and I don't even know everything that's going on—I really only have need-to-know—but it's safer if you don't have intel they can extract from you."

"Okay, fine. So you said it isn't traceable. But what about me? I am carrying around a tracking device inside me. I know we want them to see me enter Zone 9 and board this boat. But what happens after that? What about the chip thing?"

Charlie laughed and shook his head, "Seriously? You're just now thinking about that?"

Hunter was feeling a bit defensive still after essentially having his hand slapped when he reached for the phone. "It's not like we haven't had plenty of other things to consider."

"Sure, but that's pretty essential to the whole plan."

"Okay, mister need-to-know. Is that on your list of vital info? And why didn't Cady include that in my briefing?"

"Because it's a non-issue."

"How so? My fishing cover story makes sense to a degree, but it won't explain why I'm all over the map."

"By the way, that was a really nice touch. Good idea."

"Thanks. It helps to have an estranged son you need to theoretically reconnect with."

"Yeah, you might want to do that in practice at some point too."

Charlie let that hang in the air for just a moment—long enough to drive home the point, but not so long as to invoke Hunter's ire, just his annoyance—before moving on.

"Anyway, the reason it is a non-issue is that the chips that were injected with the vaccine have limitations. First, they don't widely transmit your location like a GPS. You are only detectable when you pass a scanner, and those are only at points of entry, like airports, train stations, bus stations, and ports. And now at the Red and Blue Zone checkpoints."

"Why is that? Doesn't that kind of defeat the purpose?"

"I'm sure they'd like to have that capability, but for an RFID chip to be able to maintain an active transmission, it needs a battery, and for a chip to be small enough to inject with a needle, there is no space for any kind of power source."

"Wait, so how did the Special Ops from America find us then, if they weren't tracking a beacon?"

"Because you passed through some checkpoints that helped our military triangulate your location. That and some pretty effective spy craft and intelligence gathering helped us get a bead on you."

"Okay, so that means they can't follow me like a little red dot moving on a map. But I am still passing through ports along the way. I'm gonna get picked up there."

"That's where the other limitation comes in. These chips degrade pretty rapidly. Yours hasn't been in quite long enough to break down completely, but it's probably start-ing to lose its transmission strength. The fact that you live in the neutral zone of DC and the expiration date hasn't come up on yours yet, you haven't been 're-inoculated,' so we have a fortuitous window of opportunity here to help your chip along in the degrading process."

"What the hell does that mean?"

"It means that after you board your floating tourist trap, you're going to take a capsule in your kit—the kit I will give you when we get there—that will accelerate the dissolution process."

"I don't like the sound of that. You mean I'm going to have something corroding in me?"

Charlie looked at Hunter, surprised by his concern. "I mean, you might have some pretty fierce indigestion . . . seriously, the tracker is microscopic, so you aren't even going to notice. You haven't felt it up to now, right?"

"Okay, okay. No need to be a smartass. This technology was just a myth in my day. Remember, I'm an old fogey."

"Sorry, just having a little fun to break the tension."

"Does it all have to be at my expense?"

"No, sorry, man. I need to be more sensitive."

Hunter sighed heavily. "No, I need to be less sensitive. I'm just a little stressed over all of this. I know there is a lot on the line, and I'm out of practice."

"You'll be good. As I said, we've got your back."

CHAPTER FIVE

The two men rode in silence for the next hour. It wasn't an uncomfortable silence, so much as it was two people recognizing there was no need to force conversation out of some social obligation. Hunter had been watching the sun creep up over the horizon through his side mirror, wondering if that would look different in the other places he was about to visit. Then he wondered how many sunrises or sunsets he would actually see, since he had to stay out of sight most of the time. Charlie had his eyes trained on the road before him and behind him, never losing sight of his responsibility to deliver Hunter safely and without detection, driving cautiously, but not so cautious that this too would arouse suspicion.

Finally, Hunter spoke, but Charlie wasn't sure at first if he was supposed to respond, or if Hunter was just thinking out loud.

"Well, here we go."

Charlie muttered a "hmm" without much inflection, just in case Hunter wasn't actually talking to him.

"I haven't been out of the neutral zone since I went back to Marshall. The world has changed so much. Hell, this country has changed in ways I never imagined possible. I am sure we are getting a very sanitized version of it in this bubble, and I'm afraid to find out exactly how bad it is out there, and I'm at a bit of a loss for how to navigate it."

"What's troubling you, boss?"

"Charlie, I am not your boss."

"No, I know that. It's just something I say. Like some people use man or dude, I guess."

"I get it, but I still don't like it."

"Cady said something about that. What's the deal? Why don't you like being treated with respect?"

"Short answer is those titles aren't where the respect is, and they are often thrown around in place of respect around DC."

"I get it. So what do I call you?"

"Hunter works."

"Got it. But don't think you dodged my question. What's troubling you?"

"Not sure. It's not exactly insecurity or not feeling up to the task. I know I'll get there. I just have this unease I can't quite pinpoint. Different from the usual edginess you get going into an unknown situation."

"Like some kind of foreboding?"

"Maybe. You know, when I set out for Alpha Centauri, I knew my world would never be the same, but it was exciting. It felt like this incredible opportunity that was going to open doors for all of humanity." Hunter looked to Charlie to see if he was coming off as arrogant, but his audience just seemed intrigued, so he continued. "I don't know. This has the same kind of life . . . world . . . changing feeling, but not in a good way."

Charlie chimed in with concern, "How much more change could we possibly face? We've had the population tank thanks to unimaginable plagues and disease. Our world economy collapsed. You guys come back from legit outer space and bring a cure. Only to have this country fracture into pieces over it. And those are just the big things."

"Well, when you put it like that . . . now I'm more anxious. Got any valium in that kit of yours?"

Charlie wasn't sure if he was serious, but just in case, said, "No, all you have in there is a basic first aid kit."

Hunter laughed, "I'm kidding. I have never messed with pills and other crap. If I need it, two fingers of Macallan will set me right."

"Have you tried meditation?"

"Nah. I remember Jacob's mother was into all that hippy-dippy garbage. She tried to get me into that and using sage and crystals and shit. Thankfully, I left the planet before she had a chance to turn me into a . . ."

Charlie interrupted, surprised by this personal revelation, "So, you and Jacob's mom were actually a thing?"

"Michelle. Yeah, we were involved for about 6 months during my training in Houston. We met through mutual friends at a cookout. She was a physical therapist and personal trainer. I tried to get her on to train the team at NASA, but she didn't have all the creds and degrees they required, and she had a ding on her background check—a pot possession charge from when she was in college." Hunter seemed to be slipping into a space of reminiscing as he talked, almost forgetting where he was and who he was with.

"That's too bad. I guess that was before all the legalization."

"Well, that, and it was in Texas. They never really got on board with that. Now that they are part of the Greater Gulf, it's even more restrictive. Anyway, it was disappointing, but probably for the best. Work relationships get complicated fast." He cut his eyes to Charlie and noted the comment hit its mark. But Charlie glanced over, returning the knowing look.

Attempting to deflect, Hunter said, "So, anyway, if I had been there much longer, she probably would have started putting the screws to me to move in together. If that had happened, my place would have turned into some kind of Zen den full of incense and essential oils and pillows."

Charlie laughed at the idea and paused before asking, "So, you really didn't know about Jacob at all until you came back? You didn't even think there was a possibility?"

"Not a clue. We had kind of cooled things down for the last few weeks for several reasons. We got together a couple of nights before our launch and, honestly, I kind of put her out of my mind after that. You have to be able to compartmentalize the things in your life when you deploy a lot. Damn. I've never told anyone as much as I have you about all of this. In fact, I really haven't said any of this aloud before. I don't know what's wrong with me."

"Don't worry about it. Road trips make strange bedfellows. And nothing said leaves this car . . . which is bugproof."

Hunter leaned back in his seat and stared out the window, watching the landscape slip by in a blur. He hadn't thought about Michelle this much in a long time. Jacob had informed him in the big reveal that she had died from breast cancer while he was in his third year of undergrad. He had lost touch with his grandparents after the funeral. He heard from his grandmother when his grandfather passed a few years later, but he didn't go back for his burial. His grandmother spent a decade on her own before taking a bad fall that put her in a nursing home where she lived until her death three years after. Jacob had no other family he knew of on his mother's side, so there was a longing for connection with Hunter, but he determined quickly that wasn't going to be an easy path to forge, if at all. Hunter knew he should try, but hadn't the first clue of where or how to start. He pondered all of this as they sped toward the first stop on his epic journey.

They were about 4.5 hours into the trip and the sun was creeping up over their shoulders when they passed the northeast side of Pittsburg. They were about forty miles out of Petersburg, OH, where the Zone 9 checkpoint bottlenecked, and Charlie felt it was time to begin his briefing. Hunter was taken aback by how much he downloaded because he was under the impression Charlie was just transport.

"Okay, you have your itinerary, and, trust me, it's correct."

"How do you . . ."

"Hunter. Need to know. Now, we don't have much time, so listen up. You won't encounter your first contact until you are on the fishing boat in Port Clinton."

Hunter nodded grimly, not thrilled to be in a hostile environment, and hostile was not referring to being in a Red Zone, but his being on a cruise ship.

"So, once you board the boat for the cruise, you can move about freely. In fact, this is a perfect cover for your departure because it ties in nicely with the fishing trip story. It's a day trip to Pelee Island where you'll drop off the radar."

"How does that work?"

"You'll be detected at the pass point when you board, and in Pelee you are going to switch to a smaller boat and they are going to skirt the north coast through St. Claire into Lake Huron. You'll be in good hands. Now, even though you'll be on the Zone 13 side of the waterways, which are neutral, it's best that we keep you in friendly territory where we can rely on allies for transport. Once you hit Lake Michigan, it's not as easy. We have arranged for safe connections, but some of them are hesitant. Actually, you shouldn't even try to talk with the crews once you change hands in Mackinac. These guys owe us one, but they aren't happy about the risk they are taking. Just stay out of their way and everything will be fine."

"Okay, but that doesn't answer my question about how I avoid detection at the other entry checkpoints."

"Once you reach Pelee, take the capsule, which will disable your tracker. No one is going to get curious because your cover camping trip is supposed to take you into New

France where they don't really check Zone passports so much, and you won't be expected to be popping up on scanners when you're scheduled to be in the wilderness. It's a good plan."

"Okay. So, as far as they know I'm out in the Algonquin wilderness in a tent, bonding with my kid."

"Exactly. We got really lucky with this. It was a stroke of genius for Cady to come up with it. New France is one of the most laid back Zones in this whole reconfiguration."

Hunter scoffed a little. "Yeah, it's mostly Canadians. I'm sure you don't remember them as they were, but in my day, they were known for being the politest people on the planet, but very Socialist."

Charlie looked confused. "Why don't those things go together? I thought Socialists wanted to be nice to everyone."

"I guess that's true . . . on the surface. But some of the niceness comes at the expense of others, so I've never really bought into it."

"Okay, that will have to be a conversation for another time. But, is that something you've been really outspoken about? If so, it could poke holes in the veracity of our cover story." Charlie seemed to be shedding a bit of his cool and collected demeanor.

"Really? You think so?"

Charlie nodded fervently, and said, "Hunter, do you not realize how many eyes stay on you? It's why we are going to such great pains to sneak you through these channels."

Hunter looked at him, stunned, but with the slightest hint of pleasure peeking through. "That does not help my anxiety, Charlie. Why me? . . . Okay, now I see how stupid that sounds, hearing it out loud. Look, I keep my opinions about politics and religion to myself. The only thing I am outspoken about is everything the government does for the left or the right. If anyone is paying attention, they probably think I'm more of an anarchist than anything. So, going all survivalist in the wild will not seem unusual, no matter where I do it."

"Fair enough. That sets my mind at ease. How ya doin'?"

"I mean, I'm a little awestruck at the moment, but, I'll be okay. It's definitely reassuring to know I'll have friendlies along the way."

"Don't get too comfortable. After this first one, only your point person will reveal themselves to you for the handoff. If an agent is traveling with you, you won't know it. They will have eyes on you, but you won't know who they are or where they are. It's just as much for their safety as for yours."

"That's oddly comforting and disconcerting at the same time."

Hunter sighed heavily and leaned his head against the window as Charlie closed the distance between them and the uncertain future looming ahead of him.

Soon, Charlie was weaving through the parking lot of the pier where he would part ways with Hunter. He pulled in to a spot about fifty yards from the queue for the cruise check-in.

Hunter reached out his hand and Charlie shook it firmly in an excessively formal way to cover for the fact that the two of them had bonded in this brief time and neither knew when or if they would have another encounter in the future.

Hunter climbed out of the passenger seat and Charlie popped the trunk of the car. Without a word of instruction, Hunter knew he was supposed to retrieve whatever was there on his own. He found a blue 70L frameless pack with trekking poles, a sleeping bag, and pad attached to the outside. He lost his balance as he hoisted the pack out of the car, pulling harder than necessary, expecting it to be heavier than it actually was. It was clear to him in that moment that this was to serve more as a prop for his cover story than as actual supplies for his journey.

After he slammed the trunk lid closed, he peered into the driver's side rearview mirror and made eye contact with Charlie one last time, and just nodded before heading over to the pier.

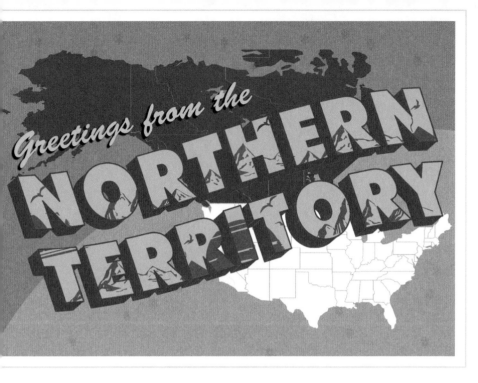

ZONE 1 - THE NORTHERN TERRITORY

Wide open wilderness is yours to explore when you come to the Northern Territory. Still largely unsettled and fertile soil for new ideas and lifestyles. If you want a place where you can just live and let live, we have all the room you'll need to do just that. Life isn't easy in this rugged terrain, but if you have what it takes to be self-sustaining, this is your kind of country.

ZONE I

THE NORTHERN TERRITORY

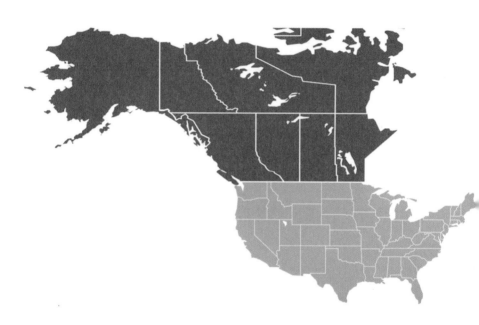

- ALASKA
- WESTERN CANADA

CHAPTER SIX

The 65-foot, 2-tiered boat bobbed at the harbor and was already buzz-ing with activity as eager travelers, decked out in rubber boots, fishing vests adorned with ornamental lures, and hopeful smiles, were staking their claims on optimal spots for casting their lines. The boat capacity was 60, but for this afternoon excursion, there would be roughly 45 people, including the captain and the crew of 3.

Hunter clung to the rail, trying to keep his stomach from betraying his cool demeanor. He felt someone squeeze in next to him and his irrita-tion mounted because there was no reason for such an invasion of his personal space. He turned his head slowly toward the stranger, careful not to move too quickly and set his head spinning. As their eyes met, he was greeted with, "Hey, Dad."

The shock was enough to make Hunter forget all about the rising bile in his belly. "What the . . .?"

Jacob grinned tightly and muttered through his teeth, "Don't make a scene. We are being watched." Then, in a more "natural" voice, he said loud enough for any nosy ears to hear, "I'm really looking forward to this trip. I think it will be good for us."

Hunter tried his best to smile genuinely and jerked his head to the side, signaling for Jacob to follow him, quickly regretting the move. He fumbled toward the bow where there were fewer people congregated.

When they were out of earshot of the others on the excursion, Hunter said through a forced smile, "You are not going with me. This is not okay."

"Hunter, relax. I am only here now to support your cover. Once we get to Pelee Island, I will disappear."

"Oh. Um. Well, I guess that makes sense." Hunter fumbled over a non-apology, and then continued to hold his position. "But, why didn't Cady . . . or Charlie give me a heads up? It's still a big risk. I don't know why you are wrapped up in all of this."

"They didn't tell you because they knew how you would react and we needed this to happen to help sell the story. And I'm in this because I believe in the same things you do . . . or I believe in the mission of the Resistance anyway. I know we have a weird relationship. You're my dad, but not really, and I'm your son, but not entirely. The thing is, I'm not going anywhere, and I am a grown-ass man, so you are going to have to figure out how to put your paternal instincts into a proper perspective so we can do what we are here to do."

"I'll try, but I'm not making any promises."

"I guess, if that's the best you can do, we'll have to work with it."

"So, where are you planning to lay low once we split up?"

"I have friends in New France who have a small co-op community. They said I can stay there for as long as I need to, and they are off the grid, so I don't have to worry about being detected. I'll show up on the border crossing scan, and then essentially vanish."

"Is it some sort of hippy commune or something?" Hunter asked with a scoff.

"I guess *you* would call it that."

"Wow. You are so much like your mother."

"You did *not* know my mother," Jacob said in a tone that clearly communicated she was off limits as far as their conversations were concerned.

"Hey, no judgment. Just making an observation."

"Well, maybe don't for now. We aren't there yet."

"Fair enough."

The two men stood in silence, Jacob staring out across the water, Hunter fixated on his whitened knuckles gripping the railing. It was less awkward than one might imagine as they both appreciated the reprieve from forced conversation.

After roughly half an hour, the captain announced they soon would be approaching the zone where the passengers would have the opportunity to drop their lines. The other travelers aboard began shuffling into place, eager to find what they believed would be the sweet spot for a good catch. Hunter and Jacob remained where they were until Jacob suggested they might be a little less conspicuous if they at least made an effort to appear interested in fishing. At that point they edged back toward the port side where there was an opening just past the cabin door.

Two members of the crew began distributing poles and containers of bait to those who were renting while the novices who hoped to pass themselves off as pros began fumbling with the over-priced gear they didn't know how to use. Hunter watched smugly as the deckhands barely above drinking age, yet already seasoned, exchanged glances of annoyance as they helped more than one red-faced faux angler untangle his line. Hunter reveled in the thought that he wouldn't be caught dead pretending to know something he didn't or be something he wasn't. And just as that reflection formed itself in his head, he realized the irony of his situation. It also crossed his mind that maybe he should be trying to fake it, but it occurred to him that this type of behavior would probably draw more attention to him and Jacob than the reticence that came so naturally.

Jacob was somewhat more engaged in the excursion. He was passionate about outdoor activities—an interest he actually shared with his father, water sports notwithstanding. Being an investigative journalist took him into some challenging environments, so he had become quite adept in the skills required for wilderness survival beyond the average camping trip. Another thing he had in common with Hunter, though he wasn't sure they would ever have an occasion to truly bond through these types of activities.

Hunter took the news that he had a son better than expected, especially considering the fact that they were nearly the same age when they met. However, if he could wrap his brain around losing forty years of his life and returning to his home planet only to find that the population was decimated and he held within him a cure for what caused the crisis, then a long lost son probably wasn't going to be the life disruption it would have been for others. That said, he had not gone out of his way to cultivate this new relationship.

Jacob struggled to know how to reach him . . . and whether he even wanted to reach him. Something inside tugged at him—a longing that he knew he needed to acknowledge and explore—but that urge was easily pushed to the side by more pressing matters of international import.

Since their kinship was revealed in the midst of the turmoil around the usage of the crew at the Center in Kaikoura, a true father and son reunion was tabled until Hunter settled in DC with the president. And even then it was difficult to navigate. The agenda of the Resistance seemed to prevail over every aspect of their lives. Personal relationships were sacrificed on the altar of the greater good. Jacob had a feeling that Hunter and Lydia might have pursued the chemistry between them but for the mission taking precedence. And if he was being honest with himself, he was a little wounded by the suspicion that his father would have made time for a woman he barely knew before he would have made time for his son . . . whom he also barely knew, but deserved to be a higher priority.

This is why Jacob had not yet taken the vaccine even though it had been available for a year. After the excitement around the crew's return died down, the cure that was developed out of what they discovered in their testing became the new focus of global attention. Jacob had grappled with the decision for months, and his tenuous relationship with his dad was a significant factor. The cure promised to reverse the inability to conceive male children, which was helping to rebuild the world's population. Jacob wasn't sure he wanted to contribute to that effort, in no small part because he didn't know if he was prepared to parent a child when he had such a complicated and new relationship with his own parent. Not that he had a partner for reproduction. His romantic prospects, such as they were, had also been deprioritized in favor of the demands of the Resistance.

They were three hours into the journey, approaching the coast of Pelee Island, when they crossed into the waters between Zone 13 and Zone 9. In a time far removed to the past, this area was on the Canadian side of the border that bisected the lake, but those lines were irrelevant now and replaced with new ones that were harder to ignore.

You see, as the United States and its annexed regions of Canada and northern Mexico split radically along political party lines in the wake of the Alpha Centauri crew return, the map was unofficially redrawn, though permanence for the new boundaries is imminent. States aggregated into Zones based on regional interests and needs, motivated by the desire to isolate with like-minded citizens. Gone are the days of diversity within communities. No more is the "out of many, one" ideal embraced. Leftist Dems and Right-wing Repubs retreated to their corners, taking their divisive labels with them.

Traveling between Zones of the same color was not a significant problem, but a passport and travel approval were required for a resident of the Blue Zone to cross over into a Red territory as their aims to keep the opposition out were heavily reinforced at all highways, ports, docks, and other commercial travel points of entry. The erection of physical walls was no longer a hotly contested issue. It was a foregone conclusion that simply had not had time to manifest, but was underway.

The complexities of passage through "unfriendly" Zones made it impossible for Hunter to make this journey by land and stay off the radar; but, fortunately for him, waterways were not governed by any Zone. They were free territory, which made this mode of transport ideal. That is, except for Hunter's distaste for this method. Still, passing between Zones, even by boat, would present challenges. The citizens of Zone 9 and Zone 13 used Lake Erie for recreation, commerce, and transportation, but Zone 9—The Greater Lakes—is a Red Zone. Though it wasn't common, conflicts did occasionally arise, so the lake was patrolled by the Coast Guard more than other areas. No other major waterways were shared by differing Zones, which didn't necessarily make them safer, just less likely to have neighboring conflicts.

The states of Michigan, Indiana, Ohio, and Wisconsin made up Zone 9. Of the Red Zones, it was one of the most Centrist. They were not as strident in their enforcement of border restrictions and were open to some left-leaning ideas about laws and regulations and social programs. This, along with their proximity to the Blue island of Illinois, made them about the safest Red Zone Hunter would encounter on his journey.

Zone 13 was named New France—what once had been the eastern portion of Canada and the distant, yet culturally connected, city of New Orleans. Louisiana had become part of the Greater Gulf (Zone 7), but because of the predominantly Blue ideology of this major port city, there was significant pushback against coming under Conservative policies and practices. Other Zones had faced similar challenges with a segment of the region not aligning with the prevailing ideology, but none of those had successfully broken away to affiliate with other Zones.

This division tended to fall along urban vs. rural lines, and while it might be expected that the preference of cities would prevail, some states had enough population in outlying areas to overrule the choice of those in the metropolitan areas. This was especially true with the states of Texas and Tennessee. They each joined a Red Zone and allowed Conservative ideology to rule despite large cities like Austin, Houston, and Nashville being predominantly Blue. Conversely, Chicago took the state of Illinois in the Blue direction. The rural parts of California, Oregon, and Washington held little influence over the way The Left Coast (Zone 2) went. The eastern portions of these states did split in an ill-advised effort at asserting some independence. They formed Zone 3, The New Frontier, but they remained Blue (if a slightly more purple hue) at this point, though there had been rumblings for some time of a shift. The primary factor holding them back so far was economy. This was not new. The financial viability of various states contributed significantly to the reasons for people aggregating into population centers for decades after the pandemic.

Separating into these Zones had some positive results. It tempered a great deal of the animus within the citizenry of the country, but it created unanticipated problems that are still unfolding. After the cure was introduced and hope came along with it, many of those who had migrated to the cities for survival were discovering the land that had been ruined by the crisis around the Apollo-VI-24 corn was now viable again. Lying fallow for more than thirty years had had a remarkable effect on the soil and groundwater of those areas. A citizen redistribution began, and the rural parts of the country were being repopulated. But, these groups did not bring with them capital for revitalizing the depressed areas. The money stayed in the cities. One of the things that made this country successful throughout its history was that every region offered unique agricultural and industrial products to the economy, and it was a cooperative environment. After the pandemic, the areas hit hardest had to be vacated, and few people remained there. These regions could come back, rebuilding the infrastructure for the agriculture and commerce they had produced, but it would take time. This was a critical factor in how states aligned to form the Zones. Within each Zone, states attempted to join with nearby states that would complement what they had to offer and prop them up in the areas where they fell short. But, as with The New Frontier, they were still so dependent on what the more populated areas contributed, that breaking away entirely was not yet a viable option.

The trip was progressing without incident, but Hunter was on high alert anyway. His discomfort was painfully obvious, but he was able to use seasickness as his cover when the excessively jovial, mountain of a man, who had announced that his name was Wendell the moment Hunter was squeezed in next to him, ribbed him with his elbow, encouraging him to put on a smile and have a little fun. When Hunter reluctantly explained his nausea, the middle-aged intruder guffawed and asked, "Then why the hell are you out here?"

Hunter did not want to engage, but knew he would not get out of this conversation without giving him something, so he offered, "My so . . . um, my brother really wanted to catch a Marlin or something for his wall."

Wendell chuckled again and Hunter, beginning to resent how much he seemed to be a source of amusement, asked with disdain, "What's so funny?"

Wendell released his beefy right hand from his rod and slapped Hunter on the back with enough force to knock him overboard had the railing been any lower, saying, "Buddy, I hate to disappoint ya, but you ain't gonna catch a Marlin out here! That's an ocean fish."

Hunter shrugged and said, "Whatever. I don't think he's reeling in anything, period. Either way, it's okay with me. I'll just be glad when we are back to land."

With that, Hunter told Jacob he was going to find a seat in the cabin and slipped away before Jacob could get out his warning that sitting down if he was feeling seasick was a bad idea. But it didn't take long for Hunter to find out on his own. His head began spinning within minutes of settling onto a banquette near the equipment room. The motion of the boat was more pronounced as he leaned against the wall of the cabin and the waves rocked him more viciously than when he was propped against the railing. Soon, he was stumbling into the lavatory, the smell of the composting toilet nearly knocking him backward. Hunter spent the next twenty minutes in the closet-sized room, relieving himself of the remnants of the breakfast he had grabbed with Charlie on the way there. Eventually, his stomach settled and he was able to maintain some level of composure for the last hour of the trip.

When they reached the dock in Scudder, Hunter was tempted to kiss the ground. The last time he had felt that urge was after his spaceship (as he affectionately referred to the Alpha Centauri I) crash-landed off the coast of California. He resisted the temptation both times, but only because he was very attached to his tough guy image.

ZONE 2 – THE LEFT COAST

With a long tradition of pioneering and innovation, the Left Coast offers you the remarkable diversity of bounteous farmland, arid desert, deep forestation, scenic coast, rolling hills, soaring mountains, and every other terrain you can imagine, providing opportunities for all professional, recreational, and lifestyle pursuits. Join us on the Left Coast for all the possibilities you could hope for. Bring your imagination and your ambition and be ready for growth in the land where dreams come true!

ZONE 2

THE LEFT COAST

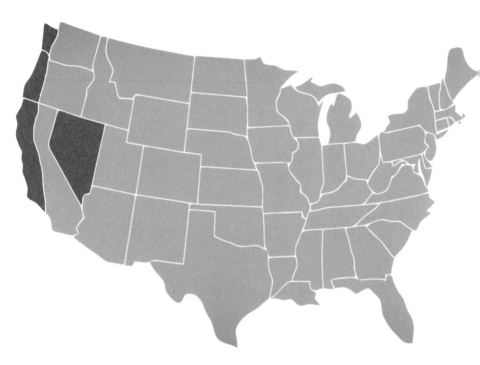

- WESTERN CALIFORNIA
- WESTERN OREGON
- WESTERN WASHINGTON
- NEVADA

CHAPTER SEVEN

The captain instructed the passengers to disembark from the port side of the vessel and make their way to the visitor stand at the land's end of the pier where Vanessa, the group guide, would give them their excursion packets that included hotel keys and restaurant vouchers. He thanked them for choosing Erie Experience and reminded them the boat to return to Port Clinton left promptly at 6:30 a.m. each morning and they would find the return ticket they purchased based on the length of their trip in their packet as well.

Hunter was champing at the bit to get off the boat and nearly fidgeted his way out of his skin while waiting for the captain to finish and the deck hand to drop the ramp to release them. He had positioned himself right next to the gateway so he could escape as soon as possible. He did not bother to check on Jacob's location. He figured they would find each other on dry land.

When Jacob was laughing and shaking his head when he caught up to him.

"Man, I never figured you for such melodrama."

Hunter scoffed, "You know, I've been through some shit. I should get to have this one thing that I don't like without people giving me a hard time about it."

"Hunter, what is going on with you? You have been really off. Not at all like the cool and collected guy I interviewed two years ago."

"What? The seasickness? It's just different. In a plane or a rocket, you don't feel the ground moving under you. It's not so much any motion. It's about the kind of motion that makes me sick.

"No. I mean everything. And I'm not the only one who's noticed."

"What's that supposed to mean? Are people talking about me behind my back?"

"See, that's exactly what I mean. The guy I first met wouldn't have cared what people thought. He would have just stepped up, sussed out the mission, and done what had to be done. You seem hesitant and insecure. It's . . . well, it's kinda freaking me out."

Jacob pulled Hunter away from the crowd and found a bench where they could sit. Hunter's head fell into his hands and he rubbed his face vigorously, as if trying to restore the blood flow to this deprived area. After a few moments of heavy silence, Hunter raised his head and stared out at the water.

Finally, he said, "I don't know, man. I guess this whole thing has just undone me. A little over two years ago, I was heading out on this incredible and impossible mission, and all of a sudden everything goes completely sideways. I thought I was a goner only to wake up drifting in space somewhere else. Found my way back home to discover the world I left behind was decimated by this horrible plague that came from the very thing that sent me into outer space. And not only that, it was forty years older too. I missed my whole life . . . your whole life."

He and Jacob made eye contact awkwardly for just a moment, and then Hunter stared out at the water again as he continued.

"Um . . . anyway, if that wasn't enough, my captain dies, my colleagues and I get turned into guinea pigs and become sperm factories, and we are treated like property of the entire world. And what happened to poor Lucas. That still tears me up. I guess it's just been a lot. Add to that the whole Marshall thing. I have absolutely no idea what I'm doing there, and I don't like not knowing what I'm doing. Give me a specific goal and a deadline, I'm great. I can make things happen under the most challenging circumstances. But everything is so abstract and undefined there. I don't even really know what my damn job is."

"Sounds like you've been bottling that up for quite a while."

"Guess so. Popped the cork and it all came spewing out."

"Well, I hope that helps you get back on track because . . . and I can't stress this enough . . . you are going to need your wits about you. We are safe here, but as soon as we leave this location, there are no guarantees. Don't be fooled into thinking the Blue Zones are a safe haven because they allow for open passage. I know they seem like they are peaceful, happy places, but there is a dark side to all of this. And they are not our friends. Remember, we are the Resistance. That means we are pushing back against all of the establishment, against all of the institutionalized ways of doing things. It's a mistake to think the Red Zones are on our side because they believe in small government, and it's a mistake to think the Blue

Zones are on our side because they are liberal-minded. We are challenging the status quo on all fronts, and that means challenging the power that matters above all else to some very influential people. That makes us persona non grata everywhere. That is why we work so hard to stay off the radar. That's why you have to shake off whatever is going on with you and get your head in the game. Got it?"

"Yeah. I got it."

"Great. Now, let's grab our packet and find a spot for some food . . . unless the green hue of your face means you aren't ready to eat."

"I'll be fine after a few more minutes on steady ground. And I lost my breakfast, so I'm starting to get hungry. But . . . wait. Why do we have packets? We aren't staying here."

"Trust me."

Jacob approached Vanessa and gave her their names. She thumbed through her stack and pulled a manila envelope for each of the men and handed them over with an abundance of cheeriness that made Hunter want to hurl again. He thanked her curtly and walked away before she had a chance to chat him up any more. Jacob apologized for his behavior and excused himself.

Hunter and Jacob found a tavern near the pier and settled into a booth near the back of the restaurant. It was dark and quiet, which suited Hunter just fine. A young woman named Robin approached them and introduced herself as their server and asked for their order. In almost eerie unison, both men ordered fish and chips and whatever beer they had on tap. She nodded and disappeared through swinging doors to take the ticket to the kitchen.

Hunter opened his envelope and slid the contents out onto the table. He had a slip of paper with a location typed on it, a smaller envelop holding some currency, and a larger sheet of paper with instructions filling approximately half the page. Jacob opened his and peered inside. He pulled out a small square of paper with only a time written on it. Hunter looked at him a bit bewildered, not only because his material didn't match in scope or size, but because Jacob didn't seem surprised by the disparity.

Jacob noticed his expression, but at that moment, Robin reappeared with two pints of an amber lager. They quickly swept their documents off the table, out of sight, and without any indication that she took notice, she laid small square napkins down before placing the glasses on top of them. She told them their food should be up in a few minutes, that they made it fresh, so it took a bit longer. Hunter nodded and watched as she went back to the server station near the bar to make sure she was out of sight before lifting his papers again.

Jacob took a big gulp of the beer and then said, "I already know what I need to know."

Hunter looked up from the page and stared at him.

"The envelopes. Mine has less because I already know what I need to know."

"Oh. Yeah, I guess that's true. Then what's on that piece of paper?"

"Just the time to meet my transport to the mainland. I'll be leaving from the same dock where we arrived and heading due north to Leamington, Ontario."

"Says here I'm leaving from West Dock. I'm taking a Catamaran up to Lake St. Clair by way of the Detroit River and that's gonna get me to Lake Huron, which lines up with what Charlie told me. I'm supposed to give this white en-velope to the person I meet at the dock. Think it's a bribe or something?"

"Call it compensation."

It was at this point that Robin barreled through the swinging doors with two platters of food that she slid in front of them. She pointed to the end of the table against the wall and said most condiments they might need were there, but to holler if they wanted anything else. Jacob said everything looked good and they should be fine.

Hunter gazed at the golden fried mound of food on his plate and found himself laughing, almost in tears. This went on for far longer than seemed fitting given the circumstances and Jacob pressed him for an explanation, saying he couldn't start eating until he knew what was wrong.

Finally pulling himself together, Hunter sighed heavily and said, "Are you aware of the code they used to communicate my itinerary?"

Jacob shook his head and explained, "They keep things as compartmentalized as possible to protect everyone involved."

"Oh, yeah. Charlie said that too," Hunter said before stuffing a fry in his mouth. He chewed quickly and con-tinued, "Well, they sent me a menu, from a non-existent seafood restaurant in DC."

"Okay."

"And all of the locations were denoted with different types of fish."

"Seriously?! That's bizarre and impressive and maybe a bit convoluted."

"Indeed. But we cracked the code, which was some really clever work on our parts, if I do say so myself."

"Props, pop."

"Umm . . . yeah, anyway, I don't know what kind of fish this is, but I couldn't help but wonder if it's on the list. The absurdity of all of this just kind of got me going, and I lost it a bit. Better to do that now, I suppose."

"Someday, you'll have to tell me all about it. But, for now, we should pay. I have to connect with my contact in half an hour."

"I am so glad our currency is one of the things that hasn't changed with the dividing into Zones. That's one complication we don't need. Especially since all I have is old dollars."

"Yeah. It looked like it might not work out that way. Some people in the Blue Zones wanted to revive those alternative currencies that were taking off in the 20s. Crypto, I think it was called."

"It was a big mess about the time I left. Glad it didn't hang on."

"I kind of liked the idea. Wasn't it pretty revolutionary—trying to pry control of the wealth away from those who had always had it?"

"That was the theory. And don't get me wrong. I think the stock market was a sham, but the way they were going about it didn't just stick it to the man, it destabilized things for everyone. And it's a good thing everything else collapsed the way it did. We were heading toward entirely electronic transactions, which, of course, made businesses and politicians happy. They could see where everyone was spending every dime, and that gave them a lot of power. There wouldn't have been any coming back from that."

"The pandemic set us back 100 years in technology on a lot of fronts. That has some benefits, and some challenges. I think people are wanting to build back the infrastructure we had, but I'm not sure that's for the best. As for the currency, I think both sides agree it's not something we can change on a whim."

"At least they agree on something."

They let that last comment lie and dove into their food. Hunter paused long enough to swallow the pill Charlie had given him, and then began inhaling the rest of his meal. In short order they had filled themselves to discomfort. Robin had left the check for them while their mouths were full and Jacob simply gave her a thumbs up. After wiping his greasy hands on his third napkin, Hunter picked up the paper to see the total and pulled out his wallet. Jacob started to object, and Hunter told him he had it. He slapped two bills on the table, grabbed his envelope, scooted out of the booth, and moved toward the door. Jacob peered at the bill before getting up to make sure Hunter tipped. He smiled slightly, noting that his dad had treated her quite fairly. He hoped in that moment there would be opportunity to learn more of these little things about who his dad was.

Hunter and Jacob stood awkwardly on the sidewalk in front of the tavern, not sure of how to part.

Finally, Jacob said, "Look, I'm sorry I got in your face like that earlier."

"No, you were right. I needed that kick in the ass. I had not been feeling like myself and couldn't figure out how to break out of it. Thanks for the tough love."

"Any time."

"Yeah, that's not permission to go off on your old man whenever you want though."

Jacob laughed at the thought of it. Here was this man who looked like he could be his brother but should be wrinkled, feeble, and spending his days fishing off a pier or watching old Westerns. Instead, he was stowing away on boats, traveling across country, and facing a harrowing journey into an unpredictable fight. The thing that occurred to Jacob in that moment that was even though the body was still agile and healthy, the mind had already lived a couple of lifetimes, and that changed everything. It was then that he decided to let Hunter be his dad in whatever way came naturally.

The silence between them as they were each lost in thought had become uncomfortable, and they realized they needed to get moving. Even with this new connection, it was still too soon for hugs, yet handshakes felt conspicuously formal so they resorted to a friendly slap on the back and a "See ya soon."

Jacob headed back to the pier, and Hunter watched for a moment and wondered when their paths would cross again. He knew he should be more intentional about making that happen, but for now he had to focus on the journey ahead of him. And that didn't even take into account what situation he was walking into in Jarbridge, NV, where Lydia was waiting for him.

Knowing he was going to be confined to small spaces for the next three weeks without many opportunities to stretch his legs or breathe fresh air, Hunter decided to walk the two miles to the western port. He tried to just enjoy the exercise and keep his mind from racing over what he was in for and the uncertainty of his future. That wasn't a particularly successful task, but he at least managed to shift his thoughts at times to the pleasure he would take in seeing Lydia's face again. Picturing her helped the time and distance pass so quickly that he was at the pier before he realized he'd worked up a sweat.

The West Dock was not what he expected. It was an old military dock that did not appear to have been in use for decades, but there were a handful of small boats moored on the pier. As he approached them and scanned the landscape, he realized that what he had incorrectly assumed was the name of the contact was yet another code. Franc Tireur was not a Canadian guy with a French-sounding name who would take him to his next connection point; it was the name of the boat—franc-tireur—which he would learn later was the name of a resistance group in the French Revolution that helped fight against the Germans during World War II. Hunter was intrigued by the word-play and wondered if they had clever revolutionary references for all of the subterfuge, and that thought left him feeling insufficient for the ongoing task of deciphering secretive language. He wished for access to Cady's brain and worried about what this tactic might mean for the rest of the trip and his success on it. He knew the clandestine methods were necessary. It just had him experiencing a relatively unfamiliar emotion: insecurity. He made a practice of staying in his lane where he knew what his strengths were and how to make them work for him. He was—pun unavoidably intended—a fish out of water, and it had him uneasy.

He approached the vessel—a small cuddy cabin—and knocked on the side, knowing enough about protocol to wait for someone to appear, and then he said, "Permission to come aboard."

The man who emerged from the cabin fit every description of a weathered, old seaman you could conjure. Leathery skin, shaggy white hair stuffed haphazardly under a typical white captain's hat, and had it been colder weather, he surely would have worn a navy pea coat. He grunted and waved his arm in a gesture indicating welcome, though Hunter did not feel particularly welcomed. He climbed over the edge onto the deck and the man grunted again, looking Hunter up and down.

Finally, with an exhale that reeked of tobacco, in a painfully gravelly voice he grumbled a few brief words: "Down below. Lock your pack in the cabinet. Don't want nothin' spillin' around if we hit hard seas. Should be some cans of beans in the galley if you get hungry. I'll sleep up top tonight."

Hunter, who was not a man for lengthy conversation either, simply nodded and disappeared below deck. He did not expect to be accumulating friends on his journey, but he at least thought the friendly Canadians would be . . . well . . . friendlier.

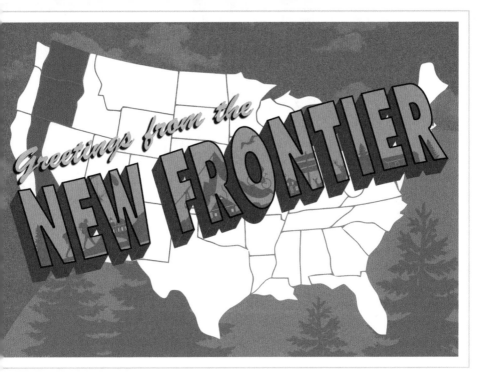

ZONE 3 - THE NEW FRONTIER

The West without the Left. We share the same wide-ranging landscape and access to uncompromised land and waterways as the Left Coast, but are more Conservative in our governing and economic policies. You'll find a happy medium here where opportunity abounds and regulatory restrictions don't.

ZONE 3

THE NEW FRONTIER

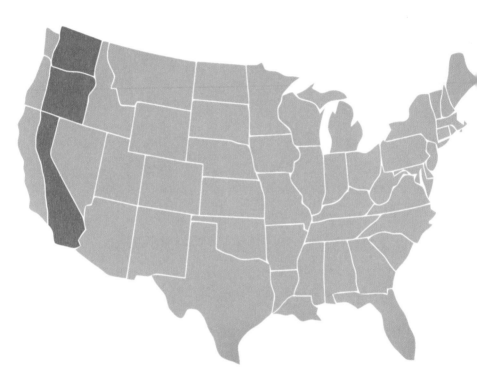

- EASTERN CALIFORNIA
- EASTERN OREGON
- EASTERN WASHINGTON

CHAPTER EIGHT

Hunter settled into his bunk and took in his surroundings. The dimly lit cubby offered barely enough room for his wingspan and several inches shy of enough head room to stand fully erect, but it was private. He was grateful for that. Charlie had admonished him to not interact with the crew on other segments of the trip, but he saw that he would have to follow the same advice for this leg. He'd had no intentions of being chatty with anyone, regardless of the instruction, so the quarters, close as they were, made it easy to keep to himself.

He had been lying on the bunk for maybe fifteen minutes when he heard the low rumble of the engine surge and the vessel jerk forward. As if the undulation of the water weren't bad enough, he realized he was probably in for an even rougher ride thanks to aging propulsion. He closed his eyes and tried to focus on something other than his physical discomfort.

Two hours later, Hunter found himself face down on mildewed carpet. It was a rude awakening from the much needed sleep he was surprised to achieve. He had drifted off pretty quickly, no doubt thanks to the undulations of the boat moving across the water, which was unexpected for him. He never imagined finding such motion anything other than nauseating, let alone soothing enough to rest. But, something had disrupted the flow of the craft to such a degree that he was tossed from his bunk.

Pushing himself up to a semi-standing position, he crept out of the cabin and poked his head up to see if he could determine what had happened without being seen. His captain was stretched out over the bow with a spotlight in hand, scanning the water lapping against the hull.

Hunter cleared his throat and the man turned to glare at him over his shoulder. Hunter simply shrugged, attempting to convey his feeling that he was entitled to know why he ended up on the floor. The man scooted on his belly back to the deck and grumbled, "Hit a sturgeon."

"A fish stopped us in our tracks?" Hunter asked suspiciously.

"Those bastards can grow big as a Buick."

"Really? That's incredible."

"Don't think it did any damage to the hull, but we need to get moving all the same."

"Okay, I'll go back below."

"Eh, it's black as pitch out here. If you want to stay up top until daybreak, that's probably safe enough."

"Oh, okay. You think so? It is pretty cramped down there."

"Might as well. Guess I didn't introduce myself earlier. I'm Henry."

"Good to meet you, Henry. I'm Hunter."

"I know about you."

"You do? Did they brief you?"

"Son, you really think there is anyone in the world who don't know who you are?"

"I guess I never really gave that much thought. I guess I kind of hoped . . . "

"Not a chance. If someone like me that spends most of his time alone out on the water and tries to avoid talking to everybody. . ."

Hunter couldn't help but interject, "Yeah, I noticed."

Henry resumed without acknowledging him, ". . . has heard of the spacemen that dropped out of the sky and seeded the world, you don't have a prayer of being anonymous."

"You're probably right. Um, so . . . sorry for making assumptions, but you look to be about the age that we were around when we left. Do you remember it?"

"That's not a stretch. I'm seventy-six. I definitely remember. I was in the Navy then—a Chief Petty Officer on the USS Cleveland, a Littoral combat ship."

"Wow. Those were pretty new when I was in the Air Force. Since I was flying planes and not helos, I never got on board one, but always wanted to."

Henry chuckled slightly, revealing a bit of personality. Hunter smiled, in part because he was glad to have some connection, but also because he realized why Henry was laughing. It was at him. At his expense.

"Okay, yeah, I know. But on a craft that big, you can barely tell you're moving. It's different. Anyway, I think I'm starting to find my sea legs."

"Hope so. You're gonna need it."

"You know about my travel plans?"

"Not beyond my role, but it don't take a genius to figure out what's going on."

"That's not reassuring. I'm supposed to be incognito."
"As I said, don't expect you will ever be anonymous, so put that out of your head. But, most people, geniuses or not, ain't paying attention to anyone but theirselves, so you can slip by. Although, if you're trying to not be noticed, going by boat is probably your best move.

"Well, Henry, I just hope certain people don't come to the same conclusion you did."

Henry just nodded and leaned back on the banquette and stared up at the blanket of stars above them. Hunter mimicked his movements and found it unexpectedly pleasant.

The men reclined in silence watching the constellations pass overhead and Hunter found himself searching the sky to see if he could identify any of the celestial bodies he'd seen up close not too long ago. As he gazed out into space, he felt a strange tugging at his soul, almost like a homesickness. He definitely had not felt at home since his return. Maybe out there is where he belonged.

Eventually breaking the reverie, Hunter asked Henry how he came to be in a position to be hauling him across a lake. Henry explained he had retired when the military was down-sizing in the pandemic.

"It's all women now. Guess you noticed that?" Hunter nodded and read on Henry's face his disgruntlement and decided not to comment.

Henry went on, "They ushered us out, said we were a protected class all of a sudden, but for men like me, we don't want that kind of protection. I'm a man of the sea. Being on land didn't feel right for me, and my options were limited."

"I get that more than you know. I was just looking out there," he said, pointing toward the abyss above them, "and wishing I could go back."

"Maybe you will someday. Might join you if things don't get better. Anyway, I spent a few months trying to fit into a desk job in town—Port Clinton—but it wasn't for me. I used every dime I had saved and bought a Sport Fishing boat. I did those day fishing trips for tourists," He glanced at Hunter, knowing he had just suffered through a similar excursion, and Hunter just shook his head and laughed.

Henry laughed with him, and then continued, "Well, that dried up the longer the plague went on. I managed to sell the boat just before the bottom dropped out of the economy and got enough out of it for this old girl. I've been living on her ever since, and I do off-grid jobs from time to time."

"You mean smuggling?"

"That's *a* word for it."

"Hey, no judgment. Just clarifying. So, you must stay on the Zone 13 side of things most of the time then."

"Well, I operate out of there, but most of what I transport goes to The Greater Lakes and is distributed to other Red Zones."

"Seriously? That's surprising. Don't they tend to isolate from the Blue Zones?"

"In a lot of ways, yes. But Blue Zones have things they can't get in their region. That's been one of the biggest problems to come out of all of this division. I'd probably live in a Red Zone. I like them better, but I couldn't pass the citizenship test."

"Why?"

"I was all good until they got to the question about secured borders. I need to be free to move about as I please. It was too restrictive."

"Well, what did you like about it? Guns are a big one. Can't get one to save your life . . . literally . . . in most Blue Zones."

"Oh, yeah. That is tough. I don't feel the need to own one, even though I was in the military . . . maybe because I was . . . but I do think a total ban is a bridge too far. What else?"

"The basic economy. Lower taxes. In fact, Blue Zone taxes are way too high for their citizens. It's why I can't do better than live on a boat. It's also why I do what I do.

"How's that?"

"Well, as I said, Red Zones sometimes need things only available in Blue Zones, whether it's raw materials, produce, sometimes services. The thing is, while Blue Zones export that stuff, the export tariffs are so high, only the super wealthy in the Red Zones can afford it, so I transport things and people to help out."

"You don't feel like you're cheating New France?"

"Not really. It's all getting out of hand, what they charge the locals and how they jack up the prices even more for the Red Zones."

"But if they have something another Zone wants, isn't it just capitalism to get what you can for it?"

Henry laughed for the second time in their brief relationship, and both times Hunter felt he was mocking him. This time he was not as accepting of the degradation.

"What?! Am I not right?"

"Oh, no, you are. It's just that what you're talking about is at the crux of this whole split when you boil it down."

"How so?"

"Each side has things they get right and things they get wrong. You either have to decide what you're willing to live with and settle in the area that is closest to what you want, or you have to figure out how to play both sides against each other."

"I guess you picked the latter."

"Damn straight."

Hunter decided to let the conversation end there. He knew he would be encountering people with differing perspectives throughout the trip and the safest bet was to not get sucked into debates where he could avoid it.

As the edges of the sky became tinged in yellow, Henry nudged Hunter, who had drifted off to sleep again, and told him it was time to go below deck. They would be arriving in Port Huron soon, and even before dawn, there would be enough people around that he needed to stay out of sight. He would make his next connection there.

Hunter sat on the edge of the bunk, pulling himself out of the fog of sleep. He quickly pulled his gear back together, stuffing in the few items he'd removed, so he would be ready to move when the time came. He did not bother to clean up beyond splashing some water on his face and running his fingers through his hair.

Just before the sun was showing itself, they wove their way down the Detroit River into Lake St. Claire. Hunter noted Henry was right about the pre-dawn hustle. Hunter recalled being taught as a child that the best fishing happens before everyone else wakes up. He surmised that a large portion of these vessels were commercial fishing and the others were commercial transport. Their little dingy—a term he knew better than to use with Henry—would have been conspicuous if any of the shore-men had time to look around.

Henry skillfully navigated the crowded passage, avoiding collisions with the larger boats taking ownership of the waterway, and finally docked in Windsor on the New France side of Lake St. Clair.

Henry rapped on the cabin roof after tethering the boat in a slip and Hunter crept out and onto the deck. The two men shook hands firmly and formally. As they did, Hunter realized Henry was slipping him a piece of paper. His stern gaze told Hunter not to look at it until he was on the dock. Hunter nodded and quietly moved away from the boat without another word and without a glance back in Henry's direction.

Once he was on the dock, he opened the folded note and on it was a single word: Rosa.

Hunter figured it was another boat name, probably another cryptic reference to something he wouldn't get without help. He was wary of walking up and down the pier searching for it, concerned about drawing unwanted attention. He saw a bench and decided to sit for a minute and collect himself.

He slumped over, resting his arms on his knees, running back through the itinerary Cady had made him commit to memory.

> Was it Husky? The clue they gave? No, that's a dog.
> Something like that though. Musky. That's it. I can't rely on
> these fish names though. I know where I am, and I know
> I'm supposed to leave here thirty minutes after arrival, but
> . . . wait, what time is it?

Hunter looked at his watch and discovered they had arrived later than planned. The collision with the sturgeon must have caused a delay they couldn't make up. He had ten minutes to find his next transport and he had no clue where to start. Just then, he realized someone had joined him on the bench. Without sitting upright, he rotated his head to the left to see a sturdy woman who appeared to be in her fifties, wearing a plaid shirt and heavy, tan trousers, obviously made for standing up to abuse. Her skin was weathered and her hands looked strong but calloused. He met her eyes and she gave him a half-smile.

"Lookin' for Rosa?"

Hunter sat up straight and smiled back. She jerked her head to the side and stood up, expecting him to follow. Hunter, relieved to learn he had not missed his connection and wouldn't have to hunt all over the dock for it, followed along behind her eagerly. She moved at a faster pace than he expected, and when she looked back, wondering where he was, he jogged to catch up.

> When he was by her side, she said, "I'm Martha. You
> almost missed us. We need to hustle so we don't fall

behind. I don't expect you are going to have much wiggle room between hand-offs, so I'm going to relay a heads up to my contact and let them know your other dates need to be looking for you rather than letting you find them."

"You mean they weren't supposed to do that already?"

"Honey, we all have regular jobs to do. You're just along for the ride."

"Oh. Well, I'm only getting information in small pieces. It's a little hard to navigate."

"Understood. That's why I'm going to tell them to readjust. Some things work in theory and need modification along the way."

"Much appreciated."

"Well, we have our priorities, but getting you safely where you need to be is important too. The cause matters."

She slowed to a stop in front of a trap net boat. "Rosa" was painted in a script lettering across the stern. Martha jumped down into the boat and reached out her hand to take Hunter's pack, then extended her hand again to help him board. He felt a bit emasculated by her assistance, and decided then and there to suck up whatever discomfort he was feeling for the rest of this saga and to not let anyone else see him struggle.

ZONE 4 - THE HOMESTEAD

Land of the original homesteaders, our wild west heritage still runs in our veins and is a part of the land beneath our feet, the water we drink, and the air we breathe. There is no greater place for a fresh start than the land of big skies and wide-open spaces. Settle here and start over with unlimited opportunities and an unrestricted way of life.

ZONE 4

THE HOMESTEAD

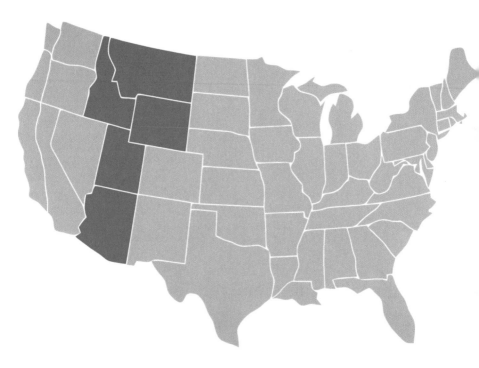

- IDAHO
- MONTANA
- WYOMING
- UTAH
- ARIZONA

CHAPTER NINE

Martha gave Hunter the ten-cent tour of the squared-off rugged boat, pointing to the areas he needed to avoid, which was pretty much all but the few square inches to the left of the wheel. It was more of a crawl space with floor access to the engine. It wouldn't realistically conceal a grown man, but it kept him mostly out of sight. Martha apologized for the accommodations and recommended he put something waterproof down to sit on or his backside would reek of dead fish.

Martha set to shaking out nets and unmooring the boat from the dock. She gave a hefty shove with her foot against the pier to push off and then went to start the motor. Hunter had settled into his cubby and watched in admiration as Martha handled herself as well as, if not better than, any other fisherman he'd ever seen.

Hunter strained against the unforgiving metal floor and dreaded the nine hours ahead of him. He hoped that once they were in open waters he would be able to get up and stretch his legs, if not be of some assistance to Martha. He was feeling more and more that he needed to earn his keep. It was probably due to carryover of the masculine ideals embedded in him from his era, but he couldn't bear to watch a woman labor so intensively while he was parked on his butt.

Once they were clear of the port activity and following the shoreline across Lake St. Clair toward Port Huron, Martha turned her focus from steering the ship and peered down at Hunter who was sitting just below where she stood at the helm, strong and sturdy.

"How ya doin' down there?"

"About how you'd imagine."

"Yeah, sorry to stuff you down there, but I think you know the drill."

"I'm getting used to the idea of being in a perpetual state of discomfort for the duration."

"Yeah, I don't expect you'll find yourself on yacht at any point."

"It's okay. I spent most of my career in tight quarters. And, make no mistake. Some of the people I shared a cockpit with smelled about like these fish."

Martha, who had been keeping her eyes forward on the water in front of her, smiled down at him and chuckled heartily. Then she let out a deep sigh that told Hunter she spent a lot of time alone and his company was quite welcome.

Martha stepped away from the wheel and said, "Think you can manage piloting this ship for a minute?"

Hunter stood eagerly and took the wheel, saying, "I think I can manage. But, is it okay for me to be visible now?"

Martha had moved to the stern where she was lifting nets and releasing them into the water. She looked over her shoulder at him and said, "Sure. We're okay here."

Hunter had been gripping the wheel tightly and eased up when he felt the tension through his arms. Martha assured him he didn't need to steer so much as keep the boat from being swept toward shore by a current.

Once he felt he was getting the hang of things, Hunter shouted back to Martha, asking, "How much do you typically haul in in a day?"

Martha straightened from where she was craned over the side of the boat untangling a portion of net. She shouted, "Well, on a good day I'll fill this whole damn boat."

"You do this all by yourself?"

"Sometimes I have a hand or two, but with the extra cargo on this trip, that wasn't an option. Can't really afford to pay them to work more than a couple days a week anyway. But, truth is, I'm not really after a catch today. This is mostly for show and just some maintenance."

"Oh. I see. So we don't look so conspicuous out here doing nothing. I've never seen a boat quite like this."

"That's not surprising. During your first life—before you went into space . . .," she looked at Hunter before continuing to make sure he was catching her drift and that he didn't take offense. Hunter just smiled and nodded.

". . . um, these boats had been regulated out of use. Things are different now, at least in my zone, and this ol' girl has been in my family for generations. Nobody had used her for a long time, but she was stored in a slip and looked after real good."

"How long have you been doing this . . . fishing?"

"Pretty much my whole life. My pappy never got the crew of sons he'd hoped for—just me and my sis—so he put us to work, sweat the girl right outta us. Not that I was much for dolls and dresses anyway. But Sis fought him tooth and nail. She left for New York as soon as she was eighteen and never looked back."

"Is she still there? Do you stay in touch? . . . Or is that a sensitive topic?"

"Nah. I'm what you'd call an open book. Mary—that was her name; my parents were real religious and got those names from two sisters in the Bible."

"Yes, I'm familiar."

"So then you know we got the right names assigned to us. Me, being Martha, and my workin' hard to take care of everybody; and, her, being Mary, focused more on the stuff that goes on in her head."

"I can see how that would be very fitting."

"Well, anyway, Mary and I did stay in touch even though Pappy didn't want me to. But she died during the pandemic. She got pregnant . . . this was before they knew what the corn was doin' to us . . . and the baby died. Mary was one of those who got sick because the corn made her body unable to fight diseases. She was always a little more sickly as kid. Got colds way more than I did. Had lots of allergies too. They said that's why the baby died. She was too sick to carry a baby. I'm not sure she would have survived that kind of loss anyway."

"Wow. Martha, I'm really sorry. That's tough."

"Yeah, the saddest part is she passed before she and Pappy could set things right. He's gone now too. Maybe they are patchin' things up wherever they are."

Martha cleared her throat and physically shook off the troubling memory. Hunter searched for a way to change the subject, trying to recall what they were talking about that led them down this path.

"Um . . . oh, you were saying you have been doing this since you were a kid?"

"Oh, yeah. I just took to it like I was born to it. It suits me. Doesn't make for a real family life, not that I've really had options in that department."

Hunter asked himself how he kept ending up on these conversational landmines and struggled to find a way out, but Martha, being the open book she had already claimed to be, went on before he could find a new topic.

"I'm sure it comes as no surprise that I don't have a line of suitors stretching down the pier waitin' for me to come back to port."

Hunter looked really uncomfortable and tried to stay focused on steering the boat that didn't need his help.

"It's okay. You can agree with me. I know who I am. It's just too bad people who don't know me think they do. That's probably the downside of living where I do. These Red Zone folk . . . for a bunch of people who want the government to stay out of their business, they sure do like to stick their nose in their neighbors' private lives. The thing is I like men. I would like to get married and, now that they have this cure figured out, maybe have a kid or two. I don't have much left in the tank, but I think if I squeeze them out pretty quickly, I could make a nice little family. But everybody assumes I am too butch to let somebody else be the husband. So, all the fellas I know ask me out for a drink, but just as one of the guys. Not as a date."

Hunter could see he wasn't going to have any luck shifting to something more neutral, but he figured she needed to get this out, and listening was the least he could do considering what she was doing for the cause. So, he just nodded and "mmm-hmm-ed" periodically so she knew he was paying attention.

Finally, he ventured a question he was sure would open another can of worms, but one he couldn't resist asking.

"If you don't like how you're treated here, why don't you move to a Zone where they would be more accepting? Aren't we right off the coast of one of those places now? Seems like the whole country is doing that these days— isolating themselves in Zones where everybody else thinks like they do."

"Oh, I couldn't do that. My family has been in Wisconsin and Michigan for generations. We've been fishing these waters going back to the time when these trap net boats were first being used. It's in my blood. I have friends here. I have a business here. Sure, I could sell my catch to other places, but they know me and give me the best rate possible because they know what I bring them is going to be the best. The other big factor is the property rights in the Red Zones.

"What does that mean? I left all of my property behind when I joined the crew, and after I came back, they gave me a place to life in DC, so I don't really know what's going on with that."

"Well, see, I inherited this boat and the house my parents lived in outside of Saginaw. Also, half the family farm in Plum City over in Wisconsin came to me since my sister passed and I only had one other cousin on that side. Another family lives on it and is trying to work the land, but it's just now coming back from what they did to it during that plague."

"So, how does being in a Red Zone affect that?"

"Taxes, mostly. If we had been in a Blue Zone, they would have taxed my inheritance so much I wouldn't have been able to keep it. Also, the land we are renting out . . . well, in Blue Zones the rent control they put in place during the collapse of everything to help people out hasn't lifted even though we are getting back to normal. If I had to keep renting all that land for pennies on the dollar, we'd lose the farm cause we couldn't keep up with what we owe on it. And it would break my heart to lose what my family managed to hang on to for generations, through all kinds of hardships and droughts and other things life throws at ya."

"Wow. I had no idea things were so different between the two sides."

"Yeah, not everybody is gonna agree with me, but the way I see it, the Red Zones get a heckuva lot right in the things that affect me. And what they don't I guess I can live with. So, ya see, I may not get everything I want out of life here, but I can't imagine life anywhere else."

"Fair enough. But if you could . . . would . . . live anywhere else. Where would you like to go?"

"Well, it would have to be somewhere with lots of water and boats. Maybe one of the oceans would be nice. I always wanted to visit Mary in New York. It just sounded too crowded for my tastes. Maybe up in Maine. I could definitely find a job fishing up there."

"I'm sure you could. The coastal towns up there are small and have strong communities. They came through the pandemic fairly well and Zone 12 is holding strong in all this division. I imagine that's because it still has one of the highest populations as a whole and a lot of diversification in their resources."

"You live there? Sounds like you know a lot about it."

"No. I live in DC, but I have a friend who spent some time there recently. I was thinking of visiting, but then all of this came up."

"Was it a friend of the female variety?" Martha asked grinning and giggling, showing the softened edges of her personality, which pleasantly surprised Hunter and endeared her to him more than he expected.

"As a matter of fact . . . but don't make too much of it. I don't know what will happen now that this mission has become our priority."

"Well, I hope you have a chance to find out. I know firsthand what happens when you put survival ahead of enjoying life and the people you share it with."

"I hope we do too."

Martha took the wheel back from him and he found himself disappointed. He was oddly soothed by the function, and it seemed to help with the seasickness still subtly plaguing him. He supposed it was due, in part, to having something else to focus on, and feeling a little more in control. He hoped it was also attributable to him just getting used to it since it wasn't likely he'd get to take the helm on the other legs of the journey.

As the sun was directly overhead, the rays bearing down on them, Hunter began to feel nauseous again and worried he hadn't come as far as he'd imagined, and then he realized he had not eaten all day. Not wanting to use one of his emergency energy bars, he was just about to ask Martha if there was anything to eat when she pulled a cooler from a compartment at the back of the boat. She offered him a sandwich and a soda pop from the box, and he eagerly accepted with a hearty thanks. Martha settled in on the side of the boat, giving Hunter a bit of anxiety as the edge was not wide enough to function as an adequate seat. But she seemed to balance herself comfortably and opened the wrap around her sandwich, gesturing with it to encourage Hunter to dig in to his own.

Within the tightly folded brown waxed paper, he found more than he expected. When she handed him the parcel, he figured he was going to get something pretty basic like a peanut butter and jelly or bologna and cheese. It turned out that Martha was quite the sandwich craftswoman as well. The sourdough appeared to be homemade, and between the slices, shaved roast beef was piled almost an inch high along with some kind of spicy green leaves, provolone, and a roasted pepper sauce. It was the fanciest sandwich he recalled ever having, and not just because he was ravenous.

Hunter didn't utter a word until he had finished the last bite, and realized Martha had been silently eating as well. He wadded up the wrapper in a very satisfied manner and let out a deeply contented sigh.

"That was amazing. Thank you so much for sharing. I hope you didn't sacrifice any of your lunch for me, but I do appreciate it."

"Hon, I'm a big girl, but even I can't eat two of those. I made it especially for you."

"Well, it's probably the best sandwich I've ever eaten."

"Aww, shucks. That's quite a compliment. I made it all from scratch."

"Everything?!" Hunter asked in genuine astonishment. He had suspected the bread was homemade, but never imagined it was from her home, and he certainly hadn't expected such culinary prowess from her. He hated to admit it where his ideas about gender roles were still embedded, but he figured this type of homemaking was too girly for her.

"Yep. The bread, roasted the beef myself. Okay, I did buy the cheese. But, I grew those greens and the peppers for the sauce in my garden."

Martha beamed with pride and revealed a smile one could call pretty that was hidden behind her grizzled exterior that was weathered by the sun and disappointment. It wasn't until then that Hunter noticed that the thick wavy locks she kept tamed in a braid, and imagined there was a softer side to Martha that would appeal to a lot of men if she let herself show it.

"That's incredible! How do you have time for all of that?"

"Well, when you don't have a husband and kids to run you ragged, it frees up a fair amount of time. And I really do love takin' care of people . . . just like my Bible namesake . . . I just don't have folks at home to do that for, so the people I meet get to benefit."

"Well, this person is beyond grateful," Hunter said with deep sincerity, not just for the nourishment, but for the obvious care and generosity that went into the preparation.

"It's absolutely my pleasure. But, now that our bellies are full, we need to tend to a few things before we close in on Port Huron."

"How much longer 'til we are there?"

"I'd say we'll be in spittin' distance within the hour. I need to pull these nets in so they don't get caught on anything as we move into more shallow water."

"Can I help?"

"Well, you should probably let that food settle for a few minutes. I'm used to eatin' on the go, but you're just getting your sea legs, so a little rest is advisable. When I have the nets prepped, you can help me drag 'em. I do it alone a lot of the time, but it sure goes smoother when you have more than one set of hands on the job."

"Sounds good, but don't go trying to do that solo because you're worried I might get a stomach ache. I'll be fine."

Martha looked over her shoulder at him and just sort of chuckled at his bravado.

Hunter leaned his head back against the metal panel behind him and realized he had eaten so fast, giving himself a little digestion time was fully appropriate. However, he did not anticipate being jarred awake by the side of the boat knocking against the pier and the clanging of harbor bells. Once he was alert enough to grasp his surroundings, he turned beet red from embarrassment and looked sheepishly around for Martha who was already on dock mooring the boat. She waved to the Harbor Master and then leaned down where Hunter could hear her speak.

> "This gal is a bit of a busy body, so just hang tight a minute. I'm gonna head her off at the pass and keep her from coming down here. I'll give you the go ahead when it's clear to come out and meet up with Jerusha."

Martha spun around and disappeared up the gangway before Hunter had the chance to be concerned. He tried to make himself as small as possible in the corner without looking like he was cowering. He knew it wouldn't matter much if someone did come down to the boat slip because there was nowhere for him to hide, so he was just hoping to stay out of view of passersby without looking like a stowaway if someone did see him.

After a few long minutes, Hunter heard heavy, booted footsteps approaching, and he prayed it was Martha. She resumed her tasks on the pier and spoke without looking at Hunter, giving him the low down.

> "So, Ronnie is distracted by something else now, but it ain't gonna last long, so you need to get moving. Jerusha is in a fishing tug off Pier 27—that's a much bigger boat than mine. We are about a football field away. Her boat is called Paine."

Hunter laughed, "That seems fitting."

Martha shook her head, "Not pain, as in an ache. Paine, with an 'e,' as in Thomas."

"Well, that confirms it. I thought I was noticing a pattern. So, is yours Rosa for Rosa Parks?"

Martha kept working and not making eye contact as she said, "No, although she was a revolutionary woman for sure. My Rosa is Rosa Luxemburg. She was part of a German insurgency during the first World War . . . and my great, great, great, and so on, aunt. But you don't have time for a history lesson. It's time to go."

Hunter jumped up and climbed onto the pier. He extended his hand for a handshake, but Martha grabbed him into a bone-crushing bear hug.

"I guess you're not much of a hugger, but I can't do it no other way."

Hunter stepped back and pulled himself together, but reached out and patted her on the back again as he was leaving, and said, "It's okay. I appreciate all you've done for me. I hope you get that family and home life you're dreaming of. Take care."

"Gosh. Thanks. Maybe someday I will. Maybe after I take that trip to New York. You take care too. You'll like Jerusha. She's a hoot."

Hunter nodded as he jogged up the slope to the walkway that would take him to his next transport. He tried to weave in with the others on the dock and walked with his head down to be as inconspicuous as possible.

The fishing tug with P-A-I-N-E in block letters on the side near the rear was rumbling and water churned from under the stern. It was a good four times the size of Martha's boat, and Hunter knew that would offer him better options for hiding, possibly even a bunk passing for comfort where he could rest since this portion of the trip would be roughly three days total on one vessel. He would not change boats again until he reached the Port of Illinois. This one would take him across Lake Huron, through the Mackinac Strait, and down Lake Michigan to Chicago. It would not be the longest segment of the journey, but it would be a long stretch without touching land, and Hunter was not looking forward to that. He hoped Martha was right and that he actually would like this woman, Jerusha, since he was going to be stuck with her for a while.

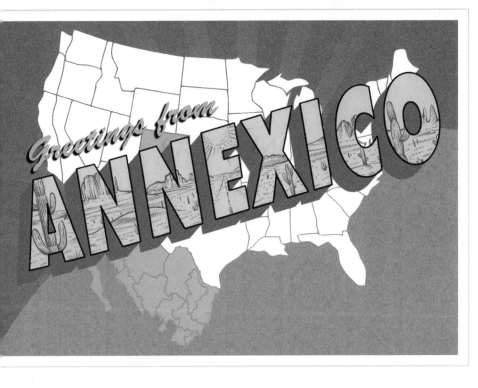

ZONE 5 – ANNEXICO

Ours is a land of expansion. Including the annexed regions of our southern border, this zone welcomes all. Our borders are open to anyone seeking a place to call home, looking for asylum from a world in turmoil, and wanting a gateway to everything this zone and those around it have to offer. There are no walls here, but you will find an open door for all those yearning to be free.

ZONE 5

ANNEXICO

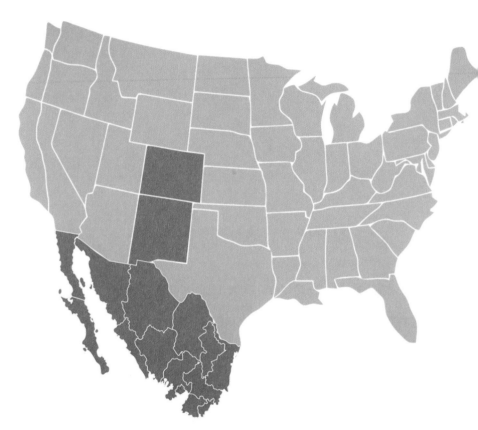

- COLORADO
- NEW MEXICO
- MEXICAN BORDER REGION

CHAPTER TEN

Hunter looked for anyone around the boat who seemed like they worked it and would know why he was there. Just as he was beginning to worry he was going to blow everything, a woman in her late twenties brushed past him with a crate hoisted onto her right shoulder and barked, "Don't just stand there. Grab something and come on!"

Hunter looked to her and then around him, then back to her. She paused before stepping on the plank affixed to the starboard side and winked at him. He wasn't sure what to make of her at all, but he realized he needed to get in gear. He saw a similar crate on a stack behind him and hefted one onto his shoulder and followed his guide onto the boat.

Once they were on board, she set the crate down and told Hunter to put his on top.

"You don't need to do anything else with that. The crew will get it below where it needs to be." She shoved her hand toward him and said, "I'm Jerusha. Welcome aboard!"

Hunter took her hand and she shook his vigorously and with a much stronger grip than her tiny frame suggested was possible.

"Hunter," he offered, while scanning his surroundings. The size of the vessel did not abate the undulation that triggered his nausea; however, he did feel he was adapting to it fairly well.

"Well, Hunter, let me show you around. My crew knows you're here, but not why," she began as she showed him around the deck.

"Umm . . . so, what do I tell them?"

"Nothing. They aren't going to be worrying about you. Sure, we have close quarters, but they have a job to do and it takes every minute of eighteen hours a day, and every ounce of concentration they have to keep from screwing something up. With what we do, there isn't any margin for error. One slip, best case scenario, just gets you a fine for violating catch regulations. Worst case, someone goes overboard, gets impaled, or some other gruesome mishap."

"You call those mishaps?"

Jerusha did not respond, but kept moving counterclockwise around the upper level of the boat. "You won't spend much time up here, but you need to watch out for flying winches . . . that's with an 'i,' not an 'e.'" She chuckled at her cleverness and looked for any sign that Hunter got the joke. If he did, he didn't let on, so she pressed forward.

"Anyway," she said, dragging it out to show her disappointment with his lack of appreciation for her humor.

"Huh? Oh, I get it."

Jerusha wasn't convinced and kept moving. Hunter moved quickly to catch up and tried apologizing.

"Look, you're going to have to give me a minute. You really threw me with that whole bit about getting impaled."

"Right. I forgot. They told me you were a chummer." She flung open the door to the bridge and went inside, laughing. He didn't know for sure what the term meant, but he knew enough to know it was a joke at his expense. Probably about his lack of experience on the water.

"Do you people have some kind of bulletin you circulate?" Hunter was getting frustrated, fearing he would not escape this stigma.

"What do you mean, *you people*?"

"This network or whatever. The Resistance."

"Okay, first of all, don't use that word here. As I said, my crew doesn't know why you're here. They won't care as long as you stay out of their way, but we don't need you yammering on about stuff they don't need to know. And, second, yeah, we kinda do. It's not an official newsletter, but there's a digital message board. You've been the headline for a couple of weeks now."

"Wait. What?" Hunter was both mortified and intrigued by the idea.

Jerusha laughed and slapped him on the back. "I'm just yankin' your chain. Not about the message board. It's how we stay off the radar and still manage to function while being scattered all over the country. I'm just teasin' about you being the headline. We do get updates about the op, but it's not really about you. But, boy is it easy to get your goat! You really need to lighten up a bit. Life out here is hard enough without taking every little thing so seriously."

Muttering only slightly under his breath, Hunter said, "Martha said you were a hoot. I don't think she knows what that word means."

"Hey, Martha is a gem. And she doesn't take things too seriously. That's why she appreciates my sense of humor."

"You're right about that. She is a gem. Look, we may have gotten off on the wrong foot here. I'm not that uptight. I'm just winging it out here, and I tend to not find gallows humor all that entertaining. But, you seem like you know what you're doing, and you have an impressive operation here. Plus, Martha thinks highly of you, so that's good enough for me. I'm also pretty beat. Is there a place I can rest for a bit?"

"Sure. I'll take you below deck where there is a bunk with your name on it." She opened a hatch and led him down a metal staircase. "We are going to pull out in the next twenty minutes or so. Just a few points to check. Once we are clear of the port, we'll be about our business and you should have some relative peace and quiet."

Hunter followed her down a short, tight corridor to a cabin that, while it didn't actually have his name on it, was clearly prepared for his use.

"That sounds great. I don't think I've slept more than a handful of hours since this whole thing began, and most of those were done propped up against something hard and metal," Hunter said while examining the narrow, but comfortable bunk.

"Well, you'll have a fair amount of alone time while you're with us. I'll wake you when we gather in the galley for dinner."

"Thanks, Jerusha."

"Everybody here calls me Ru. You might as well, too." She stepped out and pulled the door closed behind her. Hunter leaned back on the pillow and was out within seconds.

Hunter was sleeping soundly when Jerusha placed her hand on his foot and shook him awake. He was sleeping so soundly, in fact, he forgot where he was and bolted upright so quickly his head began spinning. He had to swing his feet down to the floor quickly and drop his head between his knees to keep from humiliating himself further.

Jerusha could tell he had given himself the spins and decided to resist the urge to make fun of him. She just stepped quietly toward the door, saying, "Soup's on."

Hunter lifted his head, and said, "Thanks. I'll be right up. Just want to splash some water on my face and shake off the sleep. I crashed hard."

She nodded and left him to pull himself together.

Up in the mess hall, fifteen women of varying ages and ethnicities were pressed together to make their way through the chow line before plopping themselves down at metal tables with benches bolted to the floor.

Hunter took his place at the end of the line and stood silently, knowing there was no hope of not standing out as the only man on board. Jerusha had told him they wouldn't pay any attention to him because they'd be focused on their work, but now they were eating, and not working, so he was very self-conscious and wondered what he should say if anyone spoke to him.

He accepted a tray of food that looked far better than he expected from this setting and went to sit in a corner by himself. If he hadn't been hoping to stay inconspicuous, his ego might have been a little bruised by the fact that the women, in fact, did not even look in his direction. They all had their heads down and were shoveling grub into their mouths. There were only the clinks of metal utensils against metal trays. No one uttered a word until they finished one by one and thanked the cook as they scraped any remnants of food (of which there were very few) into a barrel and stacked the trays on a table for the dishwasher to retrieve.

When Hunter was about halfway through his meal Jerusha came in, got her tray of food, and settled in next to him. She shoveled a forkfull of food into her mouth, swallowed in a gulp Hunter thought surely couldn't be healthy, and then spoke to him in little more than a whisper.

"How ya doin? Everything goin down okay?"

"Yes, I'm fine. It's actually very good. Doesn't come close to the sandwich Martha fed me, but it's still a lot better than the protein bars I have in my pack. Thank you."

"Aw, man! She made food for you? You don't know how lucky you are! . . . Or, I guess maybe you do."

"Yeah, I was in awe. She seems to have limitless talents."

"Sure does. She's a real asset to us, and a great friend. Like I said, a gem." She hesitated, and then continued as if revealing a carefully guarded secret. "Still, there seems to be a sadness in her."

Not wanting to talk out of school, Hunter simply said, "Hmm."

Jerusha could tell he was avoiding the topic, so she moved on.

"So, a couple things you need to know. We are currently about forty nautical miles north. We've shifted over to the Michigan side."

Hunter popped his head up to meet her eyes and asked with some alarm, "Is that safe?"

"Safer than not following our typical route. You're in Red Zone territory now, so there are border crossing concerns, but that's why you, my friend, are staying out of sight. In fact, I may bring breakfast down to you so we minimize your interaction with the crew. They won't have access to shore to tell anyone about you until we dock, but by then we'll be in Chicago, which is a Blue Zone, so it won't really matter."

"How does that work, anyway? Illinois . . . or what we called Illinois in my day . . . it's always been a pretty split state. I wasn't really surprised to see it go with the left, but I have been pretty shocked it didn't get consumed by the zones around it as a matter of practicality. It's like a Blue island in a sea of Red. I don't know how they hold on, especially with all the restrictions around passage be-tween Blue and Red Zones. They must be pretty isolated."

"In a word: commerce."

"How do you mean?"

"Well, first of all, you have to remember that after the pandemic wiped out so many people and the Midwest in particular was decimated in the eradication of the corn, people migrated to the population centers, and Chicago was the primary one in this region. People are just now beginning to repopulate the more rural areas. It's mostly those who lean Conservative, and while there are quite a few—especially here—they are starting over with not many resources. So, their economies are just getting their legs under them."

"Oh, yeah, that makes sense. How are they doing that?"

"As you'd expect. These areas in the middle of the country were the breadbasket at one time, lots of grains and other forms of agriculture were their way of life. Eventually they will be the primary food source for a lot of the country again, but they have to rebuild from nothing. In the meantime, they are importing a lot from the more established areas, which happen to be in the Blue Zones. That's why I said commerce is the lifeblood for a Blue island in the middle of this sea of Red. There are challenges for Blue Zone residents in moving around the country by land, but the waterways create some avenues for them that allow them to avoid checkpoints . . . unless they are going into a Red Zone. But, the big thing is that people who provide in-demand goods and services get some leniency at the borders. Like I said . . . commerce. Money still greases wheels, and if you have something to sell or barter with that the Red Zones don't have, there's a whole lot you can get around."

"I get that. But why don't they just set up shop in a Red Zone? Wouldn't that be easier? I hear they are better with taxes."

"They are, but take someone like my friend Alice. She is a beekeeper and farmer, and she cultivates stuff that doesn't grow so well in other regions, but one of the things she grows that you can't get most other places is horseradish. Did you know Illinois produces more of that than any other area?"

"I was not aware, but does that really make a difference?"

"Hell yeah, it does! I'm sure you know it goes great on a steak, but it is used in lots of natural remedies for different things. After the pandemic, a huge portion of the country stopped relying on conventional medicine and went the herbal route. Everything she grows is plant medicine, but the horseradish is hard to come by across most of the country, and the honey and honeycomb from the bees supplies a lot of the eastern Zones since the other territories where bees thrive are in the west."

"How do you know all of this?"

"Sweetie, I'm in transport. There's not a lot moved around this country, regardless of the Zone, that I don't know something about."

"So, where do you call home?"

"I'm what you'd call a Blue island girl."

"Do you like living there?"

"Mostly. Sure there are issues, but a lot of those are because of external influences, not things I dislike about the Zone itself."

"Like what?"

"Damned carpetbaggers, for one. I do wish the Blue Zones could figure out how to have free passage without letting any ol' so-and-so in. I get being welcoming to people looking for a better life, but some people are just after what they can mooch off the Blue Zone system without giving anything. They come for the benefits, but don't stay to contribute to the economy."

"That sounds like a big drain on resources. And there's nothing they can do about it?"

"Not at this point. They think the alternative is going to what the Red Zones do, which is requiring extensive background checks and interviews before they will grant a passport for travel, and regular re-screenings. My cousin works with a woman named Eleanor who was prevented from visiting her dying mother because of the stupid passport rules. Her mom still lived in what was Texas where she grew up. Eleanor lives in New Orleans—another Blue island—and they wouldn't approve her passage from there to come to her mother's bedside."

"Why not?! They have a process for that."

"Sure they do, but it's bogged down by bureaucracy and prejudice against particular Zones. New Orleans isn't just a Blue island, they went Blue while the rest of their state went Red, and they aligned with one of the most liberal Zones there is—New France. I think they are trying to make things as hard on those citizens as possible to get them to align with the rest of the Louisiana territory to make it all Red. Anyway, her mom died and she didn't get to say goodbye. It's such a tragedy; and for what? Logic tells me that there are happy mediums to be had, but this whole world has become so polarized that it seems like if something is proposed that might benefit someone you see as your ideological opponent, its' a nonstarter. It's like cutting off your nose to spite your face. It don't make any sense to me at all. But, that's the world we live in, and it's only getting worse. I think before all is said and done, we are looking at a more official and permanent split.

"You really think it will get that bad?"

"As I told you, I'm in transport. I move a lot of things and people around various parts of the country, so I see where things are headed and hear how people feel about it. So, yeah, I think it's basically already that bad. We just haven't had that final straw drop on the camel's back yet. But my gut says it's coming. I don't know what exactly is going on . . . why you are being moved in secret across the country . . . but I can't help but think it is going to lead to something big."

"I don't know what I'm heading into either, but I'm afraid you might be right."

"Well, it was nice chatting. I'd better get back to it."

Hunter nodded and said, "Same here. I mean . . . nice chatting with you."

With that, she stood up to leave. Before she left the galley, Hunter jumped up to stop her rather than calling to her across the room.

"So, um, I've kind of lost my sense of time and don't really know where we are in this leg. How much time do I have left with you?"

Jerusha smiled at his awkwardness and couldn't resist teasing him a bit. "Wow. You realize we only left port about five hours ago? I can't tell if you're ready to be rid of me or getting attached. Should I be offended or flattered?"

Hunter blushed for probably only the third time in his life, and said, "Oh, sorry . . . um, I didn't mean . . . um, I'm just trying to figure out where I am."

Laughing at his discomfort, she said, "I'm just bustin' your chops. We will make good time overnight because we can move a little faster than during the day when the traffic is higher, so by the time you wake up tomorrow, we will be on the northern end of Michigan, but still about nine hours outside of Mackinac Strait where we move into Lake Michigan. Does that help?"

"Yeah, it does. Thanks. See you in the morning."

"Remember, just sit tight and I will bring breakfast down to you. We need to keep you off the radar, especially with where we will be tomorrow until late afternoon."

"Got it. Breakfast in bed it is."

She laughed at him and just walked out.

Hunter sat back down at the table, pondering the information download he'd just received. He picked at the rest of the food on his plate that had grown cold while he was enthralled in his conversation with Jerusha and finally decided to dump it and go back to the seclusion of his quarters.

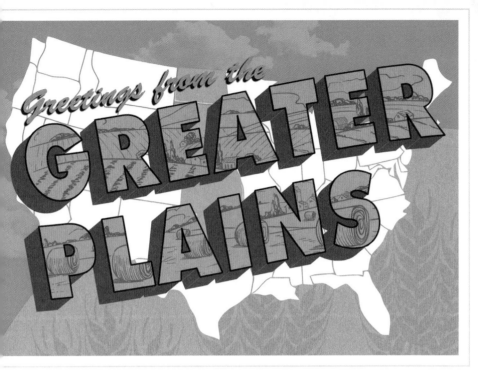

ZONE 6 – GREATER PLAINS

We're back and better than ever! Our amber waves of grain and fruited plains are ready to produce again and we want you to join us in a bountiful harvest. We need your help sowing this majestic land so we can reap the benefits of the fully recovered and fertile soil. Come be a part of restoring Zone 6 to its former glory!

ZONE 6

GREATER PLAINS

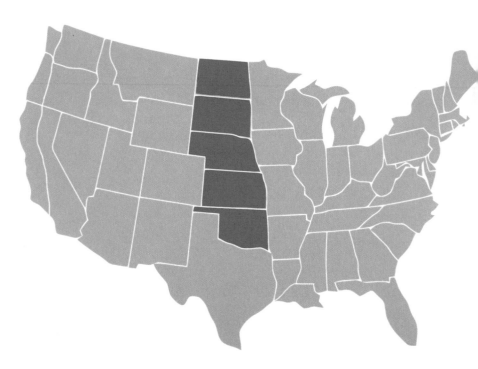

- NORTH DAKOTA
- SOUTH DAKOTA
- NEBRASKA
- KANSAS
- OKLAHOMA

CHAPTER ELEVEN

Hunter pried his eyes open at 6:00 a.m. and realized he hadn't moved from the position he was in when he passed out at around 9:00 p.m. He didn't recall having slept that long since his long sleep in space. His limbs felt heavy and stiff. As he stretched himself upright he remembered Jerusha had told him she would bring his breakfast to him. The thought of food immediately made his stomach gurgle and groan. He hoped they had an early call so he wouldn't have to wait long to eat. He realized in that moment that he hadn't had much of an appetite since this journey started, but it was beginning to come back with a vengeance.

He pulled his dopp kit from his pack and began freshening up and it wasn't but a few minutes before a forceful rap on the door startled him out of his routine. Not bothering to remove the toothbrush tucked in his cheek, he shouted, "Come in!"

The door creaked open and Jerusha stepped in, carrying a tray she nearly dropped when she saw her shirtless stowaway, back to her, rinsing his mouth at the tiny sink in the corner of the cabin. Hunter turned to greet her. Completely unaware of the fact that he was not just a man in an ocean of women, but an extremely attractive one, he was oblivious to the flush creeping up her neck. He gave her a wink and a smile over the meal she presented and told her he was starving and her timing was perfect.

Jerusha excused herself, saying, "I'll leave you to it. I have things to see to on deck. I'll come back for the tray later. Remember, stay down here until I tell you otherwise."

Hunter nodded, already having a mouth full of food. He did not notice her lingering for a moment longer, as he had already turned his focus back to the sustenance he'd been craving.

The remaining time on board the PAINE passed as a blur for Hunter. There were a series of brief encounters with Jerusha as she brought his meals and returned for his empty tray in between her duties overseeing the bridge and the crew. Hunter sensed she would have liked to stay longer each time she visited, but he knew this was not an engagement he could indulge. He suspected she knew as much. He had already experienced firsthand what happened when women became territorial. They returned from their outer space travels to a world where there was a shortage of men, period. As one of less than a dozen worldwide who was not affected by the pandemic and was still fertile, he was a hot commodity. That didn't change much with the cure. Being adrift on vessels where men were even more rare made him a unicorn, and that was not lost on him as he accurately assessed he was the subject of all the chatter on board. He understood the temptation he must present, which made him believe Jerusha wasn't just trying to keep him hidden from cargo inspectors.

Hunter had a lot of time to himself and his mind tilled the fertile ground of conspiracy and mistrust around how the government had handled the manufacture of the cure. There had been many problems with it and with the insemination of women since the repopulation program started. Just as the cause for the collapse of the world's population took years to determine, the problems with the efforts to rebuild it also took time to emerge. Things seemed to be going well for a while, but eventually there were signs that the experiment was going sideways. In some cases, pregnancies failed, but the rates were not out of line with historically average figures for miscarriages. The big surprise was in the continued birth defects that began to present in larger numbers. Some of them were minor, but some were proving to be fatal. There were increased occurrences in illnesses in infancy, but a significant portion did not reveal symptoms until the children were older. Because of the incremental nature of the data coming in, they were just beginning to identify trends. Hunter had come across some early reports before he left DC, and was carrying them with him to share with Major Statham once they met up in Jarbridge. He did not know what she planned to show him there, but his gut told him these things were somehow linked.

Because there wasn't much else to do as he awaited his arrival in Chicago, Hunter spent his time over the remaining two days thinking about Lydia and how much he looked forward to seeing her in person again, then worrying about what she possibly could have gotten herself into that required this incredible passage over land and sea that was making him feel like a relay baton. He hated not knowing more about what was in store for him, but there was a part of him that felt it was better that he didn't know. Had there been confirmation rather than just a nagging feeling she was in real danger he likely would have made a beeline to her straight through forbidden territory and wrecked their chances for remaining in the shadows. All the same, knowing he had two more weeks in these aquatic catacombs before he met up with her kept him on edge.

*****

At roughly 3:00 in the afternoon on September 9th, nearly five full days after he left DC, Jerusha banged on the cabin door and flung it open, not waiting for a response. She merely leaned her head in and announced,

> "Heads up. We are about to dock and you need to be
> ready to roll."

Hunter was on his feet with her first word, grabbed his bag that he'd already prepped in anticipation of this moment, and straightened the blanket on his bunk.

"Whoa! Slow down, Sparky. I didn't mean right now. You have a few minutes."

"Okay. I just don't want to delay my connection."

"You're okay. Remember, you're staying the night here and leaving predawn."

"Oh, right. It will be nice to have more than a few minutes on land."

"Enjoy it. Once you hit the Mississippi, you won't set foot on land again for probably ten days."

"Don't remind me. I can't think about it that far in advance. I have to take this one step . . . or ship . . . at a time."

"Well, good luck with that. Look, I'm not going to be able to be able to see you off because I'll have too much going on once we dock, so I'll say my goodbyes now. We are coming in to Calumet Harbor. You are going to head up to the pier when you disembark. Keep in mind this marina is much bigger than any you've seen so far. It's strictly industrial and is a maze of shipping containers and warehouses. It's easy to get lost, so pay close attention to your surroundings and follow this map that will guide you to the perimeter. We will be in the Port Authority district, so you need to be careful. Even though this is a friendly area, you are supposed to be camping in Canada, so we can't risk you popping up on a different radar. You're going to need to find your way to a rail station just on the other side of the Port Authority offices. There will be a young man waiting for you inside the terminal. His name is Joshua. He is going to take you to the hostel where you will spend the night and get you to your transport in the morning.

"Are there any identifying features you can provide so I'm not walking up to every boy in the station? Talk about drawing attention to myself."

Jerusha laughed at the image that conjured, and said, "He looks like a younger, more masculine version of me. He's my kid brother."

"Oh. I guess I should have made that connection. Joshua, Jerusha. I'm really losing my edge."

"Don't be too hard on yourself. That's not an obvious leap. Anyway, it was good meeting you, Hunter. I really appreciate what you're doing for the Resistance. If our paths cross again, I hope the next time it will be under more enjoyable circumstances."

"It was great meeting you too. You are an impressive young woman, and I do hope our paths cross again at some point. I appreciate the safe passage you provided as well as the insights and great conversation."

"Okay. Well . . . I better get going. This beast isn't gonna park itself. Just hang tight here for fifteen minutes and then come up on deck and someone will help you get to the pier. See ya around."

Hunter nodded and sat back down on his bunk to count the minutes.

*****

The hostel was a misnomer it turned out. Hunter had imagined what that word meant in his youth—a boarding house of sorts with rooms full of bunks and lots of barely bathed, wide-eyed adventurers barely old enough to vote. The place Joshua took him was actually his apartment. It was a simple but tidy two-bedroom, two-bath flat in Joliet, outside the city. Joshua explained that his place was owned by the Resistance and he managed it as a way-station for members trying to move about the country without passports. At the moment, Hunter was the only guest, which was prearranged for security reasons, but they have had as many as fifteen travelers staying there at any given time.

Joshua had prepared dinner ahead of time and told Hunter he could heat it up whenever he was ready. Even though it had taken two hours to get out of the port, find Joshua, and get to the hostel, it was still a bit too early to eat.

Hunter said, "I'm hungry, but if I eat now, it will be a long time until my next meal based on this schedule I'm on. I think I'll take a real shower and relax a bit, if that's okay with you."

Joshua smiled and said, "You know, I'm not going to put a lock on the refrigerator at 9:00 p.m. If you get hungry in the middle of the night, you are welcome to leftovers or there's deli meat and some other stuff in the fridge. I want you to make yourself at home here. But take your time and chill out. I guess you probably haven't had access to a hot shower in days."

"I haven't, and I'm surprised you were able to tolerate being enclosed in a car with me."

Laughing, Joshua confessed, "You know, I was going to suggest a shower if you hadn't beat me to it. But, honestly, you smell fresh as a daisy compared to a lot of the people who come through here."

"I can imagine! Okay. Well, I'm going to take your advice and get cleaned up. It may be my last chance to be fully clean until I reach my final destination."

Hunter thanked Joshua and retreated to the guest bedroom where he unpacked his bag and gathered his toiletries and a change of clothes.

While he was in the shower, Joshua took the liberty of gathering his discarded clothing and putting it in the washer. When Hunter emerged from his steamy retreat, he found a note on the side table along with a bottle of water and a bowl of popcorn.

> *Had to run an errand. Will be back by 7:00. Thought you might like a snack to hold you over til dinner. Feel free to use the television or library.*
>
> *–Josh*

Hunter wandered around the apartment, investigating the space, and then plopped down on the worn but sturdy sofa. He leaned back against the surprisingly plush cushions and was tempted to kick his feet up and stretch out, but wasn't comfortable being quite that "at home" as an overnight guest. He leaned forward and sifted through a stack of weathered books piled on the sleek metal coffee table in front of him. They all were published long ago, many before he was born. He had noticed during his self-guided tour that the furniture was good quality, but a hodgepodge of styles and ages, which supported his supposition that everything in the place was furnished through donations, but donations that came from people of means.

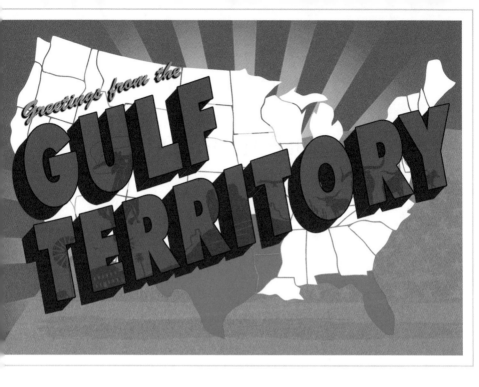

ZONE 7 - GULF TERRITORY

The Gulf Territory is the last bastion of sovereignty and the first line of defense against those who want to infiltrate our land from southern regions. We stand firm in our convictions and if you share them, you'll find comfort and aid within our borders. A hard day's work is what we expect here, but if you're up for it, that will take you far. If you have what it takes, try us on for size. All others need not apply.

ZONE 7

GULF TERRITORY

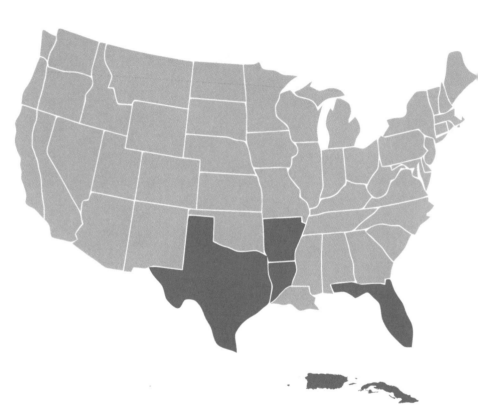

- TEXAS
- FLORIDA
- NORTHERN LOUISIANA
- PUERTO RICO
- CUBA

CHAPTER TWELVE

Hunter was deep into a biography on Lee Iacocca when Joshua returned, carrying a box full of donated pantry items and canned goods. He hauled it into the kitchen and began unpacking. The opening above the sink afforded him a clear view of Hunter who had put the book down on the table and was trying to straighten up and, it seemed, cover up his choice of reading material.

Joshua laughed and said, "Sorry we don't have anything more contemporary, but we get by on what people decide are leftovers or cast offs. Sometimes we score big. Sometimes not so much. I guess people like to hold on to the books they really loved or the ones they think will make them look smart to guests."

Hunter looked up and said, "It wasn't too bad. I just don't read a lot of fiction and this was somebody I'd heard of." He had come to the kitchen door and was leaning against the doorframe. "Can I help with that?"

Joshua pulled his head back out of the pantry where he was stacking their windfall and said, "Oh, no that's okay. It's cramped quarters in here and I kind of have a system."

"You sure? I hate to not earn my keep."

"Yes, I'm sure. And, besides, you are earning your keep by going on this trek to do the work of the Resistance."

"Yeah, I guess so. Have you been involved long?"

"Pretty much grew up in it. I was born after the pandemic had spread pretty wide. Jerusha was ten when I came along. It took both of our parents when I was pretty young, so she basically raised me. She joined the Resistance as soon as they'd let her, and we've been working with them in different capacities ever since."

"I haven't really met many guys born during that time. In fact, most of the men I've encountered since I came back are much older. You young guys are a rarity. That must be weird."

"Well, first of all, I'm old by this world's standards. I was born in 2034."

"Wait, so that means you are among the last of the male children born, until they made this cure! And, wow. That means Jerusha is about my age . . . well, my age without the gap. She definitely doesn't look it."

"Yeah, she got the good genes. And, yeah, I am part of what they call the last generation. And so many of my peers were sick in infancy. Many ended up dying."

"I heard somethings about that in our early briefings. Things like heart disease and cancer?"

"Yeah, but there were some really weird disorders too that they learned are anomalies only attached to Y chromosomes. We also learned later that there is this disease called Swyer Syndrome. It's a mutation of the Y and it affects sex organ development, which causes infertility."

"Is that how all of this happened?"

"No, but it didn't help."

"How do you know all of this stuff?"

"I don't just run this hostel. Part of why I took this gig is because I'm studying to be a geneticist and epidemiologist."

"Wow! That's impressive."

"Well, it's pretty personally motivated."

"Makes sense. Hey! Maybe you can help me decipher some reports I have."

"Sure, I'll try. What kinds of reports?"

"Stuff I shouldn't be showing you, but since this whole expedition is breaking the rules, I guess it can't hurt."

Hunter went to retrieve the documents he had tucked away in his bag, and Joshua finished putting away the supplies. They sat down on the sofa together and Hunter began explaining what he had and how he'd come by it.

"I guess you know, I've been working for the president in DC. I have a pretty high level of clearance, but I was still surprised to see this come across my desk. They seem to be data summaries of the birthing statistics and occurrences of diseases."

Hunter handed the file over to Joshua who began skimming the pages, and with each one his eyes grew wider.

Hunter was getting concerned and couldn't wait for him to finish. "What is it?"

"It looks like we have not solved the problem."

"What does that mean?"

"It means the cure turned the Y-chromosome back on, but the same diseases are showing up all over again, and in high numbers."

"What?! Why is that happening?"

"My guess . . . which does happen to be a very well-educated one . . . is that we didn't fix the underlying problem with the initial gene mutation related to the corn. I don't know how they screwed that up, but it's spreading like wildfire. It doesn't help that in their efforts to boost the male population as quickly as possible they were doing a lot of embryo selection to prioritize male babies."

"Why would that make things worse?"

"Basically because they were limiting the gene pool. The odds are greater that you will come across zygotes with mutations if you don't have as many to choose from."

"I think I understand. But don't the odds stay the same regardless of the size of the grouping?"

"You're thinking of ratios. We are dealing with probabilities and odds."

"Aren't those the same thing?"

"No. Think of it this way: say you have a bag of marbles. Five of them are red, three are blue, and two are yellow. So, a probability is the number of chances something could occur. The probability that you pull out a blue marble is three divided by ten which is 30% or 0.3. Now, odds are the number of times something can occur compared to the number of times it can't. In our bag there are three blue marbles, but there are seven marbles that are not blue, so the odds for drawing a blue marble are 3:7, or in probability terms it would be about 43% or .43. Got it?"

Hunter nodded and said, "Yeah, I got it. But, translate that for me into the impact on our repopulation project."

"Well, the smaller the number, the closer the probability and odds numbers will be. Since we are talking about the world's population, we are working with significantly higher numbers. There are so many people in this set that there is a low probability of these mutations showing up because they don't happen all that often. We're talking numbers like one in 400,000. But, if you, for example, extract all of the embryos without a Y chromosome—or, to use our previous example, remove the red marbles—you have just jacked up your odds for pulling a blue marble. Make sense?"

"Okay. Yeah, that does. Thanks for explaining it. You are a good teacher. Is that what you want to do with this?"

"No, I want to be in a lab solving the problem rather than talking about it."

"Fair enough, and really admirable. How much longer do you have in school?"

"I am finished with my coursework and now am starting medical rotations."

"And you don't want to be a doctor and treat infectious disease or something?"

"I already did that."

"Wait. So, you already had a career as a doctor? Why did you leave that and start over in school? That seems like a pretty drastic decision."

"It is. It was. But it was necessary. Our healthcare system is a mess, and I just couldn't be a part of it any longer. I didn't feel like I was accomplishing anything, helping anybody. This seemed like a more direct route to making a difference."

"What happened? It seems like being on the front lines would have been precisely the place to make a difference."

"You'd think," Joshua said, somewhat absent-mindedly, standing up to pace as he looked over the reports again.

"Hey, Joshua, come back to me."

Joshua looked up and realized he had zoned out. "Oh, sorry. I get sucked into data so easily. Yet another reason I'm better in a lab."

"Okay, but why did you leave your practice?"

"Because there was no practice." Seeing Hunter was confused and frustrated, Joshua sat back down and continued, "Look, I'm sure you know that the Blue Zones have free healthcare, and the Red Zones have limited liability. I went to school at Vanderbilt in Nashville, TN, which was an incredible medical school, so I joined a practice there after I finished interning, which was in a Red Zone."

"Yeah, each one uses it as their big selling point. Seems to me the Red Zone would be an ideal place for you as a doctor. Why are you in a Blue Zone now?"

"Here's the issue in a nutshell: doctors don't want to be in Blue Zones because they can't make any money because healthcare is free and they have much higher liabilities—malpractice insurance is astronomical. That means they migrate to Red Zones. But, no patients want to use them because most can't afford it, so they go to Blue Zones for free healthcare. And the ones who can afford it still don't want to use them because they're afraid that if something goes wrong, they can't get fair compensation for it and it will take too long to get any kind of judgment. And the thing is, without liability hanging over their heads, there are doctors who will take short cuts and the care they give is not as effective or holistic."

"Man, I thought the limited liability thing was a good idea because of how many frivolous lawsuits there are. Before I left for Proxima b, that was a huge problem. But it sounds like that isn't solving the problem and nobody is winning here."

"Limited Liability has its place, but the way it's being executed at the moment isn't working. Still too much abuse. There has to be a better way than running to both extremes, but I'm not sure if we will get people to set aside their personal interests long enough to see where there is balance. I hope that if I can find cures for the things that are causing the biggest health problems, the demand might decrease, and then we can talk real solutions. Anyway, that's what drove me back to school, and Chicago is home, so that's why I moved back to a Blue Zone. Education is also cheaper here."

"That's very ambitious. But, I gotta tell you, we may need someone like you in the meantime who can explain what's going on and why we need to take a step back from this aggressive campaign. It kind of feels like we are in a law of diminishing returns in this repopulation project where they think the more they push out the better off we'll be, but I don't know if that's true."

"Hunter, you don't have to be a geneticist to figure that out. Just a human being."

"Well, we are dealing with politicians and business people, so . . .," deciding to let that lie, Hunter moved on, "So, what are we looking at in terms of . . . I hate to put it this way . . . but, what are we seeing in terms of failures."

"I can't really tell from what you have here because the data is incomplete, but if this trend line continues, I'd say we could quickly undo all that we've achieved in the last two years."

"Seriously? That would be devastating . . . and a big fucking waste!" Hunter was really alarmed at the possibilities that washed over him.

"Oh, that's right! You could be the father of quite a lot of those kids."

"No, I only have one as far as I know. I gave them plenty of samples when we first returned for all of the testing they did on us, but I wasn't part of the group that signed on to stay on the stud farm. I considered it, but I was called to DC and never made it back there. Of course, I don't know what they did with anything they had leftover, so there's no telling, I guess."

"Wow. That's quite a lot to consider. But, back to your comment. Yes, it would be a huge waste. Too much loss. I was afraid of this when they started rushing out the cure."

"Yeah. Explain something to me. Why were things looking so good for the first two years? This data looks to be really new."

"Again, I can't say for sure because I am limited in the information I have, so this is a guess, but, first you have to remember that these sorts of things do take time to show up in numbers high enough to get attention. That said, I think the numbers you're seeing there for birth defects, diseases, and deaths are children fathered by men with the cure, not ones that are offspring of the crew."

"Oh, that has to be it. Man, I have so much to tell Lydia and I don't know if it can wait until I get to Nevada. But I'm not supposed to make contact. I have a number, but it's a one use only kind of thing."

"I can get this information to her through the pipeline. The rest of us can still communicate. You are incommunicado because no one is supposed to know where you are."

"Hey, that would be great! I don't know if it is relevant to why I'm meeting her, but it would be good for her to have this info anyway while I'm still traveling."

"Absolutely. This is a major problem and it will be of urgent interest to the Resistance."

Hunter sighed heavily and released the tension he'd been holding in his
whole body since the conversation began. Joshua patted him on the
shoulder and told him to relax while he pulled together some dinner.

ZONE 8 - THE HEARTLAND

At the center of the country, The Heartland is the heartbeat of America. We are proud, salt-of-the-earth people and welcome anyone wanting to join us in a simpler way of life. If you're looking for an escape from the hustle and bustle of the coastal cities, we've got room for ya.

ZONE 8

THE HEARTLAND

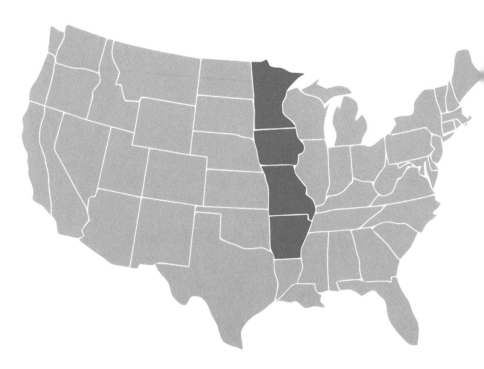

- MISSOURI
- ARKANSAS
- IOWA
- MINNESOTA

CHAPTER THIRTEEN

Joshua drove Hunter to Peoria, IL where he would make his next connection. There were no toll roads or check points along this very Blue two-hour stretch, so it was safe to travel by road, and this allowed him to skip several tedious hours of passage through the channel and lock system that connected Chicago to the Mississippi River. In Peoria, he boarded a grain barge that went through Grafton, IL, where the Illinois River opened into the Mighty Mississippi. From there it would be a straight, but arduous and sometimes treacherous journey where he would be flanked on both sides by Red Zones until he reached New Orleans. Hunter knew this posed the most threat, so he was not eager to wade into these waters.

The car-float barge Hunter boarded looked like all the others in the harbor and was loaded with rail cars, but the tug out front of it was stamped on its flank with simple block letters, Harriet, and he was sure he knew what this referenced, though he was curious about why they chose this particular name. He would soon find out.

There was little communication with his contact who was operating the tug. She guided him between the two rows of railcars, to a ventilated boxcar that he prayed would not be his home for the next nine days. She slid the side door open and told him to stay out of sight unless instructed otherwise. Before he could ask she confirmed there were no other options, that this was the safest as it would provide him with air, even if it wasn't the freshest, and he would have access to potable water here, which the other cargo boxes did not provide. She told him he would have roommates, but they were temporary as they were being unloaded at a port about two days down river. Hunter thanked her, and figured she would let him know when he was supposed to find other accommodations, so he began looking around for a manure-free corner where he could settle in. Even with the venting slats that allowed bars of light to come through, it was still pretty dark, so he fished his flashlight out of a side pocket and nudged his way past a cluster of dairy cows none too happy to have a human traveling companion. He found a stack of hay bales in one corner that he determined would be the best place for him to set up camp and tugged a few into a platform of sorts where he could stretch out and store his packs.

The space provided to him was not intended for human habitation, but it was full of great bedding and he discovered Joshua had included a camping blanket as well, which would be all he needed for a decent night's sleep. He definitely felt like a train-hopper, and it stoked a bit of the adventurous spirit that led to his joining the Alpha Centauri crew in the first place, and the nostalgia that arose made him a little less resentful about this trip and fueled his sense of purpose. He decided from that moment until whatever end might come, he would give this everything he had. What he was doing was important, and too many people were taking big risks to support him in this endeavor. It had to come off without a hitch.

With this new sense of pride in what he was doing, Hunter began nesting a bit, sorting through his supplies and bundling them into plastic bags Joshua had included according to the type of meal—breakfast, lunch, dinner, snack. Joshua had filled a pack with portable rations—protein bars, instant soup packets, and a mixture of government issue Meals Ready to Eat that Hunter was sure predated his time in the military and freeze-dried meals for camping. There were the basics that made a simple camp kitchen, including a compact gas stove with a small propane canister, a collapsible bowl, utensil set, and 32 oz. bottle filled with filtered water. The water wouldn't last him the whole trip, though there were enough food supplies to survive a zombie apocalypse. Having access to a water source helped, but he realized he would have to save the food requiring heating until he wasn't sleeping on kindling.

He knew better than to leave his supplies accessible because grain plus hay plus dark, warm corners equals rodents. He was already worried they could chew through the canvas of his pack, but he figured being mostly dried goods, they would not emit much odor. Still, he searched the room for a hook or something that would elevate his goods. The best he was able to do was string a length of the climbing rope he brought with him as a prop from one side bar to another, careful not to leave much visible from the outside. He felt good about his set up and settled in for a rest. It was still very early in the day when he felt the jolt of the tug pulling the barge into motion and Hunter could tell this newfound energy around his mission would not let him sleep. He pulled down the pack Joshua had given him and retrieved a protein bar and he discovered Joshua had also slipped in the book Hunter had been reading the night before and a couple other selections. Hunter had tried to reject the supplies, not wanting to be an imposition or to be weighed down, but as he inventoried the bag, he was beyond grateful that Joshua didn't take no for an answer.

*****

In the dark of night Hunter was poked awake by a shadowy figure who told him to get his things because he had to move. He stood, shook out his blanket and folded it before stuffing it in his personal pack. He had anticipated his relocation was coming, so he had untethered the cord stringing up his goods and had them ready beside him for when the call came. He followed the figure out the door and breathed in the cool, crisp air of predawn that was a blessed relief from the barnyard aroma he'd been inhaling. She was already several paces ahead of him and looked back for him to catch up. She heaved open the side panel of another car not slated for removal until New Orleans. He had another week on this vessel and figured this is where he would remain for the duration. It was not as ventilated as the cattle car, so the air had its own musty, languid quality, but at least it wasn't saturated with the stench of ammonia. Although, Hunter did come to enjoy the gentle lowing of the cows through the night. It was somehow soothing to him.

This new space was full of pallets loaded with cotton, hemp, and other processed feed grains loaded there in Memphis, TN, where they had stopped into the third day of their journey. He found a stack of cotton bales that weren't as comfortable as they appeared and settled in. As he was unpacking he heard the faintest, most delicate sneeze, so insignificant he almost second guessed himself, but then he heard a slight gasp and knew he was not alone. He sat for a moment, deciding what course to take. He was supposed to be staying off the radar, but something told him whoever was hiding in the recesses of this boxcar was just as intent on not being discovered. He decided to acknowledge their presence and try to disarm the situation. He spoke in a clear but barely audible voice.

"Look, I don't know who you are or why you're here, but I'm guessing we're both concerned about privacy. I won't bother you, you don't bother me, and we'll get along just fine as long as this ride lasts. Okay?"

For what seemed like several minutes there was an electrically charged silence. Then a soft, quivering, very Southern voice spoke up.

"Okay, Mistah, I don't mean no harm. We just tryin to get to Nawlins without no trouble."

Hunter was completely taken aback, not expecting to hear from a young girl. He had figured it was a vagabond hitching a free ride or maybe a comrade in arms in this still to be defined revolution. A fragile teenager was not in his calculations, and he did not know how to proceed. Eventually, he gathered himself and tried to address her more gently.

"Hon, I don't know what circumstances brought you here to this . . . this hard way of travel, but this is no place for a child. Why don't you come out and let's find you a more suitable form of transportation?"

Panic rising in her voice, "Naw. Mistah, I can't do that. Please don't tell nobody I'm here. Please. You'll be killin' me for sho."

"Wait, wait. Calm down. I'm not reporting you to anyone, but . . .," Hunter was beginning to think he was creating a big problem, so he stepped toward the voice slowly, and said, "Look, I don't want to upset you. I'm just concerned. Listen, can you just come out and talk to me face to face? My name is Hunter. What's yours?"

Hunter heard her suck in a deep breath and then she whispered, "Felicia."

He asked her to repeat it. "I . . . I'm Felicia. And my friend, Cassie, she here too, but she more shy than me."

The voice grew louder and Hunter could tell she was moving closer. Then a tiny frame with a very round belly emerged from the shadows and a shadow of her own just as slight and nearly as pregnant followed her. It took everything he had for Hunter to not gasp himself.

He tried to be as comforting as possible, but he knew he was way out of his depth here. He fumbled around and tried to find somewhere the two could sit comfortably and patted the surface like he was trying to summon a dog to sit.

"Here, why don't you get off your feet."

"Thanks, Mistah. I am tired. We had to walk to the port from Egypt.

Hunter laughed, thinking she was being hyperbolic. She looked at him with confusion and a bit of hurt.

"Why you laughin'? That's a long ways to go on foot, especially when you walkin' for two."

"I'm sorry. It's just you said Egypt and that sounded funny to me."

"Yeah, Egypt, Tennessee, north side of Memphis. We walked nearly all night."

"Oh! I'm so sorry. I just . . . never mind. You must be exhausted."

"You ain't from around here, is you?"

"No, I'm not. I've been traveling for quite some time. But, at least I didn't have to walk it."

"I'm pretty used to it. We don't have no car and I had to get to work somehow and can't always afford a bus."

"Felicia, is it?" She nodded. "Well, Felicia, I think you could use a break. Do you have anything to eat or drink?"

"Well, I had a couple a sandwiches I packed for the trip, but the baby got real hungry on the way, so I only have half left. And Cassie, she only had an apple."

"Oh, that's no good. I have plenty of food here. You need some better nourishment, especially in your condition."

"Thank you, Mistah. I'm sorry, I forgot your name already."

"It's Hunter."

"Well, Mistah Hunter, Cassie and I thank you from the bottom of our empty stomachs."

Hunter handed each of them a protein bar and promised they would share some hot food later once they were moving out of the port and he wouldn't have to worry about the smells attracting attention. He watched them inhale their food and exchange glances of reassurance that this was okay.

After they finished eating, they sat for a moment in silence, and then Cassie leaned over and whispered in Felicia's ear. Felicia shook her head fiercely, but Cassie nudged her persistently until she sighed and said, "Okay!" with the most exasperation she could muster.

"Mistah Hunter, Cassie wants to know . . .," Cassie shoved her hard enough to shift her body over a few inches, and she pushed back gently before continuing, ". . . okay, *we* want to know how come you is in here too. Why's you hidin'? You look like somebody who could tell anybody where he gonna go and what he gonna do and they can't do nothin' about it."

Hunter had a feeling some form of this question was coming and he had been rehearsing an answer, but her last comment made him rethink what he had prepared. He laughed at her characterization of him and realized she might be put off by his sense of humor again.

"Felicia, you flatter me. I've learned that there is always someone who's going to be able to tell you where you can go and what you can do, no matter how tough or powerful or rich you are. The truth is, I'm going somewhere I've never been before, never even heard of, because a friend is in trouble and needs me. The trouble is, there are people who would want to cause more trouble for her if they knew I was coming to help, so I have to do it in secret."

"So, you're like a hero or a knight in shiny armor, ain't ya?!"

"Well, I don't know about all that, but I am trying to do whatever I can to protect my friend."

Felicia let a coy grin creep across her face and said in a very sing-songy tone that signaled her youth, "Is she your *girl*friend?" putting extra emphasis on "girl."

Hunter blushed a little, much to the delight of the girls who didn't miss a beat. He let them revel in their giggles for a moment and then said,

"Well, Felicia, that's not really your business, but since we are travel companions, I'll just say that I don't know what kind of friendship it is right now. We've been really busy with work and haven't spent much time together lately. Not even in the same zone a lot of that time. So, for now, we'll just stick with friend. Okay?"

Felicia and Cassie were clearly disappointed, but said in unison, "Okay."

Hunter whipped his head in Cassie's direction, stunned to have heard her, and said, "Oh! You *can* speak!"

She just giggled and leaned over behind Felicia to hide her face.

"Well, girls, now that I've told you about me, how about a little give and take? Why are you on this barge, hiding in this car?"

The merriment seemed to dissolve instantly. Felicia looked up doe-eyed and Cassie stared at him with renewed insecurity.

"I'm sorry. I just can't say. I know it's not fair after you

shared your food with us and was so nice to talk to us.
But, it's just . . . it could be dangerous to say out loud."

"Felicia, what kind of trouble are you in? I'm not trying to
hurt you or make problems for you, but I think you need
someone. It's not safe for girls your age to travel so far
under these circumstances."

"We fine! And we ain't girls, by the by. I'm nineteen, and
Cassie's eighteen and a half!" Felicia shouted indignantly,
more over the accusation that they were children than
the suggestion they needed help. She turned in a huff
and said over her shoulder, "I think we best stay on our
side and you on yours."

Hunter suspected they weren't nearly that old, but he regretted the
hard press and decided to let them initiate the next conversation . . .
which he knew would come because, their trust issues notwithstanding,
they wanted to talk and they needed guidance . . . and food.

ZONE 9 - GREATER LAKES

Here, you'll find all kinds of options to earn a living and even more ways to enjoy living at the end of the day. The Great Lakes are as diverse as they are large in the kinds of catch you'll haul in and the types of boating you'll enjoy. If hunting is what you prefer, our big game is abundant. With many forms of industry available and access to the greatest channel for shipping and receiving goods outside of the coasts, you'll have everything you need to live well in the Greater Lakes Zone.

ZONE 9

GREATER LAKES

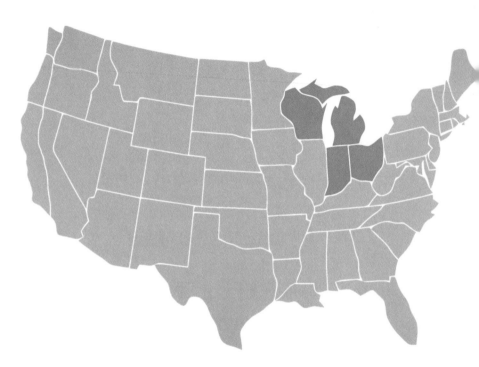

- MICHIGAN
- OHIO
- INDIANA
- WISCONSIN

CHAPTER FOURTEEN

That evening, as Hunter was heating some bottled water to mix with a pouch of dehydrated Brunswick stew, he heard rustling from the girls' corner and eventually, Felicia poked her head out from between two palettes. She stayed back at a vantage point that she thought was out of sight, but made her visible to Hunter's perspective. She watched every motion intently as he prepared his dinner, unaware that he could see her and was making more of a production of the procedure than was necessary in order to capture her attention. He was also making enough for three.

Just as he was about to eat, she stepped forward with a bit of consternation, and glared at him. Then she said, "You ain't as nice as you put on, Mistah Hunter. How you gon' make all that good smellin' food that you offered us just a while ago and then go and eat it all yoself? Just cuz we ain't want to tell you our private business."

Hunter acted as though he had forgotten she was there and said, "Oh! I'm sorry. You're right, it is impolite of me not to share. Would you and Cassie like to join me?"

"Um . . . well, you gonna be askin' more nosy questions?"

"No. I'm going to be too busy eating."

"Well, okay then. I guess if you got extry. Don't like seein' food go to waste."

"I have plenty."

Felicia turned to call to Cassie but discovered she was right behind her already. The girls sheepishly approached Hunter and accepted the bowl and cup he'd used to portion out servings from the pouch for each of them and ate what was left.

Once they finished eating, Hunter collected the dishes, sloshed a bit of water in them, and drank the liquid. The girls watched him in horror and made dramatic gagging noises. Hunter waited bemusedly until their antics subsided and then explained.

"When you are out on the trail, you can't leave any traces of food. Bears and other animals are going to get attracted to the scent, and you do not want that."

The girls looked wide-eyed at the idea of that and shook their heads dramatically.

"And if you are trying not to attract attention of the human variety, you can't leave signs they could detect either."

"Oh, that makes sense," Felicia said, but got in one more gag to make her point, "but ain't there no better way than drinkin' the swill of someone else's leftovers?"

"Under normal circumstances I wouldn't be drinking anyone else's. You'd be on your own. But since you are new to life on the road, I thought I'd help you out."

"Well, I sure thank you, Mistah Hunter, for the food and for doin the dishes. Especially after I got so smart with you. I'm sorry about that. It's just, they's people who wouldn't like what we's about to do so much so that they'd stop us anyway they could."

"Felicia, I get it. I'm kind of in the same boat. But, maybe we can figure out a way to trust each other?"

"Maybe. We still got a ways to go, so I'm gonna have to sit with it awhile. If you don't want to share no more of your food with us until we decide, I understand. My belly is about as full as a tick and will be for a good while."

"Felicia, my sharing the food doesn't come with strings attached. That's just the right thing to do."

"Not everybody does the right thing though."

"Unfortunately, you're right about that. I guess I'll just have to keep doing the right thing to make up for them."

Felicia smiled at him and yawned. "I guess I'm kinda tired. Cassie and me is gonna go to sleep. See ya in the mornin'"

"Sleep well, Felicia."

*****

Each of the next five days proceeded in much the same manner. Hunter sat on his own palette reading until meal time, and then the girls would emerge from their corner and dine with him. They didn't exist in silence, but most of the conversations were chatter about inconsequential things that Hunter had a hard time following. Still, he was trying to build trust, so he listened without outward judgment.

The morning of the ninth day, as they were closing in on the Port of New Orleans, Cassie caught Hunter completely off guard by slipping up next to him and tugging on his sleeve. He set down his book and focused on her, waiting for her to speak.

Finally, she whispered, "Mistah Hunter, Felicia, she's havin' a hard time. She won't stop cryin' and I don't know what to do."

Hunter's mind ping-ponged between the shock of Cassie's approach, the fact that he hadn't noticed a sound from their side that suggested sobbing, and concern for what he could possibly do to console her if her best friend was coming up short. But, he slid off the palette and followed Cassie to their corner. He had not ventured over there before, so he was surprised to see two pastel sleeping bags, one with unicorns and rainbows and the other dancing bears, unzipped and laid out on top of a palette of burlap sacks full of rice. Felicia was curled up in the corner and Hunter could see her heaving and shaking while silent sobs racked her body. Cassie looked up at him with tears streaming down her face and said, "I can't do nothin'. Can you please help her?"

Hunter cautiously approached the palette and reached over to pat Felicia's shoulder. She shrugged him off at first, but then rolled over in their direction and continued sobbing.

> Hunter sat down next to her and said, "Felicia, if you keep crying like this, you'll make yourself sick. Would you please talk to me?"

Felicia turned her face toward him and stopped long enough to suck in a weighted breath, then began the torrent of tears again. Hunter looked to Cassie and just shrugged. Cassie pleaded with him with her eyes. Hunter was struck by the amount of courage and concern it must have taken for this girl to overcome her fears and engage with him. He couldn't give up if for no other reason than to meet her in her bravery.

> "Felicia, look, I know you are afraid of letting the cat out of the bag here, but we are almost to New Orleans, and then you're home free. What could it hurt to tell me now?"

> Felicia sat up and through the snubbing cries of a toddler trying to tell her mother why she is melting down, she said, "That's . . . the . . . thing . . . I . . . I ain't . . . home free."

Hunter put his arm around her and pulled her close and she just wailed again into his chest.

"Felicia, hon, I can't help you if I don't know what's going on. Won't you let me be your knight in shiny armor?"

Felicia looked up at him with awe and suddenly the tears subsided.

"Mistah Hunter, I don't know what you can do to help, but I shor do like that you want to try."

"Will you let me?"

"I guess. It's just . . . well, I'm goin' to Nawlins to see a doctor."

"I kind of figured that. I know the Blue Zones have free healthcare and it didn't seem like you could afford what's available in your area."

"Oh, um . . . well, I can't, but I'm not goin' to that kinda doctor."
"What do you mean?"

"I got to see the kind that will put my baby to rest."

"I . . . uh, Felicia, I'm not sure I understand what you mean."

"I need an abortion."

"What? Why? You are pretty far along. Why would you want to do that? Can you even do that with the new laws?"

"That's why I got to be in secret . . . like you."

"But, Felicia, I'm not doing something ill . . . oh, I guess I am . . . but that's not the point. I'm trying to save lives."

Felicia turned away from him, saying, "I knew I shouldna said nothin'."

"Wait . . . I'm sorry. It's just a surprise. It's not what I was expecting you to say. I just don't understand."

"No, you don't. You don't know what's happenin' out here with folks gettin' pregnant these days."

"Probably not, but how do you mean?"

"It's bad. So many people havin' babies that's wrong, that's got bad things wrong with 'em. Hearts that don't work right, cancer . . . in babies! And even worse stuff. And the mamas is getting sick from carryin' 'em in they bellies sometimes too."

"How do you know all of this?"

"I see it all over my neighborhood. And I see it in my own baby. The doctors told me I could die if I stay pregnant because we gots different blood types that don't match, and they wants to take my baby out now and put it in one of those artificial woons."

"You mean womb?"

"Yeah, whatever it is, the thing they have to grow a baby without the mama."

"Well, that sounds like a good option so you don't get harmed and your baby gets to live."

Felicia sighed heavily, frustrated that Hunter wasn't on her side.

"But it ain't! The thing is he has some kind of tumors all over his body already and they just want him to be born so they can study him. He ain't gonna be able to live a normal life. He ain't gonna even get to ever leave a hospital bed. How do I do that to my baby?"

Felicia collapsed into sobs again and Hunter had no words to offer in comfort. He had no words for the inhumanity he was witnessing. Everything in him felt there had to be some reason to help this child into the world rather than destroying this life, but he found himself asking if it wasn't equally cruel to subject an innocent soul to a life that would be inevitably short and undoubtedly torturous.

He just stroked Felicia's hair and let her cry. Cassie looked on helplessly and rubbed her own growing belly. It wasn't until then that Hunter realized he had forgotten Cassie had her own pregnancy to consider and wondered if she was here just as a travel companion or on the same mission. As they made eye contact, he realized he knew the answer.

"Cassie. What about your baby? Does it have the same problem?"

"I . . . I don't know, Mistah Hunter . . . maybe. They can't say for sure cuz they might be something wrong they can't see yet. They say they's workin on a cure for what might ail him, but I don't know that it will be before he gets here and has to go through all of that."

"Don't you think it's worth finding out?"

"I . . . I don't know. I just . . . "

"Mistah Hunter, please don't bother Cassie with that. She made her decision and she got right with herself about it. It wasn't no easy choice to make like people think. They act like we's just out here throwin' babies in the trashcan so we can go la-ti-da about with our lives. It ain't like that."

"Felicia, how old are you really?"

"I told you, I'm . . ."

"Come on, Felicia. I have known plenty of women in my day, and there is no way you are nineteen years old. Be honest with me."

"Why does it matter?"

"Because it does . . . to me. If I'm going to be helping you, I need to know you are being completely honest."

"I'm fourteen."

"That's what I thought. And, Cassie?"

"I'm fourteen too, but I'm four months older. Her birthday is in July and I was born in April."

"Okay. Now that we've corrected the record on that, let's talk about where your parents are and how you ended up pregnant at such a tender age."

"Well, it ain't like you think! I ain't no slut!"

"Felicia, I wouldn't dream of calling you that. It's just this is a lot for someone your age to be burdened with, and it seems like you are and Cassie are alone. Are there parents back in Memphis who are wondering where you are? What about the fathers?"

"Um, Mistah Hunter, you don't understand. We come from a group home. They ain't no parents. We's all the girls who came along after the sickness got all the boys and nobody wanted us. We's been there since we was babies. And as for the fathers, well, I don't know. We don't know them."

Hunter had a sickening feeling creeping over him of realization, horror, and dread. "Felicia, what are you talking about? You mean you had a one-night stand?"

"Naw! Mistah Hunter, I'm a virgin. I ain't never even had the sex."

"How is that possible? I mean . . . maybe you aren't clear on . . . um . . ."

"Oh my gosh! I may be only fourteen, but I *know* what it is. The people who run the home, they make the babies for us."

"Okay, Felicia, you're going to have to explain this to me right now."

"Well, I was tryin' but you're interruptin'."

"Sorry. I'm just . . . I can't believe what I think you're telling me."

Hunter was glad he was sitting because he began to feel weak in the knees. Cassie had climbed onto the palette as well and had just laid her head on her friend's shoulder. Felicia seemed to find her bravado again in having the freedom to tell her story.

"Well, if you're thinkin' that they put babies in us and make us have 'em and then give them to other families, then you'd be thinkin' right. I heard them call us inkabators."

"Incubators."

"Yeah, that. Only, we have to be good ones or else we get kicked out. Once we start havin' menstration, if we don't have good . . . um, healthy babies . . . we don't get to stay there no more cuz we ain't earnin' our keep."

"Felicia, please tell me they are not forcing you to have sex . . ."

"Naw, Mistah Hunter, like I told you. I'm a virgin. I don't know where they gets the stuff from, but they just bring us in to the clinic when we ripe and shoot it up in us. Then they watch us and make sure it took. If we got a baby growin' then they real nice and give us lots of food and vitamins and take good care of us. But if we don't, they send us back to the regular part of the home with the younger girls until they can try again. If you don't get a baby in you after three tries, they kick you out too."

"I really don't know what to say. I had no idea this was happening."

"Well, why would ya? You's a nice man and wouldn't have dealins with people like that."

"Thank you for saying that. But I come from a place where I have access to information and should know about things like this going on. I just haven't been paying close enough attention to how this cure is affecting everyone. But that changes now. Felicia, Cassie, I still wish you could give science a chance to help your babies, but I understand you have an impossible decision ahead of you. I can't go with you once we reach New Orleans, but I don't want to leave you alone to fend for yourself there. I'm not really sure what to do. I suppose I could call someone and see about delaying my connecting boat."

"Naw, Mistah Hunter. You think we got on this boat by accident? That lady drivin' the boat—Caroline—she Cassie's mama's cousin."

"I thought you said you didn't have parents."

"Nuh uh. I said we wasn't wanted. Cassie's mama and daddy gave her away and it made her Auntie Caroline real mad, but they wasn't nothin' she could do about it then because she couldn't take care of no baby. She stayed in touch as Cassie grew up and sent her a little money when she could and came to visit a couple a times. So when we both wanted to get away from the home, we gave her a call and she said she'd help."

"I'm really relieved you have someone to keep you safe."

"Well, I don't know how safe we'll be if they find out what we did and that we ain't comin' back. They only see us as dollars, either for the good babies they sell to old people who can't have babies of they's own or for the bad babies they can sell to the science people who use 'em for learnin'."

Hunter sat in silence and Felicia studied him for a few minutes and then gently reached over and patted his shoulder, offering him the comfort he wanted to provide her but felt ill-equipped for. There really wasn't anything he could say. He was consumed with guilt for dropping the ball, getting lax in his signature suspicion of everything. He knew it was unrealistic to think he could have known about such unconscionable opportunistic behavior, but the old Hunter would not have been so surprised by such callous disregard for the rights of the vulnerable. The old Hunter would have been looking for this sort of abuse of the cure and the rebuilding of their society at every turn. He would have anticipated it. But now, he was caught completely unawares and it not only made him mad at himself, it broke his heart, and he did not like that feeling at all.

Hunter told the girls to pull their things together because they'd be in New Orleans soon and they needed to be ready to move when Caroline gave them the signal. He went back to his area and pulled his kit together. As he did so, he decided to give them the food supplies he had remaining and the bit of cash he had on him. He also wrote down the office number where they could reach Cady if they needed help Caroline could not provide.

Three hours later they arrived at the port and Caroline slid open the gate and told them to move quickly. She saw Hunter's face and knew he was finally up to speed. He saw from the look she gave him that she knew exactly what she was doing in putting them there together. They just exchanged nods. Felicia and Cassie both wrapped Hunter in hugs and told him they'd miss him. He stiffened a bit at the excessive affection, but secretly cherished every squeeze until Caroline urged them to get going. Hunter handed the bag to Caroline and said, "I hope this helps." She nodded and shook his hand. Then she disappeared, following after the girls.

Hunter realized she had slipped him a piece of paper with instructions on where to go next. He hadn't even thought about those next steps, so he was grateful for the finely-tuned operation that had his back.

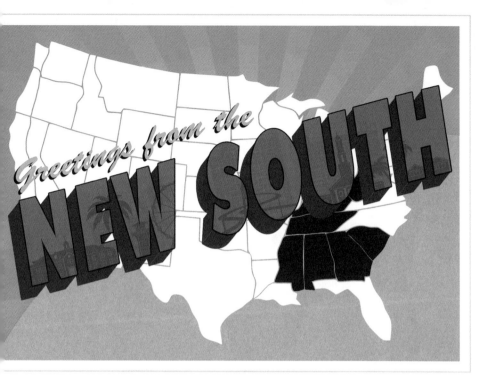

ZONE 10 - NEW SOUTH

Is there anywhere in the world you'd rather be for pursuing your God-given right to life, liberty, and the pursuit of good ol' harmless fun? The New South has all the agriculture and culture we've been known for throughout our history, but we are new and improved because we are stronger than ever, united in our ideals, and empowered to protect what we hold dear. We ain't for everyone, but if how we do is right for you, come on down; we'll save you a seat.

ZONE 10

NEW SOUTH

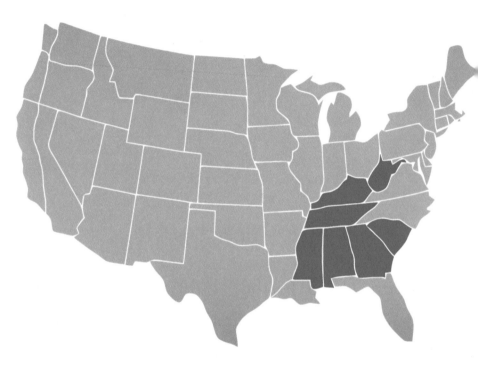

- WEST VIRGINIA
- KENTUCKY
- TENNESSEE
- MISSISSIPPI
- ALABAMA
- GEORGIA

- SOUTH CAROLINA

CHAPTER FIFTEEN

Shortly after three in the afternoon Hunter reached the shrimp trawler that itself looked like a spiny sea creature with its many outriggers, winches, and nets shooting in various directions. The starboard flank was christened *Claire* in a simple script lettering. The Port of New Orleans sat inland from the mouth of the gulf, so the ship he would take to cover his last aquatic leg of this journey had to wind its way through roughly 100 miles of narrow waterways before breaking free into the vast expanse of the sea.

Hunter boarded the ship and nodded to the woman who greeted him with a firm handshake and a smile that welcomed him in a way that touched him more deeply than he expected. He dismissed it as being overly sentimental due to the rigors of the long journey and isolation. Though he had been with a chaperone through each stage, he had been laser focused on his purpose and remaining incognito. The young girl peeking out from behind a crate shared the same smile and then ducked back into hiding. The grin that had crept up on him fell away as he was struck with the fear that he might be encountering a similar tragic circumstance as the one he just left.

The woman, who was weathered in spaces around the periphery, still held the brightness of youth at her core, and Hunter guessed she could be no more than late twenties. Noticing the sudden shift in his demeanor, she reached for his bag and introduced herself.

"Ma name Hélène, me, . . . and dat dere . . .," jutting
her thumb back over her shoulder in the direction of the
girl, ". . . dat my daughter, Céleste, and . . .," raising her
voice to communicate the instruction to the sheepish girl
emerging from cover, ". . . her gon take yo bag below
deck and git you settled, ya."

Hunter blushed with delight at hearing the thick Cajun accent that
rolled across her words unlike any he'd heard in real life conversation.
Céleste came closer and curtseyed, properly extending her imaginary
skirts outward. They had the same café au lait complexion and wiry
curls, though Hélène's were more tamed than her daughter's. Hunter
suspected that was indicative of her personality as well.

Céleste took his bag, which he extended reluctantly as he had not allowed other hands to touch it since he had retrieved it from Charlie's
trunk in Erie. But, he figured she was not likely to run with it and conduct
any sort of subterfuge with what was tucked inside. She wobbled with
pride as she lugged the pack that was too big and too heavy for her tiny
frame as she led him into the cabin. She cast a glance back over her
shoulder to make sure he was following her lead and shifted to a stern
countenance before warning,

"*Allons*, and mind yo head and yo steps, mistah, or it be
no *beaucoup* for you!"

Hunter chuckled, which caused her to stop in her tracks and glare at
him, letting him know he should take her seriously. He cleared his throat
and nodded with all the somberness he could muster. Not entirely satisfied, but knowing she'd better not dawdle in getting him to his quarters,
Céleste gave him a contemptuous harumph and continued down the
steps into the hold.

Hunter worried he had ruined what seemed to be a great start by mocking the girl and attempted to make amends since they would be sharing
a small space for nearly three days.

"Um, so, Céleste, how old are you? You must be pretty grown up to be helping your mom on the boat."

"I'm seven, me, and way mo grown dan you tink."

"Oh, I'm sure that's true. You are handling my bag like a champ, but if you want, I can take it now."

"Nah, sir. Ma mere, she tell me I spose to deliver you, and that what I be do."

"Okay, then. I wouldn't want to get you in trouble."

"It no trouble. We just gon do right by de *pauvre ti bête*."

"What does that . . . pove Tibet . . . mean?"

This time she chuckled, giving back as good as she got. She shoved open the passage to a compartment of the hull that had been equipped with a cot, blanket, and lantern. She placed his bag on the cot, curtseyed again before turning on her heels and making her way back to the stairs.

Hunter sat on the cot and began unpacking his bag. After lining up his toiletries on the back of the sink, he shoved his pack under the cot and sat down to absorb his new surroundings. He realized as he assessed the room that Hélène and Céleste had given him their quarters, which made him feel guilty and honored at the same time. His pride nudged him to insist they take back their space—that he would have no part of kicking a little girl out of her bed. But his growing awareness told him that regular people, especially those committed to a cause, live by a code where personal sacrifice is a gift and he needed to receive it without objection. He could see how everyone he'd encountered on this journey was giving what they had to offer. They may not have money to finance an operation or expertise and connections to make things happen, but they could still be of service, and they deserved to have that sense of purpose for themselves, regardless of how it affected Hunter's need for self-sufficiency and propriety. Also, he already had a pretty clear sense of Céleste's temperament and knew she would have none of his resistance to what she had deemed to be her duty.

*****

Several hours later, a rather forceful, yet small banging on the door of the cabin roused Hunter from the sleep he'd drifted into during his deep reflection.

"Mistah Hunter, you gon sleep all de day and night or you come up and et, ya?"

The stern, admonishing plea from Céleste permeated the metal door at a volume Hunter found surprising. He sat up quickly and opened the door to find her standing with her hands perched on her hips in a manner that fully reflected the attitude that came through her voice. He knew better than to let her see his amusement, so he nodded slowly and courteously.

"Thank you, Miss Céleste. I think I might have slept the day away had you not come for me. You saved me from a sleepless night and an empty stomach for sure."

She found his acknowledgement to be acceptable and softened her stance a bit, but turned without a word and moved toward the steps. Sensing he wasn't as hot on her heels as she thought he should be, she turned and summoned him with a glance over her shoulder and a flick of her hand. Hunter closed the distance quickly, suspecting she would deny him his supper if he dallied.

Up on deck, Hélène was in the galley stirring a pot of something that started Hunter's stomach rumbling, letting him know he was far hungrier than he realized. She looked up from the stove and smiled at him with that same warmth she radiated when he boarded her boat.

"Come on in. We bout to sit to some fine gumbo!"

"Oh, I love gumbo. But it's been a long time since I've had any. In fact, I guess it's been close to forty-five years."

Céleste grew wide-eyed and exclaimed, "How old you be, Mistah Hunter?"

Hélène snapped her head toward her daughter and scolded her, "Céleste, mind yoself, you! Dat ain't how we speak to our elders! And why you be standin around dere not settin' da table fo to et?"

"Sorry, mamá."

"Not to me, you say you sorries to Mistah Hunter."

"Sorry, Mistah Hunter. You not *dat* old, ya?"

Hélène was ready to jump on her again, but Hunter just laughed and squatted down to Céleste's level.

"No, I'm not *that* old, but I'm pretty old . . . actually a lot older than I look. See, the reason I haven't had gumbo in so long is the last time I had it was when I lived in Houston and was training to fly a spaceship. Well, that spaceship and all of us in it disappeared for forty years! Can you imagine that?"

"Mistah Hunter, I ain't dumb. I knowd bout de Centaree. Ma mere and me, we read bout it in my school books, we did."

"Oh! So you go to school. How do you do that when you're on this boat?"

"Ma mere, she my teacher."

Hunter looked back to Hélène with confusion. She was transferring the gumbo to individual bowls and held one out to Céleste to place on the table she was setting for dinner.

"I homeschool her. It not zactly legal in da Greater Gulf, but we skate by seein' how I work mostly from de New France satellite." Seeing Hunter's confusion had not abated, she asked, "You know bout de Zones, right?"

"Oh, yeah, sure. I'm learning on this trip that they are becoming more of a reality than anyone imagined. We've been keeping an eye on it, but for the most part it's just seemed like people retreating to their corners, kind of isolating in their echo chambers, but that it wouldn't really catch on. But as I travel through these zones, it's becoming clear this separation is something everyone seems to be all too comfortable with and they want it to be more permanent."

"Ya, dat de truth. People don't want no mo' of live and let live. Dey want to be wit dey own kind. I don't see how dat gon' last. We all need each other and we need difference to make it all alright."

She handed her daughter the last bowl and pulled a pan of cornbread from a tiny toaster oven. Hunter was astounded by what she managed to produce from such compact accommodations. They sat down at the table and Hélène and Céleste took each other's hand and closed their eyes, breathed in deeply, and sat silently for a moment. Hunter observed quietly, unsure whether to join them in some fashion or just let them be. Before he could decide, Hélène nodded her head and said, "Amen."

She lifted a spoonful of the gumbo to her mouth and inhaled the aroma, but put the spoon back into her bowl, and said, "See dis here gumbo? I see it like de way we used to be. If I make dis and I say, 'You shrimp, you of de sea, so you gon stay over here wit you kind; and you okre and tomatoes, you vege-tables, so you gon stay by yoself. Don't you go mixin in wit dat shi-ken dere or dem shrimps. Dey not like you. Dey don't see tings yo way. If we do dat, den we ain't gon have a fine meal like dis one here. You see?"

"Sure. It makes sense to me," Hunter said, finding her utterly enchanting. "I do understand why people get afraid of what's different and why they want to be with people who agree with them, but it does cheat you out of variety and the things that make life interesting. But how does that relate to Céleste's education?"

"Well, I was askin dat you knew about de Zones because we, Céleste and me, we from de bayou and it Zone 7. Nawlins be de only part dat not. Greater Gulf is Red, and dat mean dey ain't no public schools. Dey want all learnin' to be in de private schools."

"Isn't that a good thing? I know public schools have a hard time providing as good an education as private ones do. And they are giving vouchers to make it more affordable, right?"

Hélène laughed heartily and Céleste laughed with her, though it was clear she didn't totally understand why. She just knew they were making fun of something the old white man had said.

"Oh, chere, dere so much you don't understand bout how dis work. Ya, dey give de vouchers, but it only cover de tuition. Den dey gon git you wit de uniforms and de books and dis dat and de other. Po folks can't do it all, and den dey kids gon suffer on one hand by not havin what dey need to learn and on de other hand by de kids dat have it and make fun. It sho easy to sit dere an say easy peasy and wipe yo hands. You has to see beyond de stuff that looks right and good on paper. You git me?"

Hunter pondered what she had said and tried to imagine what his experience would have been like if he'd had a young child to educate, which led him to thinking about the son he did have and wondering what kind of experience he had in school, and then wondering where he was at that moment. His reverie was interrupted by the girl to his right muttering under her breath the words he'd heard earlier and couldn't translate. *Pauvre ti bête*

Hunter said, "There it is again! What does that mean? Pove Tibet?"

Hélène tried not to reveal her amusement to her daughter and set down her spoon in a subtle but all-too-familiar gesture that let Céleste know she had overstepped.

"Mistah Hunter, I do must apologize. My Céleste, she tink she a bit too grown fo herself and she use words she ain't know too well sometimes."

"So, what does it mean?"

"*Pauvre ti bête* it be French Cajun. It mean 'po little creature.' She sayin you a pity. But you ain't notin like dat, so don't you worry yoself none."

"Oh. Why would she think . . . ," Hunter stopped himself, realizing Céleste would not respond well to their talking about her in front of her, so he turned to her and said, "Céleste, why do you think you should feel sorry for me?"

Céleste looked at her mother for help and Hélène nodded indicating she could speak for herself.

> "I told you I know bout de Centaree, and ma mere, she say you need help gettin to see yo bonne amie, dat you tryin to do somethin good fo all de people, but it be a hard job to do. She say it be harder dan pullin in de traps by yoself, and dat de hardest job out here, so I tink you be a po ting and in a might tough spot."

Hunter felt something he hadn't recalled feeling ever in his life. The affection that welled up in him for this little girl was almost more than he could handle. Her mother beamed with pride, but tried to conceal it. It was clear she was cautiously reserved in the emotion she allowed her daughter to see in her.

Hunter didn't want to belabor the tender moment, so he decided to circle back around to their earlier topic.

> "I understand that there are issues with the private school and voucher program, but it does create options you don't have in public school systems. It still seems like, if they could work out the kinks, it would be a better way to make sure you had meaningful input in the kind of education your child gets. And it seems like you have very strong ideas about that."

> "May-haps be. But dem private schools, dey have de best for some, but you got special needs, and dey don't gon do notin. I make sho Céleste, her get all de learnin she need. We have books here and at home for her to read what she need to know. She read above most children her age."

> "I'm sure that's true. I was impressed she already knew about my ship and crew. And you don't live on the boat all the time?"

"Nah, we out here two day at de time and den home a
day or two. We bring in de haul and sell it. Den we take
a bit to rest and make groceries. We mend what needs
mendin and tend to business. Den we head out again."

"May I ask, where is her father, and what about the rest
of your family?"

"My kin all gon, mostly durin de pandemic. Céleste papá,
dis was his boat. He got caught in a storm swell and took
under. His crew can't do notin to find him, but dey bring
his boat back to us. Dat tres annes . . . um, tree year
ago."

"I am so sorry to hear that. It must have been so hard for
you . . . for you both."

"We make do and git each other tru. Me and Céleste, we
make fo a good crew just de deux."

"I can tell she is the best first mate you could have. Quite
capable."

Céleste nodded with pride and sat up a little straighter in her seat to
affirm how capable she was.

As they wrapped up dinner, Hunter helped them clean the dishes and
put things away. He was more of a hindrance in the tight quarters, but
they let him assist anyway. As a way of making conversation while they
worked, he asked more about Céleste's schooling.

"Where do you get the books you use to teach her? Is
there some kind of curriculum you follow?"

"Nah, I just make sure she gettin all she need to know. I
give her de mathematics and readin and science. Out

here de best classroom anyway cause she have to know how to count and measure and add or subtract. She learn bout science by learnin de weather and sea animals and much many more. De books, dey be harder to come by. You know dey make it real hard to get readin now."

"Really? How so?"

"Well, everybody, dey want to tell you what you can or canna read."

"In New Orleans?"

"Nah . . . well, ya, everywhere. Dem Blue people, dey want to make sho you ain't readin notin dat might hurt yo feelins and dem Red people, dey want to make sho you ain't readin notin dat might make you mad and want to change somethin."

"You mean they are censoring books?"

"Ya! Dey make it all so if you po, you can't get notin but what dey want you to see. You got to have spendin money to buy de real books."

"So, how do you get them?"

"It all part of de movement. De Resistance, dey help me git what my girl she need."

"Oh, so you are part of the Resistance. I wasn't sure if you were a member or just a sympathizer. Or like some, just needing the money. So, does your boat name have anything to do with that?"

Céleste jumped in, proud that she could contribute to the conversation, "Ya, sir, it do! *Claire* she name for Claire Lacombe."

"Who is that?"

"Mistah Hunter, maybe you need come to my class time tomorrow and git caught up wit me on learnin!"

"Céleste mind yoself, you."

"Sorry, mamá. I just want him can learn too."

"Céleste I am sure I could learn a lot from you. How about you tell me about Claire while I have this cup of coffee and get ready to turn in?"

"Well, I can tell you real quick. She be *femme française* . . . um, she live in de old France a long time back. Even before you was *bebe*. She be a girl and fight strong to make de men treat de women equal. Ma mere, she be like Claire. Dat why we name our boat for her."

"That makes perfect sense to me. You both are very strong women and are doing good work."

*****

Hunter did sit with Céleste the next day while she did her studies and the day after that, though the second day involved some actual trawling to contribute to their cover as they approached the harbor.

As they docked, Céleste moved about the deck pulling winches and securing lines, obviously well-seasoned in the trade at a tender age. Hunter watched the mother-daughter team as they worked with precision to bring the vessel safely into a slip.

Once the dropped anchor, Hélène shouted to her daughter, "Céleste, catch me dat bundle you made up."

Céleste ran to the galley and brought back a bag with some boudin balls and hoecakes and a slip of paper tucked in with them.

As she handed over the parcel, Céleste informed him, "Ma mere, I tell her you need beignets, but she say dey don't travel. I say beignets always beaucoup, but she say no. So, you come back and we have beignets at home. Oui?"

Hunter smiled as he put the bag in his pack and said, "Yes! Oui. I would love to do that. And thank you so much for the treats for the road. I am really grateful to both of you for your hospitality."

"Pshaw! Our pleasure it be. You take care Mistah Hunter, and give Miss Lydia our best!" Hélène said as she lowered the gangway for him to cross to the pier.

Hunter found himself disappointed to leave them, but quickly shifted his focus to finding his next connection. He was closing the distance between him and Lydia, and with the longest portions of the journey behind him and only two more days of travel ahead, he was eager to reach his destination and find out exactly what this whole saga was for.

After exiting the port, he fished the paper out of the bag Céleste had given him, and he moved quickly to the location detailed in her childish but precise penmanship.

ZONE 11 – APPALACHIANA

Scenic mountain villages, quaint coastal towns, and historical sites make Appalachiana an ideal retreat for those who are tired of the survival rat race. Come claim your little piece of heaven before everyone else decides to leave the cities for a more peaceful way of life.

ZONE II

APPALACHIANA

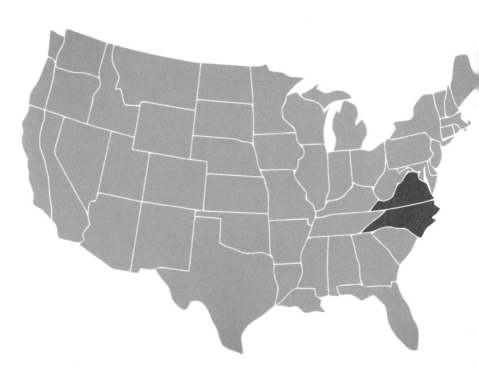

- NORTH CAROLINA
- VIRGINIA

CHAPTER SIXTEEN

Hunter found the green and white VW bus waiting at their designated meeting place, just as had been described in the note. The sun was just beginning to slip from its position overhead, and he was grateful for the remainder of daylight as the area was not lit with streetlights and he sensed this wasn't the best place to be stranded after dark. He knew the remainder of his journey would be by land, but this was a change in the plan Cady had laid out for him before he left, and this definitely didn't look like a US port. Though he'd been getting some additional instruction from each contact along the way, he was a bit unnerved by this disruption to the plan. He was expecting to cross the gulf to Port Isabel, and someone to take him the three hours to Matamoros where he would change to a different mode of transportation to travel through the Mexico border region—now called Annexico—over to Calexico. The note he got from Céleste read: *Route change. Meet Manuella outside Hotel Las Delfines. Green bus. Bon Voyage.*

He was concerned about those words—route change. *Hadn't the route been carefully mapped out to avoid detection? What could have gone wrong? Is Lydia okay?* Those and a million other thoughts raced through his head as he assessed the van, and he was tempted to use that emergency number to make sure this was on the up-and-up. If not for the fact that it was stressed to him this was a one-use thing and the change had been passed along by people he trusted, he would have made a call and diverted. Instead he walked cautiously toward the van, and as he opened the door and stuck his head in, he found a middle-aged Latina woman behind the wheel. She smiled but urged him to get in and not mess around.

> "I'm Manuella and I'm going to be taking you across the desert to Calexico. It's a long, treacherous trip, and we have more than a few challenges, so buckle up and let's get going."

Hunter climbed in on her command, but was bewildered and alarmed. He settled in and sat in silence as he watched the mere traces of civilization disappear in the rearview mirror. Unmarked miles of desert ticked away and he sunk deep into his thoughts. Manuella expertly wound through the labyrinth of streets that would get them out of town and on the road to their destination.

*****

A couple of hours into the trip, Hunter had finally had enough of trying to unpack this mystery on his own and the rabbit hole of catastrophizing that consumed his mind, and he decided to simply ask.

> "Manuella, what's going on?"

Startled by the abrupt interruption to her own internal musings, she muttered a "hmm?" with thinly-veiled annoyance. Hunter repeated his question, matching her level of irritation.

> "What's going on? With this new route? With whatever these challenges are that you mentioned?"

> "Um, yeah. Well, what do you know about Matamoros?"

> "Just that it's a border town . . . or a town on what was the US-Mexico border in my day."

"Okay, in some respects, things haven't changed much there, except that there is no border anymore. But because of the location—being coastal and south of US Customs—it has always had a lot of piracy and smuggling. Well, now, along with that, there has been a recent rebellion rising up. It's in response to Texas joining Zone 7 and the borderlands becoming Annexico. A lot of the tensions surrounding the border that died down when we acquired those areas are starting to bubble up again."

"Is that why we are diverting course?"

"We're trying to avoid the fray, but we couldn't take the risk of you going through the port that is now under Zone 7 control, so Hélène had to drop down to Carboneras, Mexico. The trip is going to take a little longer because we are going to have to wind through some mountain roads to steer clear of Zone 7 and keep you off the radar, but we can't go too deep into that territory or we will be too far off the grid and could encounter insurgents."

"Wait. So, we are in real danger here. This isn't just a precaution?"

"Unfortunately, during the time you've been dark, the strain of the growing division is reaching a fever pitch and it's gonna get dicey."

"Okay, so, we're armed, right? Please tell me your little hippy bus has more than flowers and good vibes to protect us."

"Hunter, this is Annexico, not the Left Coast. Yes, we are a Blue Zone, but we still recognize the importance of the Second Amendment—probably even more than the rest of the country. After all we were appropriated without getting a vote."

Hunter looked around to the back where the seats had been removed. The van had been retro-fitted with cabinets and a kitchenette. It was clear Manuella lived out of her vehicle, and it seemed to be quite well-appointed for an extremely compact space. He figured each compartment served more than one purpose and was likely engineered for maximum efficiency. He saw no trace of weaponry, but was ready to give her the benefit of the doubt that she had what they needed and that having them out in the open was a piss-poor idea in those parts.

Hunter conceded her point and said, "Fair enough. As long as they are easily accessible if we run into any trouble."

Manuella nodded while keeping her eyes on the road before her, expertly maneuvering the winding road illuminated no more than ten feet ahead by the meager headlights.

"Hunter, trust me, if we get anywhere near trouble, I will have a gun in your hand before you even know you need it. Because if you see trouble coming, it will be too late to go fishing for a weapon."

"I guess you know this area pretty well?"

"You know those pirates and smugglers I mentioned?"

"Yeah. Why? Do you know them or something?"

"I am one."

"Wait. What? You're a criminal?"

"Hey, maybe dial back the judgment a bit, okay? Don't forget you are counting on me for safe transport."

"Sorry. It's just those aren't the most reassuring terms. I guess I shouldn't be surprised. The first boat I was on was operated by a guy who did something similar."

"See, we aren't all bad. And, I like to think of myself as a post-apocalyptic Robin Hood."

"Oh, this guy was an opportunist for sure—called it capitalism—but not a bad person. He just wasn't charitable in his trade. What makes you Robin Hood?"

"Well, I guess I'm both—a pirate and a smuggler—because my crew and I help liberate resources destined for excessive and wasteful purposes and redistribute them where they will be more effectively used."

"So, you steal things from the people who paid for them and give them to people who didn't."

For the first time she took her eyes off the road and glared at Hunter long enough that he almost reached for the steering wheel to make sure they didn't veer off the road. But she had traveled this path so frequently that she knew every bend and dip by heart, even in the dark.

After turning her head forward again, she scolded, "That's really reductive. The people I help are desperate in no small part thanks to the people I . . . um, *encourage* to give their surplus to worthy causes.

"Look, I believe you believe you are doing what is right . . . and maybe you are, but law and order still matter."

"How the hell did you get hooked up with the Resistance with that authoritarian mindset?"

"Now, hold on!"

Hunter was feeling unsupported for the first time in his journey. He had grown accustomed to at least being left alone if not congratulated on his efforts.

He continued with his bruised ego on full display, "I am a far cry from a government shill! You must know Lydia, and she wouldn't have brought me in if she thought I was afraid to break the rules. Hell, that's why I've devoted the last three weeks to traveling in cramped spaces, hiding from god knows who might want to stop me, and all without having a clue why."

"Well, how is what I'm doing any different? It's all for the same cause."

"Okay. Explain it to me. Why do you think it's not stealing? Why do you feel entitled to decide how much is too much for someone to have?"

"For one thing, you have it backward. It's not about deciding how much is too much for one person, it's knowing what is too little for one person to have to get by on. There are fundamental needs for survival that are not being met for too many people in this zone because of greed in others."

"How so?"

"Do you think it's okay for hundreds of children to starve while a few miles away a fat cat politician holds a party for a hundred of his nearest and dearest supporters and donors, charging enough per person to feed all of those children for a month?"

"I am not suggesting the children should suffer. Of course they deserve to eat. But if you're saying you steal the food off one table to put it on another, is that fair?"

"Yes, if they only have to miss one meal so a child can eat for a month. Things shouldn't be that out of balance."

"I do understand what you are saying, and those kids should have what they need, but there are legal and ethical ways to make it happen. Capitalism is designed to inspire people to reach further than their current circumstances and to work for better conditions."

"Oh, spare me! The reason these kids are starving is because of Capitalism run amok. The Cabal has no interest in making things fair and equitable. In fact, they are working hard to see that they aren't. You'd better make sure you are clear on that before you get to Jarbridge because they—,"

Manuella stopped short and reached with her right hand to open a panel in the floor between her seat and Hunter's. Maintaining her speed and without looking away from the road, she strained to access the metal case in the compartment. When Hunter realized what she was trying to do, he tried to intervene.

"I can help. What do you need?"

"Pull that box up. Punch in the code 5-3-0-7-8. I am sure you'll know what to do with what's inside."

"Okay. Is something happening that I should be aware of?"

"Maybe. Maybe not. Just get ready."

Hunter opened the lid and found two Smith & Wesson .357 handguns tucked in foam padding. He lifted the pistols and inspected them carefully. He flipped open the cylinders and gave them a spin to make sure they were full of rounds. The familiar heft of the heavy steel in his hand gave him a feeling of satisfaction he didn't realize he'd missed.

"Why? What do you see?"

"Nothing specific . . . it's more what I don't see."

"What does that mean?"

"Normally, at this time of day, I'd be passing commuter buses taking people home from working in the city to their homes in the outlying villages."

"This late at night?"

"The people who live out here work in the city at factories, and they clock out when the foreman says so. That usually means when they hit their quotas, and that's a moving target. So, late night journeys home are common and there is enough demand for bus evening service that you usually see two or three making this run. Just be ready. It may be nothing, but out here, it's usually something."

"Okay. But, I sure hope you have more firepower than this. These are solid pistols, but something tells me they don't hold a candle to how they—whoever they are—will be armed."

"Trust me, if it comes to that, we have what we need. These are more for show."

"How does that work?"

"For this area, doing a little saber rattling—waving a handgun around—lets the *bandidos* know you aren't an unfortunate tourist who ventured too far off the main road."

"Gotcha. Now, you said this Blue Zone is different where the Second Amendment is concerned. Does that mean these are legal?"

"Let's just say we won't get in trouble for having them."

"That sounds pretty sketchy to me."

"Look, technically there is a gun ban in Annexico, but it is not enforced. All the *policia* look the other way because they understand what it is like out here. And it's not just about the crime; this is very rural country and there are lots of wild animals that are dangerous, and bows and arrows aren't enough. Most people have them for that reason, but protection is equally important."

"But they're still illegal here, right?"

"Yes, technically, that's true. But try getting away with it in another Blue Zone. There they make no concessions."

"Tell me again how you're different from the *bandidos*."

"Because I don't rob people at gunpoint for one, and I don't take from average, everyday humans. I 'skim resources' from corporate stockpiles to assist those truly in need. Are we really going to rehash this?"

"I'm just trying to understand where you draw the distinction and why. To me, taking something that isn't yours or that you didn't pay for is stealing. Even if it's altruistic. I don't like the control corporations have over this country and its politicians. And, believe you me, living in DC, I see more corruption than you ever will out here. But, I also don't think the solution is taking matters into your own hands. Mostly because I don't think it fixes the problem. It's putting a band-aid on bullet hole."

"Okay. So what do you suggest?"

"Well, the lawlessness that seems to be rampant down here is only adding fuel to the fire for why the people in the Red Zones want tighter borders and restrictions on passage. That can't help your access to resources. I know it's unrealistic to say just stop the crime-ing and wait for things to get better."

"You got that right!"

"But, it seems like you know what . . . and who you're dealing with down here really well. I'm guessing you have some influence, and you are obviously very resourceful. Can you try to work through legal channels to change what is happening? Work with the powers that be and help them see the benefit in meeting the needs of every-one?"

"I like that you think they are open to reason. That's cute."

"You misunderstand me . . . and you really don't know me. I'm not cute or doe-eyed about this. I just have come to realize that if you can convince someone that what you want or need is their idea and that it's to their benefit to give it to you, that goes a lot further than forcing your will on them with violence. It takes a special kind of leader to do that, but the results are far more lasting and effective. That's why people will follow Lydia into the trenches and go wherever she asks them to go. She has that leadership quality."

"Uh huh. I see. Do I detect a certain something between you two? Some affection in that grizzled heart of yours?"

Hunter blushed in spite of himself and was just grateful for the dark night to conceal it.

"I . . . um . . . she definitely has my admiration and respect."

"Mmm-hmm."

"Don't go making this into some dime-store romance novel. She's just . . ."

"Yeah, yeah. I'll let you have that. I don't think there's anything wrong with it . . . I'm just sayin'."

Hunter let that lie and trained his eyes forward on the road ahead of them, pretending to be singularly focused on spotting any trouble.

The next several hours passed without incident. In the pre-dawn hours Hunter saw the halo of city lights and he asked Manuella if it was safe to stop there and stretch his legs and find some facilities.

"That's Ciudad Juarez. We should be okay there. From there we are about 10-12 hours out, so it's a good place to take a pit stop and fuel up."

"It just occurred to me, we haven't stopped for gas in all this time. How is that possible?"

"Two things. My bus is a hybrid and runs on electricity and biofuel . . . oh, um, not that kind."

"No, I didn't imagine you meant the Apollo fuel. I know they got rid of all of that when they made the connection to the pandemic."

"Right. Also, I have a reserve tank, so I can make lots of trips across the desert safely. It's an important feature given how few and far between the towns are down here."

"I get the sense this van has lots of features designed for survival."

"Yep. I've spent several years fine-tuning it to meet nearly every need I have encountered or could anticipate. It may seem like a cramped space, but it really does quite a lot and is cozy."

"I can get behind the minimalist, off-grid lifestyle. The apartment they give me in DC is way more than I need. To be honest, I spend most of my time at the office and only go there to catch a few Zs and to shower and change clothes. They say it's for appearances, which couldn't matter less to me, but I'm not paying for it, so I guess I can live with . . . or in it."

"That's the kind of government excess we are fighting against. Don't you see that?"

"Yeah, I do. But, maintaining this cover is important to what the Resistance is trying to accomplish, so it's a necessary byproduct. Can you see that?"

"Yeah. But I don't have to like it."
"No, you don't. And I can't imagine anyone could make you."

Once they reached the outskirts of the city, Manuella found a 24-hour service center and pulled up next to a charging station. She told Hunter to plug the charger into the port on the side of the bus while she went in to get a key for the restrooms, which were only accessible from the outside of the building. Even though they were in friendly territory, she felt it best that he still keep out of sight and told him he would need to move to the back of the bus where the windows were covered when they left so he wouldn't be visible once daylight was upon them.

When she came back out with the key, Hunter ducked into the women's restroom since she couldn't ask for the key to the men's room. Manuella crawled in the back of the van and opened a compartment door that lifted up into a cushioned seat and revealed a recessed space for legroom. She also pulled out some packaged meal options that could be heated quickly and easily in her solar-powered microwave. She set them on the work surface of the kitchenette and when Hunter poked his head in, she scooted back to the front and let him climb in. She gave him instructions for how to warm up whatever he wanted to eat while she unplugged the charger and got them ready to get back on the road. Hunter was busy preparing food for them both as she moved back out onto the road that would take them the rest of the way to Calexico. As she drove, Manuella shared what she'd learned while inside the store.

"It turns out my safety concerns were unwarranted in one respect, but spot-on in another."

"You mean there weren't *bandidos* lurking in the shadows and hijacking the commuters?"

"No. I mean . . . yes, they are there, but that's not why the buses weren't on the road."

"What happened? And how did you find out this far away from there?"

"The buses didn't run because all the uprising I told you about in Matamoros has expanded and the factories were either shut down because of outside protestors or by workers striking. Not enough people showed up to work, so no transport was necessary. I found out because the clerk was watching the news on TV while I was in there, and that was the lead story."

"Wow. That's escalating quickly. I wonder if the unrest is spreading through the other Zones."

"I wasn't in there long enough to see what else might be in the news reports, but I wouldn't be surprised. Everyone is over it, over each other, over all of the having to band together for survival. We are becoming more and more unstable each day."

Hunter just nodded agreement as he had held off as long as he could in eating, but his stomach was rumbling with increasing vigor and he was beginning to salivate. He ate the breakfast burrito that was remarkably good for reheated eggs. When he finished, he leaned his head back against the wall and felt a slight twinge of guilt as he felt his eyelids drift downward, but told himself he couldn't be up front and visible behind the wheel, plus he was probably seeing the last sleep he would get for the foreseeable future.

Hunter woke with a start as he sensed the vehicle slowing its pace significantly. He leaned forward and tried to peer out the windshield to see where they were. They were moving into heavier traffic and the daylight was beginning to fade.

"Wow. How long was I out?"

"Long enough that we are about an hour outside of Calexico."

"Unbelievable! Guess I was more tired than I thought. And who knows what the next
several days hold."

"Exactly. You think the trip has been wild so far, but you ain't seen nothin' yet."

"Hey, I just remembered something. You got cut off from telling me something about
the Cabal and that I needed to understand something about them before I get to
Jarbridge. What did you mean by that? What aren't you telling me?"

"I think you'd better get that from Lydia. Just suffice it to say they are behind
everything."

"What *they* do you mean and what are *they* behind?"

Manuella shushed him and said it wasn't her place to dole out information she wasn't authorized to give. Hunter was frustrated, but understood the protocols, so he settled back into his seat and began to prepare mentally for this last stretch that would conclude the thousands of miles over weeks that he traveled to find some important answers . . . and probably a lot more questions.

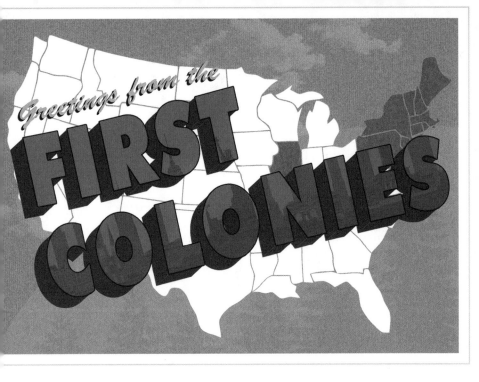

ZONE 12 – FIRST COLONIES

The first in industry, art and culture, business and finance, and forging this great country, we have everything you're looking for. Whether it's in our rural enclaves or bustling cities, The First Colonies Zone is leading the way to success, leading us back to being our best. If you're ready to thrive and grow again, Zone 12 is the place for you.

ZONE 12

FIRST COLONIES

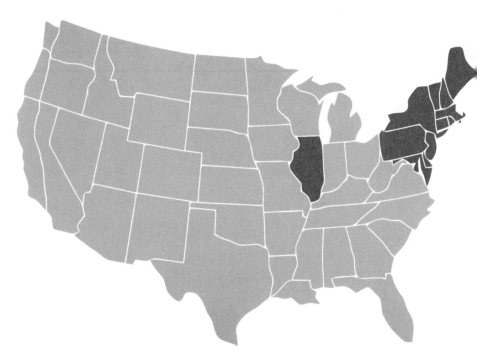

- CONNECTICUT
- DELAWARE
- ILLINOIS
- MAINE
- MARYLAND
- MASSACHUSETTS
- NEW HAMPSHIRE
- VERMONT
- RHODE ISLAND
- NEW YORK
- NEW JERSEY

CHAPTER SEVENTEEN

Manuella pulled up beside a well-maintained Jeep Renegade with tinted windows, but faced the opposite direction so the passenger door was next to the side door of her van. They were safely in a Blue Zone in Calexico, just on the other side of the Annexico border—one of the most liberal and open to free passage—but because it was still crucial for Hunter to stay off anyone's radar, they sat in the parking lot of a shopping center until the sun had set completely before he exited the van and quickly slid into the back passenger seat.

He and Manuella did not belabor goodbyes, but he thanked her for her protection and wished her the best. She told him to give Lydia her best. After settling into the Jeep with his pack and securing his seatbelt, he looked up, prepared to introduce himself to the driver, and simultaneously jolted from shock and found himself close to tears. There was the familiar massive form of his first protector and friend.

"Charlie! What are you doing here? How did you get here?"

Charlie laughed and turned around and extended his hand to shake Hunter's. He was about to answer his questions when Hunter interrupted with more. Charlie headed out of the parking lot toward the interstate as he let Hunter finish.

"Hey, wait. Why did I go through all of what I did to get here—weeks on boats, often without even basic necessities—if you could have just driven me out here?! What the hell, man? It's been brutal."

"Hunter. You gonna let me get a word in edgewise?"

"Fine. What's the deal?"

"You have to remember a few things. First, you are way more recognizable than I am and people are paying attention to everything you do. I am trained to blend in and not be noticed. It's one of the most important parts of my job. You had to go deep underground or you'd have been detected and that would have been it for this whole operation. Second, I had other things to tend to for other parts of the plan while you were making the trip—things I couldn't do if I was chauffeuring your sorry ass across the country. Last, I have a cover story of my own."

Charlie paused and Hunter saw a wry grin in the rearview mirror, which piqued his curiosity.

"Okay. All of that makes sense. And what's the cover story. I get the sense there's a story behind it."

"Honeymoon."

"What? You? And Who?"

"Cady."

"You've got to be kidding me! But, it's really just a cover story right? I mean . . . so, is she here too?"

"Slow down, partner! No, I'm not kidding. No, it's not just a cover story, but it worked out well. And, yes, she is waiting for us with Lydia in Jarbridge."

"When did this happen? And how did I miss that?"

"About a week ago, and you probably missed it because you have your head up your own ass . . . and you were incommunicado."

Hunter's head was spinning and it wasn't just from the surprise. He was actually excited for them, which was unsettling for him as he never imagined he even had the capability to be a romantic or sentimental kind of guy.

"Well, I remember thinking something was up in the way you talked about her when we were en route to Erie. I guess I was just so focused on the road ahead and how much I hated boats that I didn't give it much more thought."

"Yeah, speaking of that. How have you managed? Did you find your sea legs?"

"Eventually. I had some good guidance from experienced sailors, and time helps you make the adjustment. I can't say I'm eager to jump on a cruise ship or even a dinghy again any time soon, but the seasickness didn't plague me the whole trip, so I'm thankful for that."

"I knew you were in good hands with the volunteers we lined up. Good, good people."

"Yes, they were. Impressive and knowledgeable. I learned a lot from them about what life is really like for most peo-ple, what they experience in the different Zones they're affiliated with or have to work in, and the challenges they are facing. I tell ya, Charlie, the seriousness—and per-manence—of this division happening across the country made its way to me even out on the water where I was off grid. I hope we have a plan for what to do about it."

"We have many plans, my friend, but what you are going to do with Lydia in Jarbridge isn't going to make any of that any better."

"Why? Manuella was really cryptic about all of that, and now you are. What gives?"

"Hunter, I'm under strict orders not to get into that with you. Lydia will debrief you when we get there. I know you don't like being in the dark, but you're just gonna have to wait."

"You're killin' me. What are we going to talk about for the next fifteen hours?"

"You know, we don't have to talk at all."

"Fine, if you're going to be that way about it. You have some kind of partition you can put up so you really are just a chauffeur?"

"Hey, don't get testy. I'm not saying I don't want to talk. I'm just not used to this chattier side of you, and I was trying to give you an out."

"Oh. Well, yeah, it is kind of a new feature in this old model. I guess being isolated for so long has had an effect. And I'm sorry, man. I guess this saga is starting to wear on me."

"No worries. Why don't you tell me about your trip—the people you met, what you learned, that sort of thing."

"Deal. As long as you promise to tell me what the hell I missed between you and my assistant!"

"Hunter, you do understand that she is your handler, not your assistant, right?"

This was the first time Hunter had really given any thought to the actual nature of their arrangement and he was a bit embarrassed he hadn't recognized it before and that he had diminished her role so much.

"Oh, wow. Yeah. That probably makes me look kind of stupid. Well, you still owe me the real scoop."

"Deal."

For the next several hours, as the evening crossed over into the next day, Charlie and Hunter talked about life and politics and relationships as they traversed the desert of the southern portion of Zone 2—The Left Coast—toward their final destination. It was not only the longest conversation either of them had ever had in their lives, it was the longest either had ever talked to another man about anything, but especially about real, meaningful topics. Their route took them past Los Angeles, which was still a thriving city, but not the movie mecca it had been in Hunter's day. They briefly skirted across a portion of Zone 3—The New Frontier—before re-entering the Nevada portion of Zone 2. While both Zones were Blue, the New Frontier was actually more purple. They were moving toward Red on issues such as gun rights, deregulation, and commerce. Really more like the old Libertarian ideology than anything, truly a live-and-let-live mindset. But, recognizing they were sandwiched in between Blue regions and knowing they were still very dependent on the resources of those surrounding areas, their shift toward a different system moved at a snail's pace. The struggle in that region was nothing new. The more rural parts of the Left Coast had been trying to break away from the progressive cities for decades before the Alpha Centauri crew disappeared in the '20s. But, for the same reasons of viability, they never could secede and split the states. Alaska faced a similar conundrum as it faced the decision about which Zone to align with. While there had historically been a lot of Red-leaning politicians in the region and a lot of elections went that way, the people tended to support just as many principles of the Blue Zones as of the Red. Ultimately, it came down to a matter of practicality. Being isolated from all the other states and separated by a massive region of what would become the very Blue Zone 1, they felt it best to hitch their wagon to the one that would offer them unfettered access to the resources they needed. Even though trade was open between the territories, the tariffs imposed by the Blue made importing across zone borders cost-prohibitive in many cases.

Hunter attempted to probe Charlie on what he knew about Jarbridge, but he was about as subtle as a freight train, and Charlie repeatedly deflected him. The sun was creeping up over the eastern horizon sprawled in front of them as they approached Battle Mountain, Nevada, leaving four short hours that felt like an eternity to Hunter. He fell silent as he retreated into his own mind, considering a multitude of things about what was to come next. *What the hell was actually going on? How will it feel to see Lydia in person again? What are we going to do about whatever she found there? What does it mean for the future? What are we going to do about the things I found out on my trip—Felicia and Cassie's plight, the hardships of the people who helped him, whatever that science stuff was that Joshua discovered?* Hunter had made so many troubling discoveries along the way, he dreaded what could be more life-altering than those that would require his journey.

The closer they got to Jarbridge, the more anxious Hunter became, and finally he broke the silence that had hung between them for the better part of an hour.

"Charlie, is there really nothing you can tell me about what's going on?"

"Oh, there's plenty I *can* tell you, just not much I'm *allowed* to tell you."

"Well, what are you allowed to tell me that you haven't."

"I guess we're close enough to Jarbridge that I can give you some prep."

"Fire away. You have a captive audience."

Charlie chuckled and then paused to gather his thoughts before speaking. Hunter waited less than patiently.

"Well, the first thing you should know is that Joshua got those reports to Lydia and shared with her his thoughts on what they mean."

"Great! I couldn't believe what we were seeing. I have a feeling I met some girls who are evidence of the problem. Really sad situations."

"We know about them, and you're right. Lydia will tell you more on that when you see her. Just know they are under our protection and are getting the help they need."

"That's a relief. I really felt for them. I wanted to help more, but knew I couldn't divert from the mission."

"No, that wouldn't have been a good choice. And, the reality is there is nothing you could have done to help anyway."

"I'm sure you're right, but I still felt like a heel leaving them alone."

"They weren't alone. Know that. So, anyway, back to the

download . . . Manuella told us she let something slip about the Cabal."

"Yeah, but she clammed up real quick. What is that?"

"The Cabal is an alliance of twelve billionaire families. They are the top 1% of the top 1%, and, as your conspiracy mind is probably deducing right now, they do run the show."

"I knew there was something to that! So what do they have to do with all of this?"

"Well, I can't get into all of that with you. Lydia wants to be the one to tell you about what she found in Jarbridge, but she asked me to give you some background info on the situation so you can hit the ground running when we get there."

"Okay, so what's the background?"

"The Cabal has existed for centuries, power and unimaginable wealth passed from generation to generation. They are international in scope, and they have their hands on everything—agriculture, natural resources, politics, religion, you name it. In fact, they don't just have their hands on it all. They are the ones pulling all the strings and determining who gets what, how it gets there, and how much it's worth."

Hunter couldn't believe what he was hearing and held up his hand to get Charlie to pause for a moment so he could process the information.

"You realize you are confirming the darkest fears I've held for twenty-five years, not counting the forty I was in limbo. This anti-establishment bent of mine started while

I was still in high school, but people have always mocked me as being gullible or crazy or whatever. I was dismissed, but it turns out I was right!"

"Yes, you were. Can I continue?"

"Yeah, I just . . . as cool as it is to be validated, it's still a really heady thing to consider the implications of being right."

"So, these twelve families have been controlling everything forever, and we now know they have meddled in the pandemic recovery."

"Sounds pretty typical. Capitalizing on crisis to make more money to add to the piles they couldn't possibly spend if they had a dozen lifetimes."

"It's not just about profit for them. This is about power that doesn't even necessarily tie to bank balances."

"What are you talking about? Money is power."

"True, but even more than money, subjugating other people is power."

"What are you saying?"

"Their purpose from the beginning has been to dominate the racial power structure."

"So, in other words these well-funded lunatics are white supremacists?"

"Exactly. I could give you a list of all the events in history that have been instigated or manipulated to ensure they retained the upper hand, but I'm pretty sure you can already see their fingerprints all over them."

"I doubt you'd surprise me with anything."

"Probably not, but what they are doing now is possibly the worst yet. But this is where we get into Lydia's territory, so I'll stop here and let her finish the update. We should be there in a couple of hours. We're meeting her on the outskirts of town."

"Oh, okay."

"Do you know anything about Jarbridge?"

"No. Never even heard of it until you guys told me to go there."

"It's actually a really beautiful area. Kind of an oasis in the desert of Nevada. It used to be listed as one of the most secluded places in the US. Of course, in the fallout of the pandemic, lots of places became really secluded. But it's still kind of a surprise in the sand out there—a beautiful, green valley."

"Sounds great, but I have a feeling whatever is going on there betrays the setting."

"It does indeed."

The two men rode in relative silence for the remaining miles that seemed to stretch interminably.

At roughly 8:00 a.m., they passed a sign welcoming them to Jarbridge Wilderness. Hunter's heart began to race, and he noticed sweat beading up on his forehead. It was almost "go time". He hadn't felt this nervous since the launching of the Alpha Centauri I. They wound through the mountain pass and he was awestruck by the changing terrain. It really was a spectacular little enclave.

Charlie pulled off the road and into a campground approximately thirty minutes outside of the center of town. He pulled up in front of an RV that was not terribly impressive from the outside. They both took in a deep breath, almost in unison, and got out of the Jeep. Charlie was first to the door on the side of the camper, but Hunter was hot on his heels. He was just lifting his hand to knock when the door flung open and Cady dove out and into his arms. Hunter was surprised to see such girlish expression from the woman who brilliantly supported him day after day in the most professional and confident manner. Charlie softened like a mountainous teddy bear as he held her close and twirled her around. Lydia had stepped down out of the RV and waited for Hunter who hadn't yet noticed her, being captivated by this display of young love, to turn in her direction.

When he saw Lydia, he was immediately caught up in a wave of joy and was tempted to grab her and scoop her up in an embrace to rival Charlie, but his age and his insecurity about where things stood held him back. He did reach out to give her a quick hug and told her she was a sight for sore eyes. He was too self-conscious to pick up on the subtle disappointment she registered on her face because of his seeming lack of excitement.

> "Okay you two lovebirds, let's take it inside. We can't
> be drawing attention," Lydia snapped playfully. "Hunter,
> come on in. I'll show you around the place.

Hunter found that to be a strange way to put things as there couldn't possibly be much to see. He quickly found out he was wrong, and made a mental note to stop judging books by their covers. If this tableau—

the deceptively tattered RV, the unexpected romance between Charlie and Cady, the verdant setting in the desert—was any indication, the looks of everything he was encountering could reliably be deceiving.

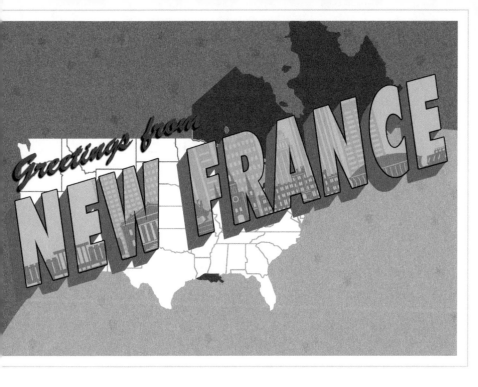

ZONE 13 - NEW FRANCE

We will give you safe harbor. We will be a beacon in the darkness. New France is the home for all seeking refuge, the space where all are welcome and not judged. From our satellite community in New Orleans to the wide expanse of the continental northeast, we embrace all who enter. What's ours is yours, and if you join us here, we will work together to build a better world.

ZONE 13

NEW FRANCE

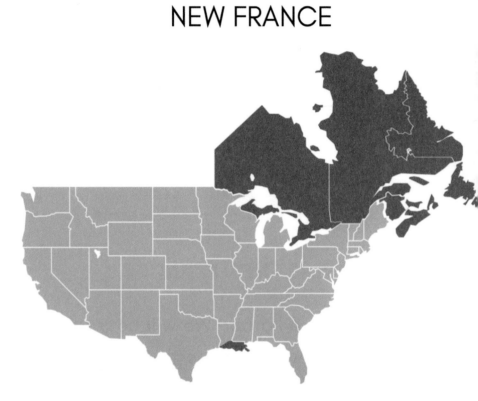

- EASTERN CANADA
- NEW ORLEANS

CHAPTER EIGHTEEN

On the outside, the RV looked like an ancient Winnebago that had seen better days. It was rusty and covered in road filth. It didn't look like it could accommodate more than one or two people comfortably, if *comfortably* was used generously. Hunter couldn't say for sure, but he suspected they coasted into the spot where it was parked and would never be able to get the engine started again to move it.

However, the inside of the RV told a different story. The finishes were sleek and modern. It was far more expansive than it appeared outside. There was a command center with a level of state-of-the-art technology that rivaled any military ops hub he'd ever seen. The two bunks on both sides of the hallway were compact, but looked very comfortable. He caught himself grinning at the mental picture of Charlie squeezing in one of them, and Lydia seemed to read his thoughts.

"Oh, he fits. It actually is a great sleep. Climate controlled, memory foam. We spared no expense in making it look as not worth your attention from the outside to deflect attention from all the amenities it actually has inside."

"It's incredible! You can't even tell from looking in the windows that it's so different."

"That's the idea. We aren't long on luxury in the Resistance, but we do recognize the need to take care of our operatives when they are in the field. Surveillance can mean long, miserable hours of nothing, and then rapid, dangerous action in a split second. People need to be well rested and equipped for that."

"That's awesome! I saw how much the creature comforts mattered on my journey."

"Hunter, that was different. We had to throw that together last minute with whatever resources were available to bring together some very complex logistics. And, don't try pretend you suffered every step of the way. I know some of the transport wasn't ideal, but I also know our people looked after you, and you were even treated like royalty in a couple of spots."

"Fair enough. I am not so sure about the royalty part, but it wasn't as bad as it could have been for sure."

"Excuse me, you were treated to the privilege of Martha's cooking, and I know Celeste gave you her bed. That is the royal treatment in those parts, my friend!"

"Okay, okay. You're right. I'm letting my cynical side skew my perspective. And yeah, everyone was at the very least interesting, if not really pleasant, so I appreciate their help."

"And their risk. You have no idea what they put on the line to transport you."

"Well, I am definitely getting a sense of that. I was pretty insulated in my office in DC, but traveling through all of those territories and learning about all the issues dividing everyone and how that is playing out gave me a rude awakening."

"It's only getting worse. And once I bring you up to speed on why we're here, you're going to see how the lid is about to blow off of everything."

Charlie and Cady had settled into the swivel chairs in the driver and front passenger spots, and Lydia told him to grab a seat on the banquette.

"Okay, so, tell me. Why did I come all this way?"

"That is going to take a little time to explain and your focused attention. Before we dive in, do you need to clean up, get something to eat or drink?"

"Honestly, Lydia, I'd just as soon cut straight to the chase. I've had nearly three weeks to wonder and worry and build up all sorts of scenarios in my head. I'll be able to appreciate a hot shower and a meal more once I know what we're facing."

"Okay, then. The reason we are here in Jarbridge is that I received an anonymous tip that there was some research being done at a secret facility here."

"What kind of research?"

Lydia leaned back and sighed heavily then put her hand on Hunter's arm and looked sternly into his eyes.

"Hunter, we do this every time, and every time I have to tell you it will go faster if you don't interrupt me. I'm going to give you all the information I have. You will absorb it and process it, and only then will you ask questions. Got it?"

Hunter smiled sheepishly. He knew she was right. He did do this every time and she always told him more than he thought he needed to know without his help prompting her. He told himself one of these days he would actually trust her to be as good as she is.

"Sorry. I'll shut up."

"Thank you. So, the tip. They did not tell me what the nature of the research was, only that it was groundbreaking and, in the wrong hands, very dangerous. They provided me with coordinates and access codes. They even went so far as to upload a biometric profile for me so I could bypass those security measures."

"What? How?"

"Well, that's how I knew we had an inside man . . . or woman . . . and that I should take this seriously."

"You didn't worry it was a trap?"

"Of course I did. But I still had to investigate. So, I came out here and got into the facility. Our mystery insider had also sent me a floor plan of the building with a path marked for where I needed to go. I went in fully prepared to be ambushed, but none of that happened. The map led me to a lab. That was about what I expected. But, what I found shook me to my foundation."

"What was it? Some kind of new weapon?"

"No. It was a cure."

"Lydia, we already have a cure. Why is that so groundbreaking?"

At this point, she slid a panel out from behind a cabinet where photographs of the lab, the white boards with notes and formulas, an action plan, and a mission statement were pinned with lines and circles drawn, making connections and laying out their discoveries. Hunter thought it looked just like the wall of a mad scientist or obsessed criminal investigator you'd see in the movies. She pointed to the formula first.

"This is what's so groundbreaking. And it ties to the information Joshua forwarded to me. You were right about the trends in birth defects and deaths. The cure the world is currently receiving is severely flawed. Whoever is running this lab has figured out that the formula is missing a key piece of information to make it fully effective."

"How could they get it so wrong?"

"Well, see this section of the formula here?" she said, pointing to a zoomed in image. "It's the genetic code for the Apollo corn. Turns out being able to study the abnormalities of the mutated strain change everything."

"I thought they eradicated every trace of it."

"Everyone did. That's what was supposed to happen. Apparently, somebody kept some, and now they are using it to develop a new and improved cure."

"Well, shit! That's a great thing! Why aren't we celebrating?" Hunter said, looking to each of the team members for what he thought was a more appropriate response. Charlie and Cady glanced at each other and then to Lydia, only increasing Hunter's confusion. When he didn't get a response, he continued.

"I met two girls traveling down the Mississippi who are getting rid of their babies because the old cure isn't stopping the defects. If this can prevent that from happening any more, we need to get it out into the world!"

"Yes, exactly," Lydia concurred without the affirmation Hunter expected.

"So, what's the problem?"

"Look at the Mission Statement," she said somberly, pointing it out on the board.

Hunter stood up to lean in and skimmed the image of the document. He sunk back into his seat stunned.

"You've gotta be kidding me!"

"I wish I were, Hunter. But it's why we are here, and it's why I need you."

"Well, you've got me and I'm ready to go bust some heads and kick some asses!"

"Holster your gun, cowboy. This is not that kind of operation. We have to move with stealth and precision. If they know we are on to them before we get this to the right people, it will be impossible to stop them."

Hunter looked to Charlie, and asked, "You knew about this the whole time we were driving here?"

Charlie nodded apologetically.

"Yeah, but come on, man, you know when Lydia gives an order, there is no second-guessing that. And, really, what would have happened if I had told you? You would have insisted I take you to the lab, completely bypassing this meeting. You would have gone in and busted up the place. I get the impulse. Really, I do. But Lydia is right on this one. We can't get caught before we get this out there. It's too critical."

"Yeah, I know. Honestly, I'm just amazed you kept it under your hat for fifteen hours."

"It wasn't easy. I almost caved when you started talking about all the different types of fish you saw on your trip."

They all laughed in that slightly excessive way that indicates it wasn't all that funny, but served as a much needed tension breaker. Lydia let them have the moment of reverie before bringing everyone back to the task at hand.

"Okay, so here's what we are dealing with and why we need you. The pictures I have are helpful, but only so far. I don't think the formula on the board that I photographed is complete."

"How do you know?"

"Well, I already sent it to Joshua and he said he isn't sure what, but at a glance, he can tell something is missing."

"Okay, so we need to get back in and find the missing puzzle pieces?"

"No. We need to get the actual serum. The vials are re-frigerated, but we can't just go in and grab one. We have to make sure we have the right version of the formula and replace it with something so they don't notice right away that it's missing. And then, you are going to take it back to DC where Joshua will be waiting. He is going to study it and see about replicating it."

"Why did you need me for that? You couldn't have brought it to me there?"

"No. I am persona non grata in those circles. I can't show up on the radar there. And,
once Joshua has confirmed it can be mass-produced outside this lab, we will be
relying on you to use the relationships you've been culti-vating there to get the word
out."

"Wait. I need to back up a few paces. Tell me, first, why this cure is working and the
other isn't."

"I just did. It's because they have the genetic coding of the corn."

"Yeah, I got that, but what is it about that?"

"Well, the missing piece in the other cure is understand-ing what made the genes mutate and how they affected our DNA. In order to reverse that and turn the Y-chromo-some back on without activating and amplifying all the Y-relaed diseases, they needed to pinpoint what in the corn makeup was triggering it. This group managed to do that."

"Okay, that makes sense. Now, about that Mission State-ment . . .," he said, leaning forward and rubbing his head vigorously as if trying to force comprehension into his brain.

"Pretty astounding and brazen, huh? To fund the support of Caucasian and Jewish peoples and their expansion in the global political, financial, medical, agricultural, and commercial space . . . ,"

"It's just . . . they really think 'tipping the scales in their direction,' as they put it, is ethical when we are talking about a global pandemic?"

"We can't let it happen. That's why you had to come out here in secret and why we have to exercise the utmost care in our next steps."

Unable to move past his disbelief, Hunter went on, "I just can't help thinking about Felicia and Cassie and how heartbreaking their situation is."

"The two girls that went to New Orleans?"

"Yeah. If these assholes hadn't been holding out on everyone, they wouldn't have had to make such a devastating decision."

"Hunter, it's worse than that. These people are funding the group homes like the one Felicia and Cassie left. They are using a form of means-testing to decide who gets the remaining specimens from the crew and who gets fertilized by tainted DNA, and who will be inseminated by the fixed material. It's all a sick sociological experiment to them. They are trying to prove the superiority of the white race with a stacked deck."

"I can't . . . I just . . . I need to hurt somebody."

"There will be plenty of time for that. Right now, I need you to come back to me and focus. We have a mission to execute flawlessly for the sake of all the Felicias and Cassies around the world."

"Okay, okay. I'm here. What's the plan?"

Lydia laid out in finite detail how she intended to get in and out without detection, what they needed to collect while they were there, how to identify it, and what would happen after that. When she was finished, Hunter excused himself to get that long-overdue shower and sort through everything he had learned.

The plan was to infiltrate the facility under cover of darkness, so they waited until the sun set and then loaded into Charlie's Jeep and drove the thirty minutes to the site in silence. As they were arriving, Lydia informed them her contact would be waiting for them there. The security access she had been granted had to be removed from the system immediately after her use so it wouldn't set off any internal alarms and alert the group.

The lab was what you would expect from a secret research facility. It was hiding in plain sight. The access point was in a tiny bed and breakfast just on the north edge of town. The Victorian-style two-story home was quaint and innocuous . . . on the outside. They could not go in through the front door, but if they had, they would have found a formal entry with a reception desk in front of a mahogany staircase, a parlor to the right and a small dining room with all the charm one would expect from a mountain getaway. It actually did serve as a functional inn and restaurant where unsuspecting guests dined and dreamed a hundred feet above an underground bunker-turned-lab. The technicians, scientists, and security came and went from the above-ground entrance disguised as employees of the inn—maids, kitchen staff, groundskeepers—all in uniforms with name tags that certified them as members of the Jarbridge Mountain Retreat.

Lydia led them to a tool shed at the northeast corner of the property, approximately fifty yards from the main building. The team followed her inside where she accessed a panel and entered a code. She told them her contact would come up to meet them and get them through the security checkpoints.

When a panel at the back of the shed slid open to reveal an elevator car, Hunter looked at Cady and Charlie to see if they were as impressed as he was. They seemed nonplussed, so he turned back to watch the metal doors open. The fluorescent lights overhead illuminated the sterility of the interior and revealed a man roughly Hunter's age and build, but less rugged and finely dressed in a well-tailored, obviously expensive suit. Hunter did a double take and then lunged at him and pinned him against the wall as the rest of his team looked on in horror.

"What the hell are you doing here?" Hunter shouted at the man. "Just what are you
trying to pull?"

Lydia charged forward and pulled Hunter off him.

"Hunter! What has gotten into you? He's here to help us!"

"Him?!" Hunter shouted incredulously. "Don't you know who he is?"

"Not really. I'm getting the sense you do."

"He's Margaret fucking Marshall's brother!"

The man sighed heavily and stepped into the shed, allowing the elevator doors to close behind him. He turned to Lydia and said, "I guess we need to talk."

CHAPTER NINETEEN

Lydia and her team found benches, overturned buckets, and anything else that would serve as a seat, but Winston Marshall remained standing. It wasn't clear if this was to maintain a position of power or because he was concerned about soiling his suit. Hunter suspected the latter as the man held no authority or even the semblance of influence beyond his power suit as far as he was concerned.

"I am about three seconds away from letting Hunter and Charlie haul you out behind this woodshed, so start talking, John Doe, or whatever your real name is."

"Lydia, I'm sorry I . . . by the way, you had to have known my name wasn't really John—"

"Insulting my intelligence is not the smart play here, buddy."

"Yeah, okay. I just meant that you shouldn't be surprised I withheld details about myself for safety reasons."

"I get that, but this is a pretty important detail, so explain yourself . . . quickly."

"Yes, I am Winston Marshall . . . President Margaret Marshall's brother. But, hold on. I promise it isn't what you think. I am on your side. I'm not trying to subvert your efforts; I'm trying to support them."

"Why?" all four of the team members asked as if on cue.

Winston was thrown off by the aggression and stumbled backward a bit, knocking a rake over and making enough noise to cause panic in everyone.

"Okay, you're going to have to trust me and let me tell you the rest on the way down. We can't be congregated in here if security decides to investigate that," Winston urged, moving them toward the elevator.

"Trust you? How do we know you didn't do that on purpose?" Hunter accused in the excessively suspicious way that indicated he was back to himself.

"I guess you don't; but then, I'm taking a risk in trusting you since you clearly aren't working in my sister's best interests, Hunter."

"Lydia, I say we get out of here and find another way in. This guy is playing us!"

"Hunter, there is no other way. This is it if we want to complete our mission. If he's on the up and up, this is our best chance. If he isn't, then he will alert everyone to our presence and it's all over. We have to take the risk."

"Lyd, I don't like it."

"No, I didn't expect you would. But, I do trust you, and I trust Cady, and I trust Charlie. And if Winston here tries anything, I know we all have each other's backs and we can get ourselves out of whatever they might throw at us."

"Okay. But if this guy," making a point to talk about Winston and not to him, "does anything I don't like, I'm taking him out."

"That's a pretty low bar, Hunter"

Whipping his head in Winston's direction, Hunter snapped. "I didn't ask for your input."

"No, but can we reserve any more comments from anyone until we are on the elevator?"

"Lead the way," Lydia said, putting her hand on Hunter's back in an effort to calm him.

Winston opened the elevator access again and stepped into the white chamber and held the door open for the others to file in. Once the doors closed and the enclosure began to move downward, Winston cleared his throat and began again.

"As I said before, I really am on your side. Margaret is too, though she's had to play all of this really carefully."

"I find that impossible to believe," Hunter scoffed.

"What exactly is she supposed to do? Nothing has been stable her entire presidency, and after you all came back, everything was in a tailspin. Now with the divisions in the country, it's not likely she will hold onto power for much longer. She has to be careful if she stands any chance of using whatever control remains to further our goals," Winston explained, vigorously defending his sister.

"How is it that you two are helping us?" Cady chimed in for the first time that night. "It just doesn't fit with what I know about you and your family."

Hunter turned to her perplexed, and asked, "What do you know about their family and why didn't you ever give me any of that in our briefings?"

"Need to know, Hunter. We thought we were on opposite sides and that really was all you needed to know to have you on board," Lydia explained

"So, what's the story?" Hunter asked, this time directing his question to Winston.

Cady looked to Winston to see if he was going to jump in, but he shrugged and gestured to her to continue.

"By all means, tell us what you know about my family."

Cady continued, "That you are part of the Cabal. Yours is one of the twelve billionaire families and that you have used your power and influence throughout the centuries to affect commerce, legislation, and, of course, politics. That's how your sister holds her office and got re-elected in the midst of a global humanitarian and ethical crisis."

Winston nodded his head, and just as Cady was about to continue, the doors slid open, revealing a long corridor lit with fluorescent tubes running the entire expanse. He guided them off the elevator, and in a whisper took charge.

"Cady is right . . . on the surface. Yes, our family is what you think, except for one significant flaw that is currently being exploited, which is why Margaret and I are working with the Resistance. I know you think we weren't aware of

you or your planting Hunter and Cady in the administration."

They all were stopped in their tracks by the shock and embarrassment this news was bound to bring. Winston urged them to keep moving, and he continued to explain.

"To be fair, we didn't know in the beginning, but as things were developing here and we were being threatened, we stumbled across your work and decided it was in our best interests to support it secretly."

"What do you mean you were being threatened? Why would the other members of the Cabal threaten you?" Lydia was growing more concerned with each step they took.

"Because we aren't really one of them."

"What does that mean?"

"Well, Hunter, it means that they have a singular purpose—to ensure that, at least for a while longer, the white and Jewish people hold onto control. They see the handwriting on the wall. They are just trying to delay it."

"And you don't benefit from that?" Lydia questioned.

"Not anymore. Someone in the group discovered our dirty little secret."

"You only have one?" Hunter shot back smugly.

"Only one that matters to them."

Winston used his keycard and biometrics to get them through several security doors that led into the lab Lydia had found in her previous entry. Once they were inside, he told them the not-so-shocking truth.

"Our blood isn't pure. During the fertility testing Margaret did when she was trying to conceive, they discovered a genetic anomaly that is unique to non-white South Africans. We knew part of our line was Dutch and that some of our ancestors settled and developed South Africa, but we did not know there was some . . . um, intermingling with the indigenous people. It was a very carefully guarded secret, so much so that Margaret and I were unaware of it until this big revelation. Someone must have found that information in my sister's records and has been threatening to expose us to the rest of the Cabal."

"So, the only reason you're with us is because they are turning on you?"

"Lydia, it's more than that. Sure, we've benefitted for a long time from the way they do things, but when it was just that they wanted to hang onto their money and power, I couldn't exactly blame them, even if I didn't like their methods. But now, they are withholding life-saving information from the entire world and choosing to dole it out only to those they deem worthy. That's a whole other level and one we don't want to be a part of."

"That's mighty noble of you, considering you've all been doing that in some way since your little elitist club formed."

"Hunter, you really don't understand. That's not why the Cabal formed initially. Yes, it was exclusive and not everything they did was honest or ethical, but the world would have been a much different place if they hadn't used their gifts and their advantage . . . and let me stop you right there before you say it . . . it would have been different, but not necessarily in a good way. Our families were innovators in industry and science and even in people. It's easy to criticize, but our money did a lot of good for a lot of people for a long time."

"Save your PR spin for someone else. I'm not buying it. And we aren't in the business of helping you rehabilitate your reputation."

"Hunter, you don't have to buy it. But I do need you to buy that our . . . mine and Margaret's . . . intentions are pure now. And we really don't have any more time to discuss or argue. We need to get what we came for and get out. We've already burned up most of the time I could square us away off the radar."

"Okay," Lydia said, clapping her hands together to get everyone's attention. "Where do we start?"

"Well, the serum vials you are going to swap out are in this case." From the breast pocket inside his coat, Winston pulled out a black, plastic rectangle just a bit bigger than a deck of cards and handed it to Lydia. Then he led her to a refrigerator with a clear door. "You need to take the first three on the . . .," he paused, and then turned to look at them. He was clearly panic-stricken, which made Lydia, Cady, and Charlie encircle him with alarm and made Hunter roll his eyes in annoyance.

"I . . . I don't know what's going on here . . . but this isn't good."

Lydia looked at him outraged. "Winston, I swear to god, if you got us down here for nothing . . .,"

Hearing that, Hunter whipped out his 9mm and trained it on Winston, and barked, "I am going to shoot the shit out of you—,"

"Hunter! Put that away!" Lydia snapped at him, and then turned back to Winston. "Where are the damn vials?"

"I really don't know. They were here when I checked an hour ago."

Just then an alarm began to groan increasingly louder and red lights above the doorways flashed. Winston grabbed the door handle and jerked on the door, obviously relieved it opened.

"This place is going into lockdown. We have to go . . . now!"

Everyone jumped to action and ran out the door and back down the corridor from the direction they'd come.

Winston shouted after them, "Not that way! They'll be sweeping from that end. We have to go out the tunnels. Follow me!"

Lydia led, with Cady and Charlie behind her, and Hunter brought up the rear, glancing over his shoulder to watch for impending doom.

Winston led the crew through the underground tunnel system that was part of an old mine shaft. It was a maze of dead ends and double backs that were designed to prevent nosy explorers from finding their way to the lab. Without a guide, they surely would have been lost, and eventually trapped in the collapsing beams and tumbling rocks and dirt that came from a cave-in clearly designed to be triggered upon detection of a breach.

Once they were out of the tunnels and a safe distance from the mine entrance, they stopped running and gathered out of sight behind the sweeping branches of a large fir tree. The first to speak through gasps of air was Winston.

"I promise you, this was not a set up . . . at least not on my part. I don't know what happened."

"Winston, I'm having a really hard time believing that," Lydia said while pacing in small circles trying to catch her breath and comprehend what had just happened.

"Who else could have taken it?" Cady asked, taking the conversation away from accusation to more productive consideration.

"I honestly don't know. As far as I knew, the only people outside those who worked in the lab who were aware of our operations were you guys."

"Are you accusing us of something?" Hunter jabbed.

"No, Hunter, I'm not. I'm saying someone else must have let it get out. Who knows, maybe someone bragging to a family member or friend blabbed it. Maybe someone who wanted to help someone they cared about promised access. And maybe that was overheard by the wrong person."

Charlie finally spoke up, "That's a whole lot of maybes. We need to move to a safer spot than just hanging out in the wilderness exposed, and then we need to go through the list of people who had access and would benefit from leaking this information. I'm going to see if I can get to the Jeep and bring it around to pick you guys up."

"Charlie, that's pretty risky."

"I know, Cady, but what else are we gonna do?"

"You're right. It's just this place is going to be crawling with their security."

"Okay, so you come with me, and if anyone stops us to ask what we're doing, we tell them we are staying at the inn on our honeymoon."

"Good idea, Charlie. Winston backstopped your cover as newlyweds when he was preparing to get access for us," Lydia informed them. "There is already a reservation under the names on the IDs I gave you."

"Nice work. Cady, let's go. We don't have much time."

Charlie and Cady ducked and bobbed through the trees surrounding the inn and made their way back to the road that ran on the west side of the property. There they shifted their posture and pretended to be taking a moonlight stroll for any onlookers who might catch sight of them. A few minutes later, they approached the Jeep, which Charlie had parked inconspicuously off the road near the inn. They climbed in and started the engine without turning on the headlights and thought they were home free until a beam shone directly through the windshield into their eyes.

Charlie through the gear shift back into park and swore under his breath as the bearer of the light moved around to the driver's window and tapped, using the flashlight in their hand.

Charlie lowered the window and said as innocently as possible, "Evening. How can I help you?"

The female officer in her mid-thirties with a very sturdy frame and few feminine characteristics, said, "Evening. We have had reports of some disturbances in the area. Where are you two heading at this time of night?"

Charlie could finally see her clearly and noted she was not wearing the standard khaki uniform of local law enforcement, though she clearly was attempting to pass herself off as such. Instead, she wore dark-colored tactical gear and had gadgets on her belt that were way beyond a sheriff's budget.

"Well, we are on our honeymoon . . . staying at the inn over there. It's such a beautiful, clear night, I wanted to take my lovely wife out to look at the stars."

"Could I see some ID, please? And, you'll understand if I verify with the inn that you are guests."

"Sure. Of course, officer."

Charlie handed her the IDs Lydia had prepared for them and she took them with her into the inn. Charlie raised the window again for privacy and turned to Cady as soon as the officer was a few feet away, exhaling deeply.

"I sure hope that holds up and that she doesn't drag this out. I don't like leaving our team out there vulnerable."

"I know. But we can't come off like we're rushing her. That will pique her suspicion and who knows what will happen then."

"Yeah. I'll play it cool. Still wish she'd hurry."

"Oh, and when we do drive out of here, take it easy. You have a lead foot."

"Wow. You are taking your wife duties seriously already!"

"Hey, you knew what you were getting into, pal."

"I did. And I would sign up for it again any day of the week."

Charlie leaned over to kiss her and was interrupted by a tapping on the glass. He was simultaneously annoyed by the timing and a little relieved because it did help sell their story. He turned around and looked at the officer with a big grin and lowered the window again.

"Well, everything checks out. But, I'd advise you to be careful tonight and not venture too far away from town."

"Thank you. We won't go too far. Have a good evening!"

She turned and walked away and Charlie wanted to floor it, but heard Cady in his head cautioning against drawing more attention, so he eased it into Drive and slowly moved out onto the road and followed the road away from the inn. Once he was out of sight and earshot, he quickly picked up the pace and took the Jeep off road, retracing their path back to where they'd left their crew.

Lydia peeked her head out from behind the tree cautiously when she saw the headlights approaching. She was able to identify the vehicle and waved Hunter and Winston out into the open to be ready to jump in when it came to a stop. Hunter had fought her on being the one to stick her neck out, but she'd explained that if these weren't friendlies, she would stand a better chance of giving a good reason for being out there than he would, so he conceded. He also took note that Winston hadn't offered, which did nothing to quell his suspicion and judgment of the man.

CHAPTER TWENTY

Hunter made a point of depositing Lydia in the backseat on the passenger side and opening the rear hatch for Winston on his way to claiming the driver's side rear seat for himself. There was significant Alpha male posturing coming off of him like a nuclear blast. What he hadn't picked up on yet, because of the weight of his journey and the ambiguity around his relationship with Lydia, was that he was more Winston's type than Lydia was. At least he would have been if not for the fact that his behavior had completely turned Winston off.

Once in place, Lydia asked why they were delayed. Cady told her about being stopped by the security at the inn and thanked her and Winston for the excellent job in creating their cover.

> "All the same, we definitely need to get moving because I don't think they are treating anyone as above suspicion," she cautioned.

Charlie took this as his cue to disregard her earlier warnings about his speed, and he floored it, kicking up dirt and launching them across the rough terrain like a bucking Bronco.

Jarbridge was a short distance south of the Idaho border, but they could not cross that line because it would put them in Homestead territory. They were already racing against the clock in being identified. Passing into a Red Zone would immediately put them back on the radar, and that could be catastrophic, so they had to backtrack south, and then west until they could shoot straight north into Oregon. There they could safely head north to Zone 1 where they could head back east.

In order to avoid coming across the security teams again, they used back roads until they were clear of the Jarbridge Wilderness, and then they picked up the highway and made better time, but it still took six hours to reach the Zone 3 entry point to Oregon. It wasn't until then that any of them felt safe to stop looking over their shoulders. They knew they were not out of the woods, but that seemed like as secure a spot as any to make a pit stop and regroup.

They pulled in to a convenience store and gas station just inside the new zone. While Charlie fueled up the Jeep, and the others used the facilities, Winston made a series of phone calls that brought him equal measures of concern and relief. Once they were all loaded back in the vehicle, Winston leaned forward over the back seat to update them on what he'd learned.

"So, I have good news and bad news."

"Just give it all to us, Winston. What happened back there?" Lydia prodded, her exhaustion and frustration loaded into each word.

"Well, someone did get there ahead of us."

"So, that's the bad news?" she interrupted.

"No. Okay, so there's bad news and worse news."

"Wait. That was going to be your good news?!"

"Well, good in the sense that at least it's out of the hands of the Cabal and might end up doing some good."

"I hate to ask . . . what's the bad . . . or worse news?"

"They know we were there and think we did it."

"Holy hell! How do you not lead with that?!" Charlie shouted swerving as he jerked his head around to see Winston.

Cady grabbed the steering wheel to right their course, but Charlie regained his composure quickly, and clenched his fists around the grips and glared out onto the road ahead of them.

"Look, I know this is a problem, but we do have a considerable lead on them because it took them a couple of hours to review outside surveillance and figure out who we were. And they don't have enough of a foothold in the Blue Zones to be able to intercept us before we reach our rendezvous point to split up."

"What rendezvous point? And who are we meeting?" Hunter asked, realizing there was a lot about this plan that hadn't been downloaded to him.

Lydia explained, "We are headed to Portland where we have a team to intercept us."

"Why? We don't have anything!" He loathed being out of the loop and decided it was time to insist on some disclosure. "Lydia, I am no help to you as long as I'm in the dark! I've spent the last three weeks—hell, I've spent the last three years showing up like a good soldier and just taking orders. I've been on a need-to-know basis that seems to not include me knowing much. I shut up and showed up out of respect for you and what I believed you and this group were trying to accomplish. But after being shuttled across the country in cubby holes by strangers without knowing why, and then to find out you are working with the guy who is supposed to be the enemy, and we are being hunted!! Well, I'm not going . . . Charlie, pull this fucking car over! I'm not going any further until you answer some damn questions!"

Lydia spoke calmly and confidently, "Charlie, we are not pulling over the car. We have to keep moving. Hunter, I will explain what's going on, but you need to take it down several notches or you really won't be useful to me."

"Lyd, I don't know what I'm doing here. At least when I'm in a cockpit, I know what my role is; I know what I'm doing. I know who the hell I am. But, being this 'political operative' and wearing a suit every day and trying to be nice to people I don't like and pretending I don't see the world unraveling around us, as if it wasn't already decimated, I feel like a lunatic. I don't recognize myself and I am damn sure nobody who knows me recognizes me. Even the little girl on the shrimp boat knew more about me than I seem to know about myself these days."

"Hunter, really, I understand, and I am sorry for all we've asked you to do without explanation. I'm truly grateful for your trust and your willingness to give me the benefit of the doubt and take big risks for us. Just know that. As for your questions . . . we were supposed to meet up with a team to hand off the serum and information gathered so they could go ahead of us to DC and get it in the right hands. That would give us freedom to make our way back safely in case anything did go wrong. At least we wouldn't have anything on us if we were caught."

"In other words, you were expecting this."

"Not really this. I just figured we wouldn't entirely escape detection. We knew they were bound to have heavy security. A lot of our plan was in place before Winston ever reached out to me to offer access."

"Well, what do we do now since we don't have the serum."

"We go to Portland and do the meet. We can't risk trying to get in touch with them right now, and we still have the formula and other data."

"Didn't you say it was incomplete?"

Winston jumped in at this point, "What Lydia had isn't everything, but I downloaded files to a secure external server before you guys arrived. We can access that and have everything we need to replicate it."

"Smart. I guess you are worth something after all," Hunter conceded reluctantly.

"I guess I am. And because we have this, I don't think we need to be too concerned about trying to find out who stole the vials."

"Oh, I think we definitely still need to know that. We have no idea what their intention is," Lydia interjected. "We don't know if this is someone just planning to blackmail the Cabal, and you know they will eagerly comply given whatever the demand will hardly affect their bottom line. And then it goes back underground. Or it could be a foreign government, which is less problematic in terms of getting the exposure we want for the cure. However, we don't know if they have the means to mass produce and properly distribute it, and aren't likely to ask the US for help. There are way too many variables to leave that question unanswered."

"Okay, I see your point. But I'm burned. I can't go poking around and ask for any information, and I doubt my sister will have any better access now that they know what role I played."

"So, how do we find out? Lydia, who do you have in the field that could safely poke around?" Cady piped up from the front.

"We're about eight hours out of Portland now, but the sun is coming up soon and I think we need the protection of night to move about. We are due to meet the team tomorrow night, so I think we can find a place to get some rest—a place with internet access so Winston can get his files and I can check in with our support staff. Charlie, see what you can find in the next fifteen or twenty minutes and—,"

"Lydia, the next town with anything resembling a place to stay isn't for about two hours," Charlie told her with concern.

"Then two hours it is. Just take the first option available."

They drove the remaining distance in silence as each of them retreated into their own heads to consider what had happened and what was next. Charlie found a rundown motel with a half-blinking vacancy sign. He pulled off the road and parked in front of the office. He went in and used the newlywed cover to their advantage once again to book a single room for the night. He told the clerk they were on their way to Cannon Beach, but had driven all night after the wedding reception and just had to crash for a bit. He was hoping that would explain renting a room in the middle of the day. He also made sure to ask for a room on the back side of the building away from the parking lot for . . . you know . . . privacy. The clerk winked and him and gave him a knowing nod. After getting the key, Charlie got back in the Jeep and took them around to their room. Everyone moved indoors quickly. Lydia closed the blinds and scoped out the room.

Winston sat down in one of two chairs next to a small round table and pulled out a laptop from a black, leather attaché. Hunter sat in the chair across from him and watched his meticulous movements.

"Where did that come from? I didn't notice that when we were escaping, and I'm a pretty observant guy."

"You weren't supposed to notice it. It's a slim line case that fits in a panel stitched into the back of my suit coat."

"Seriously? That's some James Bond, Q-level gear! Is the suit bullet proof too?"

Winston laughed, thankful Hunter was cutting him a little slack. "No, I do have a collection of Garrison Bespoke suits, but they don't have the compartment, and I figured that was a higher priority."

Hunter laughed, and paused to study Winston's unwavering expression. "Wait. You're serious! How much does something like that set you back?"

"Honestly, not much more than the cost of a good quality tailored suit."

"Unbelievable. Still, probably out of my government salary budget."

"Hunter, you should check the labels in the ones my sister had made for you."

"Why? Are you saying . . .,"

"She was protecting an asset."

"Why does no one tell me anything?!"

At that moment, Lydia came out of the bathroom where she had re-treated to make some phone calls.

"Because this part is so much fun!" she teased. "Hunter, honestly, it's not a reflection on you or what we think of you. In fact, it's kind of the opposite."

Lydia sat on the bed across from Hunter and leaned in and took his hands in hers. Winston turned back to his computer and began attempting to establish a connection so he could retrieve his data.

"Hunter, you are so valuable, so essential to us—and a lot of other people around the world—that we had to protect you. If we told you too much, you'd be at even greater risk for being taken by other interested parties. We had to position you as a trophy piece not to be taken too seriously because you've already been abducted once and nearly mauled a couple of times since you came back from the Proxima b voyage."

"Yeah, but with the cure, I'm not such a hot commodity anymore. They don't need anything from me."

"But, there is more to you—more to all of you who came back—than just what you could do for the pandemic."

"Lydia, what are you talking about? They did all those tests and gave us a clean bill of health."

She sat silent, trying to decide how to tell him what she had to share. Cady and Charlie had curled up together on the other bed, but sat up when they realized Lydia was about to spill the goods.

"You are right; the tests didn't find any problems in you. You weren't carrying any new diseases or intergalactic toxins or parasites. Nothing like that."

"Well, that's a relief. You had me worried for a minute that I was carrying some Andromeda Strain or something."

His reference was lost on the others, which made him feel the forty lost years more powerfully than he had in quite a while.

"Yeah, I'm not sure about that. But, that doesn't mean they found nothing."

"So, they found *something*."

"It's possible that whatever you experienced in that worm hole may have altered you in such a way that you are less susceptible to gravitational pull."

"What, like I'm anti-gravity?"

"Something like that. We don't know for sure, but there are studies going on with other crew members. It's minor, almost immeasurable, but we think it's there, and it could open doors for us in resuming space exploration."

"I really don't know what to think about that. Part of me feels like I am ready to leave here and go back out there where things made more sense. Another part of me thinks I'd be crazy to try that again given my track record."
"Well, it's not really a decision you have to make right now. But do you understand now why we have had to use such caution with you? It's been hard enough to keep them at bay as it is with them believing you aren't even a useful idiot."

"Wow. That doesn't sting at all."

"I'm sorry. I just mean we had to convince people you weren't worth stealing."

"And I played the part well?"

"Actually, no. You made our jobs really hard. Having you off the grid for the last three weeks and presumably lost in the wilderness was a big break for us."

"Glad I could help."

"You really have, Hunter. I know it doesn't feel like it, but now that you're clued in, you will be an even greater asset."

Winston pulled another device from his bag and plugged it into his laptop. It looked like a cylinder, but it quickly began cranking out a long sheet of paper with the data he had downloaded from his server.

"Another spy gadget?"

"No. This is just a portable printer. You can find them at most office supply stores."

"You should have gone with the flashier story, man. I wouldn't have known the difference."

Lydia was relieved to see Hunter cutting Winston some slack as she was keenly aware having him in their corner was essential to their survival. She encouraged everyone to relax for a bit because these were probably the only moments of reprieve they would have for the foreseeable future.

When the sun had set and they felt it safe to head out, they piled into the Jeep, this time with Winston in the front seat and Cady in the rear. They passed the next six hours with Winston making small talk with Charlie and Cady while Lydia and Hunter listened in silence. As they arrived in Portland, Charlie wove his way into an industrial district and located an abandoned warehouse where they were to meet the other team. Before they got out, Lydia stopped Hunter and asked him to hold back a minute.

"What's up? You're not still trying to protect me, are you?
If this situation is
dangerous, none of us should be going in."

"No, it's not that. They are our people and we know the location is secure. It's just . . .
I need to tell you something . . .,"

And just as she was about to tell him, something caught Hunter's eye and he turned to look out the window and discovered another crucial piece of information she'd been withholding.

"Jacob . . . ," Hunter whispered.

CHAPTER TWENTY ONE

Hunter struggled to reconcile his anger over seeing his son dragged further into this mess with his relief at seeing him again and knowing he was safe. He shot a look at Lydia that she deflected with a warning of the urgency around getting inside.

Once they were all gathered in the warehouse, they made their way to a table set up to the right of the door where they had maps and tactical gear laid out. Lydia got them started with some introductions.

"Hunter, this is Sam," she said, nodding in the direction of a woman who appeared to be Cady's age, but a bit rougher around the edges.

Hunter figured she'd seen some combat based on her demeanor and a fairly noticeable scar running through her hairline. She silently returned the nod and maintained her at-the-ready stance.

Lydia continued, "She and Jacob are going to take the information we found and deliver it to a team of scientists who will begin working to replicate the serum based on the formulas we have, which are now complete, thanks to Winston's quick work."

"Why is Jacob involved in this? He's not a scientist or special ops. He doesn't have training for this—,"

"*Dad,*" Jacob inserted with a strong sarcastic inflection to communicate that Hunter was overstepping, "in case you forgot, I am a journalist . . . an investigative journalist. That means I know how to handle myself in sketchy situations, and what I bring to the table is going to be really important when we are ready to expose this to the world."

Hunter grumbled, but conceded his position and let them continue the briefing.

"So, here's what we know," Winston said, stepping forward. "The Cabal has been operating through a shell corporation called Planet XY. While I was on the inside working with them, I was able to discover that the source of their success wasn't so much in having access to the strain of corn that caused the pandemic—we know other countries held onto some even though they weren't supposed to. But, Planet XY seems to be the only group to figure out that the key to the cure was held in the corn."

"What makes you think that?" Cady asked, skeptical that they were the only ones with the idea.

"Well, they were none too happy that the first vaccine to roll out held no opportunities for financial gain since it was treated as a humanitarian crisis and given for free. So, they have been watching closely to find an opening to capitalize on it. Because of that, they were the first to compile comprehensive data about the birth complications in children born from those with the cure. Hunter, the reports you gave to Joshua . . . I put those in your hands."

"Okay. That makes sense now. I wondered how we got them when they didn't appear to come from any government agency study."

"You're welcome," Winston said somewhat smugly. "With those statistics, they began working to understand what was missing. They decided going back to the source was the key, and the information they found allowed them to isolate the mutation that caused the malfunction in the Y-chromosome. By reverse engineering that mutation, they have formulated a new cure for the disease and are seeing a success rate that all but erases the plague that nearly destroyed us."

"That's stunning," Jacob said, impressed but suspicious. "But, I'm with Cady. Why didn't the original researchers think to go back to the source? Seems pretty logical to me."

"Well, I wasn't privy to their logic, but I think they were tunnel-visioned in thinking the crew held the key to the cure—that their blood would unlock things. And it was a great start, but because they hadn't consumed the corn, their DNA did not show the mutation process. Hence, the missing pieces."

"That tracks. But, what are we missing with Planet XY? What's the catch? Because there clearly is one or we wouldn't be here under these circumstances."

"The catch is they don't want everyone to have it because they don't want to eradicate the plague entirely."

"So, what is this? A money thing? Are they trying to capitalize on the sale of the cure? I mean, that's greedy and despicable, but I also am not surprised. It's capitalism."

"Jacob, if they were just profit-driven in their motives, I don't think any of us would be taking this risk."

"Okay, then, Mr. Inside Man, what's the problem?

"They aren't distributing it just to those who can afford it— though the outcome is pretty much the same; their plan is to distribute it initially just to those of a certain race."

"I'm assuming you mean white people."

"Yes, you would be right in that assumption. Well, white and Jewish. But they don't really see it as being racist, just tipping the scales to keep up with minority race growth."

"It's still wrong. They have to be stopped. Tell me what you need me to do."

Lydia took back the floor at this point, "Hold on. We'll get to that. There's a wrinkle in things you aren't aware of."

Jacob and Sam moved in closer with concern and Hunter, Cady, and Charlie also leaned in wondering what she was going to propose as a solution.

"We did not get our hands on the vials. They were gone when we got there. And we almost got caught. In fact, they are probably still pursuing us, believing we stole them."

"Well, we did take—,"

"Yeah, I know, Winston, but this puts pressure on us we weren't counting on . . . at least not this fast and this close. We were counting on at least a slight delay in their discovery so Sam and Jacob could be well on their way to DC while Hunter and I drew their attention and Charlie and Cady could split off as additional decoys. The hope for that to go off without a hitch is shot to hell. Our level of risk is exponentially higher now."

"So, what's the new plan, Major?" Sam asked, cutting to the chase. She was short on words and long on action, and all of this discussion was beginning to make her twitchy. Hunter could identify with her feelings.

"Yeah, why are we still standing around? If they are hot on our trail, we need to disperse now," Hunter urged.

"We are out of here in ten. For the most part, we will proceed as planned, but Cady, Charlie, you guys need to make a bigger splash as you attract attention on your route south. Hunter, you and I will still head north, but we are going to go off grid again in Vancouver, British Colombia for a bit. We have some friends there who can put us up at a moment's notice."

"Sounds like they are good friends to have."

"You have no idea. But you'll soon find out. Winston, I believe you have your own plan for where to go?"

"Yes, I'm going to have to disappear for a while too. I will communicate through Margaret where possible, but you may not see me or hear from me until this is settled."

"Okay. I trust you know what you're doing. Jacob and Sam, you need to hit the road now and use the credentials that got you out here through the Red Zones."

"How did you—,"

"Hunter, I'll explain that on the way to the safe house. Everyone, listen up." She waited until everyone had stopped putting on gear and collecting what they were assigned to take with them. "We don't know what they know or what they plan to do about it other than they will be looking specifically for me and Hunter, which is why we need to lay low. That doesn't mean any of you are not on their radar. Be smart. Be careful. Let's get this done."

The group split off into the pairings and vacated the warehouse, leaving Winston to sweep for any traces of their presence while he waited for his contact to arrive with transport and new travel documents.

It wasn't until they were saying goodbye to Charlie and Cady that Hunter gave any thought to the fact that they would be taking the Jeep and he did not notice any additional vehicles at the site. As if reading his mind, Lydia led him to a garage door a few yards down. She grabbed the handle and hoisted the door upward. Sunlight flooded into the cavernous space that was empty except for one thing.

"Think you can manage this?"

She pointed to a cobalt blue Dodge Challenger Hellcat that looked a lot like one he'd owned before his intergalactic adventure. He just grinned at her like a schoolboy and nodded eagerly.

"I could kiss you!" he shouted as he ran to the driver's side. Then he caught himself and fumbled over a correction. "I . . . um . . . I just mean . . . ," and Lydia let him sweat it out a bit before rescuing him by handing him the keys and getting in on the passenger side.

He eased the car out of the garage and Lydia directed him out of the warehouse district and to the interstate they would take northbound. While being on a highly trafficked road was a risk, being on the road at all for longer than necessary was an even greater one, so they did not opt for back roads on this passage. Once they were on the straight-away, Hunter cleared his throat and fidgeted a bit, clearly trying to decide how to broach a subject.

"Lyd, there are still a lot of unanswered questions, and now that we don't have distractions, I need you to be straight with me."

"I know, I know. I owe you some explanations. Is there somewhere in particular you'd like to start?"

"Well, it may not be the biggest, most looming question, but it is maybe the most relevant to me. How did Jacob get here? Last I heard he was going up into Zone 13 to hang out with some friends to support our cover story. When did he leave and why did that not put us back on the radar?"

"Good questions, all. He was there until two days ago when we knew you were in Charlie's capable hands and well on your way to Jarbridge. At that point, he and Sam took a direct flight here, but with fake IDs. Even though your location wasn't going to be revealed by his move-ments, and we felt fairly certain he wasn't a primary surveillance target at the time, we didn't want to take any chances. Also, his points of exit and entry were still in Blue territories, so there was less cause for concern."

"Okay. I guess you thought that through. But I still want to go on record as having strong objections to his involve-ment."

"Duly noted. But, seriously, Hunter, you are going to have to sort out what all of this is for you because this trying to be a father to a son you barely knew and who is bizarrely close to the same age . . . it's making everyone uncomfortable. And he is trying to be a good soldier, but his resentment still comes into play at problematic times."

"What exactly am I supposed to do? I know everyone says, 'But, my situation is different!', but ours really is. There is no one in the history of humanity who has had to deal with a scenario like this."

"Really? You think so?"

"Well, yeah! You don't?"

"Hunter, come on. Of course the details are different and really unusual, but the core issues are the same. You feel obligated to parent him, but don't really have any experience with that and trying to jump into the role without allowing for an adjustment period triggers all the abandonment issues Jacob has tried to bury."

"It wasn't my fault I wasn't there! He has to know that."

"Of course he does, but that doesn't change the fact that he has only recently come to understand why and work to release that baggage he carried for nearly four decades."

"Yeah, I guess."

"And, then there's his mom."

"What about her?"

"Well, she's a sore spot too."

"Why? I didn't do anything wrong."

"Maybe not . . . from your perspective. From his, you left his mom to carry the load all by herself and she died too early after suffering a lot."

"Again . . . not my fault."

"Hunter, you're not telling me anything I don't already know. I'm trying to get you to understand his perspective and why you need to tread lightly with him."

"So, what do I do?"

"Well, trying to be his buddy won't work any more than trying to be his father right now. As much as you hate not being in charge of things and not knowing what to expect, that's really what you have to accept. Let him come to you and dictate the terms of engagement. He may not know exactly what he needs yet, but you trying to force what you want and need on him isn't going to get you there."

"Okay. But, I don't have the first clue how to do that."

"Actually, you do. Just call on your experience when you fly."

"What do you mean? I'm totally in control there."

"But, are you? You know how to operate the plane, sure, and you have instincts for how to respond to unexpected things you encounter, like birds or turbulence—things that can throw you off course. You can't predict what's going to happen up there, but you do know you can trust yourself to adapt and make decisions on the fly based on what you have before you. It's the same thing with Jacob. Take your cues from him and just wing it."

Hunter smiled and shook his head. "You're good. Where were you when I was trying to figure out how to deal with his mother? She was a real piece of work."

"Well, since my parents hadn't even met yet . . .," she laughed awkwardly. "And I'm not sure I am the right person to be giving you romantic advice . . . conflict of interest."

"Oh," Hunter said, unsure of what to do with that, even though he'd been hoping for some kind of clue about where she was coming from in that regard.

"Um . . . anyway . . . what was the deal there?"

"With Michelle? Well, we met through a mutual friend. She was working as a dog groomer, but being a vegan, she was constantly conflicted over it."

"Are you sure you know what vegan means? Or . . . what kind of groomer was this?"

"Yes," he said with annoyance, "I know what it is. She, on the other hand, took the 'harm to animals' part to the nth degree. She cried every time she clipped their nails or trimmed their coats."

"If the job was so compromising to her principles, why did she stay in it?"

"It was her parents' business and they were having health problems, so she helped run the place because it was their livelihood."

"The things we do for family."

"I know it sounds silly, but it's also, in a weird way, what I kind of loved about her."
"Love? Both you and Jacob have always made it sound like it was just a casual thing."

"See, that's the trouble with the past. Everyone has their own take on it. Yeah, I loved her. We didn't break up because I didn't. I just felt this bigger calling and she obviously didn't fit with that plan. No one but my crew did. It wasn't an easy decision, and I know she really resented me for it . . . in fact, I think it may have tainted her account of what happened with us and why Jacob doesn't trust me. But, it is what it is. I can't go back and change it. I do wish I could have been there for Jacob as he was growing up."

"If you'd stayed, do you think you and Michelle would have stayed together?"

"Hard to say. Even though I loved her—and if I'd known about a child in the mix, I probably would have tried really hard—in the end, we were just too different. We had been drifting apart, so when we called it a month or so before the launch, it wasn't a big surprise to either of us."

"Wow. That's probably the most open you've been about any of that in the time I've known you."

"It *is* the most open I've been. Who knows? Maybe I'm finally evolving as a human being. It would be pretty ironic if that was all thanks to some extraterrestrial infection."

They both laughed and enjoyed the closeness they felt, as well as the moments of reprieve from drama. Over the remaining hours of the drive, they talked about the state of disunion unfolding throughout the country, what was likely to happen with the Zones, and how the new cure could conceivably change everything. They danced around the subject of what was developing between them, though they never came right out and expressed their feelings or what they wanted to do about them.

Just as they thought they were starting to run out of things to talk about, Hunter realized a missing piece of the story.

"I don't think you've ever told me how you got involved with the Resistance."

"Hmm . . . maybe not. There's not much to the *how* of the situation. The *why* is a much longer story."

"Well, we have time and I'm a captive audience."

Lydia laughed and looked at him with deepening affection.

"Okay, if you really want to hear it . . . ,"

"I really do."

"Well, as you know, the Resistance was forming, but had not fully coalesced into a functional group when we met and I roped you into all of this in that closet."

"Right. You took a huge risk that night."

"And I paid for it. Although, I wouldn't change a thing if I could. This work we're doing is too important, and I'm not sure I could have continued doing what I was doing and held onto my soul."

"I don't regret my service, but I do think it's time for a change."

"Oh, don't get me wrong. I proudly served. That's how I rose in the ranks as a woman. But, the higher up you go, the more you see the chinks in the armor and the more they ask you to ignore them. And I couldn't do that."

"I get that."

"There's a lot in my background that plays into that, but maybe we can save some things for future conversations. But, when I was discharged, they brought me in to begin running special ops, and that's how I enlisted you."

"You mean drafted?"

"Are you saying you are here involuntarily?"

"No . . . no, not at all. I just mean, when you enlist, you sign up having a pretty good clue of what you're getting yourself into. In this case, you asked for my help, and something in my gut told me I had to say yes."

"And I appreciate it. We all appreciate it. I know it's been tough feeling so out of the loop. I know you well enough to know that you will run into burning buildings, scale mountains, and take on mobs without hesitation . . . as long as you know why. So, really, I do understand what a leap of faith it was for you to join us without much information. It means the world to me. And I hope you know enough of what's going on now to really feel like part of the team."

"I still have lots of questions, but I think the important ones have been answered . . . except maybe this . . . Where the hell are we going?"

"I told you . . . Vancouver."

"It's a pretty big place, Lyd."

"We have a safe house there. It's run by friends."

"Okay, this is that cagey bullshit that drives me nuts."

"First, understand that we keep these things compart-mentalized for everyone's safety. Okay?"

"Yeah, yeah."

"But, I guess we are close enough now to our destination that it's okay for you to know . . . we will be with Abe and Sarah."

"What?! I had no idea . . . I mean, I knew they went to BC, but I just didn't make the connection. I am really off my game in picking up clues."

"Don't be too hard on yourself. You've been through a lot, and you haven't heard from them in a couple of years now. Which, by the way, was by design."

"Okay. Well, do you have any more surprises for me?"

"Now, that would spoil all of my fun, wouldn't it?"

"At my expense."

"Don't take it personally. Actually, I don't know if you'd put this in the category of surprise so much as just additional details, but Sean and Natalie Flemming are there with Abe and Sarah. Oh, and the miracle baby . . . he's three and absolutely amazing."

"Sounds like we are showing up to a reunion."

"Even more than you might realize."

Hunter wanted to ask for full disclosure, especially based on her last comment, but he knew he would only get from her what she deemed necessary at the time, so he didn't press. But, his curiosity was piqued to a new height. And he definitely was looking forward to reconnecting with some of his old crew.

CHAPTER TWENTY TWO

Hunter maneuvered through picturesque canopied roads into a remote woodland that seemed to be way off the grid. Lydia directed him to the compound where they would meet up with Abe and Sarah. When she instructed him to pull over, it appeared to be nothing more than an expansion of the shoulder, but as he eased into the space, he could see it was a drive that led up the side of a slope. He moved slowly up the trail that was worn, but well-concealed from the roadway below. As he followed the ridge climbing upward, he realized he would have no-where to go but off the cliff if a vehicle came from the other direction.

About half a mile up this unpaved drive, they came to a large wooden gate that covered the entire expanse of the path. The bisected panels opened inward once they were within ten feet, and Hunter continued moving slowly past them and up another 300 feet to the large cabin where Abe was standing at the end of the stone pathway to greet them, waving vigorously and joyfully. Sarah stood next to him with a small boy perched on her hip who had a head full of dark, curly locks.

Hunter parked the Charger next to a hybrid SUV in front of an outbuild-ing and he and Lydia jumped out and went over to their friends with-out bothering to unload their bags. Abe pulled Hunter into an almost smothering hug and laughed in his open-hearted, jovial way that en-deared him to everyone, even the stoic Hunter who had softened to him over the years. As Abe escorted them into the house, Sean and Natalie came out and welcomed Hunter and Lydia. After a quick hello, the twins went to the car to retrieve the tactical pack that had accompanied Hunter along his long journey and Lydia's bag and laptop case. Hunter tried to object, but Abe just patted him on the back.

> "Hunter, they will be fine. And you need to come inside and let me get a better look at you."

> "Doc, I don't think I need an exam."

> "I do not mean that kind of a look. You are a sight for these old sore eyes, my friend, and I just want to enjoy seeing you for as long as we have you here."

Hunter felt a sweet sense of nostalgia and relief in seeing his colleague and fellow adventurer, and the warmth filled him more than he ever expected.

> "It's great to see you too. I am looking forward to having a minute to catch my breath and catch up with you . . . with all of you!" He said, looking to Sarah and reaching out to tickle the belly of the boy she held in her arms. "Especially you, little guy! I can't believe you're here."

> The child wasn't sure what to make of the strange man and ducked his head into the curve of his mother's neck to hide, but peeked his eyes toward Hunter with a sly grin.

> "Zeke, say hi to Hunter," Sarah nudged.

> "Your name is Zeke?" Hunter said to him, trying to engage him while Lydia watched, amused by his efforts to be friendly, knowing he was uncomfortable around children.

> "Ezekiel Adam Tilden, but we call him Zeke," Abe announced proudly. "He is our biggest—and, of course, favorite—surprise to top off a series of shocking events."

"Hunter, Lydia, it is so wonderful to see you both, and we will have plenty of time to talk later, but I do need to get this one down for a nap. We pushed it out as long as we could, waiting for your arrival, but we are teetering dangerously close to meltdown territory," Sarah explained as she gave them kisses and retreated to the eastern wing of the rather impressive lodge.

"Come with me. Sarah laid out a spread of nibbles for us to enjoy before dinner. We can snack and chat." Just then, Natalie and Sean came in with the bags and Abe instructed them, "Kids, they will have the lower level accommodations, so just deposit their belongings down there and then join us for some refreshments."

Abe led Hunter and Lydia to a large rustic dining table between the open kitchen and the living area gathered around a massive stone fireplace. They clustered at one end of the table where Sarah had filled a charcuterie board with a variety of treats, many of which she had made by hand.

Abe began, "Okay. Tell me about your journey. From what I understand you have had quite the adventure. Have you not had your fill of excursions gone awry?"

"More than enough for several lifetimes! Life just doesn't seem to want things to be easy for me."

"Oh, but I dare say, you would be bored to tears if it were any other way."

"You're probably right. I wouldn't know what to do with myself in a quiet life, that's for sure. But *you* seem to be thriving. You have this amazing home and a beautiful family. I'm really happy for you."

"Well, yes, we have a lovely life and I am inexpressibly grateful every day for the gift of my wife and this phenomenon of a child. But, considering my age, he offers plenty of excitement and adventure. And, we have the twins here with us most of the time, except when they are running errands for our dear Lydia."

Hunter turned to Natalie and Sean as they were joining them at the table.

"I'm so glad you guys are here with Abe and Sarah. But the last I heard you were going back home to Seattle. And, by the way, Sean, I'm so glad you got out of the Reproductive Center. I know it wasn't under the best of circumstances, but it was a good thing you didn't have to be a part of that mess. Lucas didn't fare so well. I've wondered about him and hope he is okay now."

"Yeah, it wasn't the best news that I can't have kids, but I am kinda okay with it considering the alternative was making thousands of 'em. I've talked to Lucas some. He seems to be solid. He has a girlfriend and I think they may get married."

"It's not . . . um, what's her name who found us? Amelia?"

"Nah, man. That woulda been weird since he thought she was somebody else who turned out to be like seventy years old when he got back. But Amelia's cool. She's with us."

"With us?"

"Yeah, in the Resistance?"

"Us?"

CHAPTER TWENTY TWO

"Okay. Hunter, I guess it's time for the full download," Lydia interrupted.

"Ya think?" Hunter shot back at her, showing his exasperation with the piece-meal flow of information that she knew was a big trigger for him.

The lack of openness was one of his biggest frustrations when they returned from outer space and something he railed on her about then. It seemed she was still really good at that part of her military job.

"Hunter, we've talked about this and why it was necessary," Lydia reminded him.

"But it seems like I'm the only one out of the loop. Young Flemming, here, knows more about my crew than I do. And Abe . . . are you all up to speed? It sure seems like you are."

"Yes, Hunter, I am . . . up to speed. But, you have to understand, that is because Sarah and I have been operating this safe house for Resistance members since they released all of us. Keeping information from you was in no way a reflection of your capabilities or the faith we have in you."

"Then what the hell was it? Because I sure am not feeling the love or the trust."

"Hunter, you are getting all worked up again and you know how that worked out for you in the past. Shouting is only going to wake Zeke and it isn't going to get you in the know any faster. See, this is part of . . .,"

"No, finish what you were going to say. This is part of what?"

Lydia sighed, reluctant to throw a wrench in the bond they were forging.

"Part of why I held things back. You're reactionary . . . and loud about it. You have a tendency to bring all the subtlety of a ball peen hammer when you see injustice, and that would not have served our purposes. Look, you've been a great asset to us, and no one could have gotten closer to the Marshall administration; but, can you honestly tell me that if you'd known at the time you started working for her any of what you've learned recently that you could have held back from busting down her door and giving her what for?"

Hunter settled back in his chair and took his lumps, though he wasn't happy about it.

"I guess you're right. But look at what not knowing does to me! At some point maybe you can try trusting me to handle myself appropriately. At the very least, give me a chance to practice."

"That's what I'm trying to do now. Just because you're late to the game, it doesn't mean you are the last to know."

"Okay, so what do you have to tell me?"

"Let's start with the crew—where they are now and what they are doing."

"Sounds good. I've been wondering about them."

"Abe, would you like to start? You can tell Hunter about what you and Sarah have been doing. Then Sean and Natalie can share their part. Then I'll cover everyone else. Just so I'm not talking about you in front of you. That just feels weird."

"Thank you, Lydia. I would be delighted. Hunter, as I have already told you, Sarah and I came here after our release. This place was a family home and none of our extended family had taken ownership in the time we were gone, so we went through the somewhat arduous court process of reclaiming it. Once that was settled, we moved in and began doing some renovations and expansion. Because of what Lydia had enlisted us to do for the group, the upgrades to the compound included perimeter security, a state-of-the-art communications center, bullet proof glass, and secure bunkers. And then our sweet Zeke was born."

"I just have a hard time wrapping my brain around you running some kind of spy harbor. It's so . . .,"

"Youthful?"

"Hey, you said it buddy, not me."

"Well, we all know I am a bit long in the tooth, but having Ezekiel has given me the proverbial second wind in this advanced stage of my life; so why not do all I can to help the cause?"

"That's pretty great. And you and Sarah look better than ever. I still can't get over what a surprise it was to hear you were having a kid. But, it couldn't have happened to a better couple."

"Thank you. We are grateful every day for the gift of his life and how it has changed ours. Do you have any questions of me now?"

"No, seems pretty straight forward to me. It's not a surprise that you guys would be involved. Just a little deeper than I expected. Natalie, same for you and Sean. It's not where I thought you were, but it's not a big shock to find you here."

"Sean and I did return to Seattle at first, but all of our friends and cousins were so much older and we just didn't fit. We both had trouble finding work because so much had changed. The medical community in the Blue Zones was so different. It was hard to practice being so unprotected from liabilities, and there just weren't nearly as many restaurants in operation, so a kitchen job for Sean was nearly impossible. We had our settlement and back pay money to get by on, but nobody really wants to sit around and do nothing . . . especially nobody who lost forty years in the blink of an eye!"

"Exactly! I'm not exactly the kind of guy to kill myself for a job, but I want to feel productive and useful. I have to admit, I did feel some depression coming on after everything and then having such a hard time getting back to normal. Nothin' made sense."

"That is when Natalie called me and asked if they could come here for a bit to regroup. Sarah and I were more than happy to have them. They have been like part of our family for years. It was while they were here that Lydia made contact with us to host a Resistance member who was coming through the area while exploring the territories to assess how significant the rift in the country was becoming. We have now hosted roughly a dozen Resistance members or allies for varying lengths of time."

"So, what about the rest? Lucas, Kamil, Li? And Pearce? What's up with him? Last I heard he was really regretting going to Africa. Did he ever get out?"

"Okay, I'll just run down the list, starting with the ones I have the list information about. Let's see . . . the crew members who were on loan from other countries—Kenneth Latham, Daniel Cohen, and Yoshi Tanaka—they went back to their homes and we have not remained in contact. We keep tabs on them, but they are pretty much just figuring out their new lives. They have no connection to the Resistance at this point, though I think we can consider them friends. Most of the others went back to their original homes to see what was left for them. A few ended up going elsewhere, others stayed. As the division in the country has grown, a couple more have relocated to be in a Zone that suits them better, but many of the places had been leaning in one direction or another for so long that there were no surprises about the kind of place where they lived, and that was fine with them. The people in Blue Zones and in the Red Zones ended up being pretty balanced. Your navigation specialist, Erica Steele, is in Colorado working for with an aerospace company trying to bring the space program back online, Byron Rice is in New York, Javier Romero is in California. They were Kamil's assistants. They are still in the science field. Leila Tate, who supported Michael, is in Boston serving as his teaching assistant at MIT . . . and I'll give you more on Michael in a minute. Scott Jordan wasn't happy that Leila got the assistantship and took a job with a senator in Texas as his science advisor."

"Okay, so that covers the Bridge and Engineering. Before you go on, I need to hit the head and I need a minute to absorb. We kind of dove right into all of this right after coming off the road."

"Of course. Take whatever time you need. We are going to be here a couple of days, I think. And I need to check in on some things anyway and update Abe on what we learned at Jarbridge."

Hunter pushed away from the table and found his way downstairs to the suite that had been reserved for them. He took notice of the fact that though there were multiple bedrooms on that floor that were quite comfortably appointed, Sean and Natalie had chosen to put his and Lydia's gear in the same room. He figured that would require a conversation later that he wasn't sure he knew how to navigate. But, for the moment nature called.

Hunter had laid down on the bed with the intention of just collecting himself, but he quickly fell into a deep sleep and woke with a start to Lydia's hand on his shoulder half an hour later.

"Hmm . . . whoa! I didn't mean to . . . sorry. I'm up."

"Hunter, it's okay. You clearly needed the rest, and it gave me time to tell Abe the latest. Are you ready to go back up?"

"Yeah. I mean, I think I could sleep for a week, but I know we have a lot of ground to cover yet, and that's not even including what we do next with all of this."

"I've been thinking about some of that and I have some thoughts. I need everyone to weigh in, so we'll talk about it tonight, after dinner."

Hunter followed Lydia back upstairs and found everyone a buzz. The table had been cleared and reset for dinner. Abe was sitting with Zeke on the large sectional sofa, reading a book while Sarah and Natalie backed up Sean in the kitchen as he was pulling together what the senses said would be an incredible meal. Almost in unison, they all welcomed Hunter back to the land of the living. Hunter joined Abe and Zeke on the sofa, and the small child studied him with keen interest. He smiled quite self-consciously at the toddler whom he really wanted to impress for a reason that had not yet revealed itself to him. Lydia plopped into one of the oversized armchairs and tucked her legs under her. Hunter noted it was probably the most relaxed he'd ever seen her.

"Is it okay to talk about this stuff in front of him?"

Abe laughed, appreciating Hunter's sensitivity.

"As long as we are careful with our words and use gentle tones, he will be fine. While he is advanced for his age," Abe said with a knowing wink, "and his vocabulary is quite expansive, his comprehension of many of those words is not. He is mostly parroting us at this point."

"You talk about me, Papa?"

"Yes, Zeke. We are talking about you and how smart you are!"

"Okay. I can go play?"

"Of course, but let's not pull out too many toys just now. We will be having dinner soon."

"But, I show your friend."

"Not this time. He will be here for two more sleeps, so you have time."

"Okay, Papa."

The toddler ran to his room and noise ensued that indicated he had not taken the instruction to heart. Lydia took the opportunity to get back to her accounting of the crew.

"Let's see, we left off with Medical. Most of them are present and accounted for. I think that just leaves Nancy Bolton. She went back to South Carolina and works in a family clinic. The change has taken a toll on her, and she seems to be having a hard time building community there. I have people keeping a close eye on her. I'm sure you haven't forgotten we lost Harris during the abduction. His parents were elderly by the time you returned and he was an only child. Along with the payments he was supposed to receive, we supplemented funds to create a charity in his name."

"That's nice. How he died . . . it still haunts me. I'm glad he's being honored in some way."

"It was really tragic, and so unnecessary. We were proud to do what we could to recognize his sacrifice. His colleagues in communications—Brooke and Leigh—they ended up going in pretty different directions. Brooke is a conservative commentator based in Atlanta, which is an interesting dynamic. Georgia is in a Red Zone, and most of the region is very aligned in their politics, but Atlanta still has a lot of people who wanted to see it go Blue who either don't want to uproot their lives or don't have the means to move to a Blue Zone, so she is definitely stoking the fires of contention. She's one to watch for sure. Leigh, on the other hand, did something much different with her communications experience. She is actually working with Jacob at his online newspaper. It is interesting that they both went in the direction of journalism rather than the tech side of things, but it is serving us well. Sean, you've stayed in touch with your galley crew, right? Want to tell Hunter where they are?"

Sean shouted over his shoulder from his position facing the stove, "Oh, dude. They are crazy! Jeremy, Miguel, and

Lenny all took the money they got from being at the Center and opened their own restaurant down in Florida, but it has this weird space odyssey theme that definitely isn't real scientific. But since they can play up the fact that they did do space travel, the tourists just flock there and eat it up . . . like, literally. They make insane money selling $30 Galaxy burgers that really ain't anything special. I guess if you can attach the right kind of shtick to something and market it to the right people, anything sells."

"I had a feeling those guys would end up failing upward."

Everyone laughed at Hunter's assessment because it was what they all had felt on the ship and turned out to be true.

"I guess that leaves Charles DuPlessis who is serving as a security officer for us now. He's actually on his way here to be backup for us on our way to the next destination. Um, Pearce, I'm sorry to say, has had it rough. He's with us, in no small part because of that, but getting him extracted from Africa has been a challenge. We are hopeful that will finally happen before the end of the year. As I mentioned before, Michael is teaching at MIT. He's a Resistance member too, and a lot of the research he guides his students through is in support of our cause. Sean mentioned Amelia earlier. She has been a great asset, though she does still need some supervision as she does have a tendency for getting herself into trouble . . . like all the time. You may remember Audrey."

"Lucas's old flame?"

"Yes, and I'm going to assume you mean former, not old. That's just not nice."

"Yeah, you know what I mean . . . though that was a shocker."

"It was. Anyway, Audrey supports us a great deal and it's great to have someone who was a part of your expedition from the beginning, but lived through everything that happened here on Earth during your time away. That's some institutional knowledge we are finding invaluable."

"Nice. But, what about Kamil?"

"Kamil sympathizes with us, but feels he has so much to make up for with his family. He always regretted leaving them behind. And then discovering his wife had passed while he was gone was really difficult. There was a lot to repair with his children, and that has been his focus since returning. He's in El Paso with his oldest daughter and spends as much time with all of his grandkids as possible."

"Yeah, I know it was hard on him. Even though they split before we left, it really wasn't common knowledge, and he took all the blame for everything. I'm glad he is finding a life that works for him."

Sean, Natalie, and Sarah had filled the table with bowls and platters of food while Lydia gave the run down, and they were now ready to serve dinner.

Sean proudly announced to the room, "Soup's on!"

Everyone gathered at the table and Abe asked them to give a moment of silence in gratitude for all they'd come through together and to recognize those no longer with them. Sarah slid a wriggling Zeke into his high chair and spread tiny bits of cooled chicken and vegetables on his tray to keep him quiet, though that didn't quite last through the protracted moment Abe had wanted to provide.

CHAPTER TWENTY THREE

As they sat around the table, enjoying the beautiful meal Sean prepared, they reminisced about their time on the Alpha Centauri I. After Sarah put Zeke to bed for the night, which was significantly later than normal due to the delayed nap and the excitement of having a new audience to entertain, the group turned the conversation to more serious topics.

Lydia started them off, "Okay, so now that we have a better picture of what we are dealing with, we need to decide how we're going to handle it."

Abe interjected, "Lydia, I have been giving this some thought, and I have some reservations."

"About what, hon?" Sarah asked.

"Well, I do think having a more effective cure is of vital importance, if for no other reason than to eliminate the tragic rates of birth defects that are occurring. However, I have been uncomfortable with this entire push to repopulate the earth so rapidly."

"Why? Wouldn't that be a good thing?"

"Yes, Sean, in some respects. We certainly do need to re-store balance to the male population so we can procre-ate, but history shows us the issues that come along with rapid growth."

"How so?" Hunter asked, somewhat hesitantly, given the fact that he knew he was inviting Abe to deliver one of his long lectures, and he wasn't sure he could stay alert for the whole thing.

"The Industrial Revolution brought us the first population explosion of the modern era—the first ever was during what they call the Agricultural Revolution roughly around the period we think of for the Old Testament. During the latter period of expansion, we saw such uncontrolled development in the cities that we ended up with hous-ing crises, food shortages, labor abuses, and sanitation problems, just to name a few. We were adding people to the planet faster than we could accommodate them. Yes, we adapted eventually, but I am concerned that after the latest global crisis we endured and the unrest we are seeing across our land, a resurgence of those issues may have a long-term crippling effect."

"So, what are you saying?" Lydia pressed. "We let them get away with their plan?"

"No, I think their intentions are despicable, no matter how they try to justify them. But, unless we can come up with a better way to manage this, perhaps their approach would slow things fast enough for the world to adjust and plan."

"Abraham! I can't believe I'm hearing my husband say this. You know who they are trying to exclude, right?"

"Sarah, I do know, and I do not condone it by any means,

but there are other factors to consider. And from the information Winston shared with us, this is not something they want to do in perpetuity. They are simply trying to limit the growth to certain groups for a period. Now," he had to raise his voice to stop the others from jumping on him, "NOW, I will say again, I do not like the motive whatsoever, but the method does have benefits. I have raised my concerns. I would love for one of you to offer an alternative that can address them."

Everyone sat silently for several minutes as they contemplated the various issues facing them, what the goal was, and what was the best way to achieve it.

Hunter was the first to break the silence. "Abe, I respect you and get where you're coming from on this; but has everyone forgotten somebody got to it before us? We can plan and strategize all we want, but it may be completely irrelevant if whoever got the serum is already ahead of us on distribution."

"True," Lydia conceded. "I think our first order of business is to figure out who has it and what they plan to do with it. Then, and only then, can we decide how we will proceed."

She suggested they get some rest and reconvene in the morning after she'd had time to run through some channels to see what intel she could get on the theft. They all agreed a good night's sleep was the best plan of attack at this point.

The twins went to the kitchen to clean up from dinner before retreating to their rooms on the upper level. Sarah and Abe distributed hugs to everyone and said goodnight, and then went to their quarters beyond the living room. Hunter and Lydia headed downstairs and began the uncomfortable task of not acknowledging the heavy-handed hint the twins had given them by putting their gear in the same room.

"Since you're already kind of settled in here and obviously slept well in this bed, I'll take the next one over," Lydia offered, recognizing this was not the night to explore where their relationship was headed.

"You sure? I mean, I don't want to take this one if the other room isn't as nice. This one is pretty posh. It's definitely the nicest place I've laid my head in weeks."

"Trust me, it's fine. They're all really nice rooms."

"Oh, okay. Well, goodnight. Rest well."

"You too. If you're not awake when I get up, do you want me to let you sleep, or . . .,"

"Um, well, I'll probably be up. Never been much for sleeping the day away, but just in case, sure, come give me a nudge."

With that, she smiled, grabbed her bag, and left him to get ready for bed.

It had always seemed like such a silly cliché to Hunter when people referred to the pitter-patter of little feet; yet, as his awareness came to him the next morning, it was filled with daylight, the intoxicating aroma of freshly brewed coffee and something sweet with cinnamon, and giggles and tiny thumps overhead.

He took a moment to breathe it all in as it was the richest sense of what he imagined home would feel like that he'd ever known. He only had faint memories of the household he grew up in and any efforts his mother made to create a warm environment. They were so few and far between that the faintness of the recollections was actually due to a lack of them.

After a few minutes, he rolled out of bed, groaned a little more than necessary, and went to the bathroom with his dopp kit to clean up enough to be presentable and join the already vibrant group upstairs.

When he emerged from the hallway, Zeke was racing around the sofa and slid right into him. He looked up stunned for a moment, then wrapped his arms around Hunter's legs, gave as tight a squeeze as his little arms could muster, and then he turned to run in the opposite direction, expecting the big man to give chase. Hunter was a little slow on the uptake as he was still waking up. Zeke looked back, disappointed. When Hunter realized what was at stake—letting down the little boy he really wanted to connect with—he jogged after him along the circuitous path between furniture obstacles until his mother decided that was enough romping so close to the kitchen.

"Well, good morning! I see we are a lively bunch quite early," Abe announced as he emerged from their bedroom. He was fully dressed and groomed, in stark contrast to the rest of them.

Sarah and Zeke, still in their pajamas, were scooped up into his embrace with the kind of joy you don't expect to see every day, but it was how they lived. The twins, though dressed had clearly not graced their heads with a brush. Hunter had put back on the clothes he'd worn the day before as they were the cleanest set he had with him.

Feeling a bit self-conscious, seeing himself next to the others, he asked, "Sarah, would it be possible to run a load in your washer? I have gone through everything I brought with me several times over since I've been on the road, and I'm sure I'm turning a bit ripe."

"Of course! Just set out what you have and I'll take care of it. Abe, maybe you could find a pair of your skinny jeans in the back of the closet and a flannel for him to wear so he can include the ones he's wearing?"

"I would like to take offense at the term 'skinny jeans,' however," he said, patting his stomach, "there is no denying I expanded my waist line in solidarity when you were pregnant, and it has not left me like yours did. Hunter, I am sure I have something you can wear. I will be right back."

As he went back to his room, Sean chimed in from the kitchen, "I'd offer you some of mine, but you have about four inches on me, and as much style as I have, my clothes still won't work as high-waters."

Hunter laughed at him and said, "Sean, I also have a good thirty pounds on you, so it wouldn't work all the way around. But, thanks for the offer anyway."

When Abe returned with a neatly folded stack of garments, he handed them to Hunter and whispered, "I included some jockeys just in case. I know that is a rather personal item, but between friends, I think we can handle it."

"Appreciate it," Hunter said with a nod and went back down to his room to shower, change, and collect his laundry for Sarah.

When Hunter returned about twenty minutes later, everyone was just sitting down to breakfast and Lydia was at the table with them. Her chestnut hair was down, draped in waves over her shoulders. It was the first time Hunter had seen it out of her standard French braid, and he had not noticed how long it was. It enhanced her femininity in a way that took his breath away. He admired her strength and intelligence and was definitely attracted to her beauty, but this was a side of her he hadn't realized existed. He sat in the seat next to her that was quite obviously left open deliberately and smiled at her warmly. Then feeling all eyes on them, he tried to shift attention quickly by asking what they had to eat.

"Sean, here, has put out impressive spread, as usual. He made his special cinnamon rolls, which he says are a recipe handed down through generations of his family. They are magnificent. We have eggs and bacon as well. If you do not see something that you would like to have, speak up and we will try to accommodate."

"I am perfectly happy with all of this. Don't do anything extra on my account."

"I'm glad to! I haven't been able to work in a professional kitchen for a while because of everything that's happened. It feels good to use my skills again."

"So you don't cook like this for Abe and Sarah all the time?" Hunter asked, somewhat surprised that they wouldn't be taking full advantage of what he had to offer.

"When I can, but we come and go a lot. Most of the time it's grabbing a sandwich or something quick and easy. Everybody's getting the royal treatment thanks to you!"

"Well, then I am glad I could help."

As they dug in and most mouths were silenced due to being full of food, Lydia took the opportunity to share what she'd learned.

"So, the reason I was late getting up here is that I got a message from Winston. He found out that it wasn't a foreign government that stole the serum. It was another corporation."

Hunter stopped the fork on its way to his mouth and looked at her with alarm.

"How did he get that intel? I thought he was burned."

"He still basically is, but he has some friends left. We don't know who they are, but that does change the landscape of things."

"How so?"

"Well, for one thing Planet XY's attention is trained on them, and we aren't their concern any longer."

"I find that hard to believe. We may not have the serum, but we do have the formulas."

"True. It seems they are assuming we don't have the resources to do anything meaningful with it at this point, and they would be better served by going straight to the courts for an injunction against this other company. Corporate espionage is still a federal crime. And if they fail there, they can always sue for theft of trade secrets or a variety of other angles. They could keep this tied up in court long enough to still accomplish their goals."

"Okay, so, does this mean they are getting away with it?" Natalie asked, the outrage climbing with the pitch of her voice.

"Not if we have anything to say about it," Lydia reassured her and the rest of the team.

"What's our play?"

"Well, Hunter, you and I are going to leave tomorrow and are going to meet up with Jacob and Sam. They have all the data, and Jacob has been working on the story he will release to the wires. We need to sit with him and share this new information so he can incorporate it, and we can decide on the best messaging approach."

"Okay. But why are we not going back to DC?"

"Yeah. That's the other thing I learned from Winston."

"This sounds ominous."

"Sarah, it is. Let's let Zeke finish his breakfast, and then you should take him out of earshot before I say any more."

When Zeke had shifted from shoveling food in his mouth to shoveling it around his tray, Sarah wiped him down with a cloth and lifted him out of the chair. She told him to wave bye-bye to everyone and took him to his room to play.

"Okay, so what's this big secret?" Hunter pressed.

Lydia sighed heavily, "The reason we can't go back to DC is that a group has moved in to ouster President Marshall in a vote of no confidence."

"What?! You've got to be kidding me!"

"I wish I were, and I'm just so grateful you weren't there when this went down."

"Surely, we saw this coming," Abe suggested.

"We'd heard rumblings, and as Hunter saw on his road trip, things were escalating by the day, but we didn't really think it would go this far. It's been attempted in the past and failed."

"Is Margaret okay?" Hunter asked with obvious concern.

"At this point, we believe she is. The reason DuPlessis is not here already is because he was diverted to DC to assist in her extraction. He will be accompanying her to the location where Winston is laying low. So he won't be with us."

"I think we can handle it."

"Hunter, I appreciate your confidence, but this definitely changes things."

"So, the whole world is imploding again," Natalie cried with dismay.

"Nat, it's gonna be fine. I'm sure Lydia has a plan. Right, Lydia?"

"Yes, Sean, I do, but I have a feeling there are going to be objections."

Sarah had slipped back into the room, leaving Zeke happily stacking and knocking over his blocks.

"It sounds like I missed something important. What's going on?"

"Sarah, I was just telling them that there has been an insurgence in DC, and President Marshall is being removed from office. Things are shifting rapidly, but I think we can use this to our advantage in terms of the cure."

"How do you figure?"

"Hunter, our plan all along has been to use the division to get our citizens to push for fair and equal access. Now that the general outrage throughout the country is at a fever-pitch, they won't back down or be lulled into complacency by empty promises from our leaders or clever spin from news organizations and pundits. People will insist on the truth, and we will be there to help them find it."

"Lyd, I like your optimism, but I think you may be expecting too much of people. They just want to be able to live their lives the way they want without other people interfering and telling them whether that way is right or wrong."

"This cure is part of being able to live that life . . . period, and sometimes there is a right and a wrong."

"I get it. I'm with you, but are we saying we are the arbiters of that? Are we saying we are the ones who get to decide which it is? And if so, what makes us qualified to do that?"

"Hunter, some things are self-evident, and I—,"

"Lydia, take a breath. I'm not arguing with you. I'm just pointing out questions we need to answer before we go putting ourselves out front and asking the whole country, which is bitterly divided now, to listen to us."

She gave some ground, understanding where he was coming from, but she was clearly ramping up to take the fight to the next level.

"This is an alarming turn of events to be sure, and I think we need to choose our next steps carefully. It could be an opportune moment if used wisely, or it could be throwing a match on a powder keg. I think it prudent for us to take some time to game out the possible outcomes of various approaches before we do anything else."

"I agree with Abe," Hunter asserted. "Let's clear away breakfast and then start writing a list of directions we could take. Man, I wish Cady was here. She is so good at helping me see what I'm missing that's usually right in front of my face."

"Oh . . . I forgot to mention . . . she and Charlie will be here in a couple of hours. They are our new escorts."

Hunter rolled his eyes and stood up, taking his plate to the kitchen sink.

"You know, just once . . . just once, I'd like to feel like I have the full story from you."

"Hunter, that is not fair. Lydia has a lot to communicate and is trying to triage a very volatile situation."

"Abe . . .," Hunter started and then thought better of it. "Yeah, I get it. I'm just weary."

"We all are, but if we can get through the next few days, I think we'll have a better sense of what we're facing and how to restore some kind of normalcy."

"Famous last words, Lyd. I hope they don't come back to bite us," Hunter said cynically and came to collect the other plates.

After the table was clear, Abe retrieved a note pad and a pen from his office so they could begin making their list.

After a two and a half hours of grueling discussion, the gate buzzer sounded, alerting them to an approaching vehicle. Abe got up from the table and went to the security screen mounted on the wall of the entry. Seeing it was Charlie and Cady, he entered the code to open the gates

298

for them to enter. When they reached the portico at the front, Sean ran out to greet them and took the keys to move the Jeep into the garage. Charlie and Cady went inside and Abe welcomed them in with his robust embrace. Sarah was the only other one to get up to greet them. Hunter and Lydia said hello from their seats at the table, and Natalie had used the interruption to dismiss herself to her room for a break.

"How far did you run before you realized no one was chasing you?" Hunter teased.

Charlie chuckled gratuitously, and said, "Almost to Annexico. I was kind of disappointed we were called back. I was looking forward to a little time on the beach."

"No rest for the weary . . . or the wicked, my friend."

"You'd know all about that; wouldn't you, Hunter?"

"Okay, you two. Enough of that. Cady, Charlie, I know you've been driving for hours, so take a few minutes to rest and clean up. Then we need to go over a lot of stuff," Lydia instructed, still in leadership mode.

The newly arrived couple went down to the lower level, clearly knowing their way around the place. When they came back, they found seats at the table and Lydia updated them on what they'd put together as potential scenarios for action and possible outcomes.

After what felt like hours, they decided that the best course of action was to continue as planned and leave in the morning to connect with Jacob to work on the exposé that would shed light on the flaws in the existing cure and reveal the existence of a new one. Their primary goal had shifted to alerting those who had received the first one that it was causing an alarming number of birth defects and fetal deaths. They wanted to mitigate those losses by encouraging recipients to use all forms of birth control available to prevent pregnancies until a solution could be found. No one was particularly satisfied with this plan, but it seemed to hold the least amount of potential for harm, which was essential to the code of conduct embedded in the Resistance's *kalokagathia* creed.

CHAPTER TWENTY FOUR

Just before sunrise, the household moved into action. Hunter, Lydia, Charlie, and Cady collected their bags and loaded the cars that Sean had pulled to the front. Abe, Sarah, and Zeke were aligned in the entry, distributing hugs and wishes for safe travel. Natalie followed from the kitchen with a bag of items Sean had prepared to fuel them while on the road so they wouldn't have to make many stops and risk detection.

Before leaving, Lydia learned that Planet XY had preempted their plans to release the information by issuing a press release of their own. Lydia determined this was an attempt to preemptively contaminate all possible jury pools in their lawsuit, hoping it would secure a decision in their favor.

Overnight, the situation in DC had escalated significantly, and there was a call for a floor vote in the House to ratify documents that would revise the Bill of Rights with new amendments and modifications to existing ones to secure the policies the Red and Blue Zones had begun adopting.

In the first election after the crew returned in 2065, when Margaret Marshall was unexpectedly re-elected to a second term, there was a measure on the ballot to allow the Red and Blue Zones to form on a provisional basis. It was to be an experiment. In their infinite wisdom, the lawmakers thought that if they gave the citizens exactly what they were asking for they might realize that wasn't all it was cracked up to be. Unfortunately, that lesson was lost on the divided country. And now the news of the failures in the cure and the restrictions around the new one had cemented the ideological differences such that lawmakers were ready to implement a clause that would outline the procedure that would lead to a permanent separation. The country was becoming not just unrecognizable, but a new country altogether.

The tipping point truly was the issues that came to the forefront around the revelation that there was a better cure available. There had been so much to endure with the pandemic that decimated the population and destroyed immeasurable natural resources. The cure was to be their hope for the future. The fact that it was resulting in devastating defects and high infant mortalities seemed like a cruel joke. So, being presented with a better solution, still almost too much to hope for, was almost a last grasp at the promise of salvation.

As a founding principle for their governance, the citizens of the Red Zones wanted less involvement from the government in enterprise and less regulation of medical practices. Because of this, they felt there was nothing wrong with what Planet XY has planned for the distribution of the cure. Even though they did not agree with the policy of distributing by race, they recognized it was Planet XY's product, their idea to use as they saw fit, and the government should not be telling them how it could or could not be sold.

The Blue Zones believed it was dangerous not to have oversight of yet another cure that could have unforeseen consequences, just as the first one did; and, they believed it was wrong to restrict access to the cure (if proven to be effective) by race or socioeconomic status. They felt this was one of the areas where unfettered capitalism could go awry and cause great harm to many.

These fundamental differences highlighted the impasse that was emerging between the Zones. The two packages of amendments that would allow them to have the kind of government they wanted had been drafted over the course of the aggregation of the Zones. With the knowledge of the new cure, these packages were hastily refined and were formalized to be presented to the House. This was only the first step in what would be a road filled with hurdles toward complete rezoning and the most radical form of redistricting the country had ever seen.

When Hunter, Lydia, Charlie, and Cady finally reached Jacob, he shared with them two documents he had received from a contact. They were the final drafts of the amendments that would be presented to Congress two days later. They were as follows:

We the people of the Homestead, the Greater Plains, the Gulf Territory, the Heartland, the Greater Lakes, and the New South, to be collectively known as the Red Zones of America, do hereby propose the following amendments to the Constitution of the United States for the purpose of securing individual freedoms and protections not previously specified in the founding document:

Amendment 1-R-Addendum: (A) In regard to Campaign Finance, as we consider money to be speech, we seek to have no restrictions on financial contributions from individuals, corporations, or unions to fully empower the freedom of speech. Additionally, unions shall no longer be exempt from anti-monopoly laws; (2) government bodies and agencies, as well as their representatives, are in no way restricted from using references to God, but shall still be prohibited from promoting the adoption of a specific religion. Religiously-affiliated organizations, schools, and churches shall be eligible for tax payer funds where additional program requirements are met; (3) there shall be no law passed or judicial decision delivered preventing freedom of speech by any individual or other entity on any platform. The Fairness Doctrine shall be revoked, but all consideration must be given to the publication of books in physical format.

Amendment 2-R-Addendum: (A) All citizens who are not violent felons shall have the right to conceal and carry a handgun; (B) felonies classified as violent shall be the only consideration for restriction of access.

Amendment 24-R-Addendum: (A) 1) In consideration of the eligibility to vote, to cast a ballot and have it counted in local, state, and national elections, voters must have paid at least $500 in Federal Income Taxes during the prior year; 2) must have served in the military; or 3) own land of at least .10 acres or $5000 in property value; (B) all voters shall be required to pass a competency test, wherein knowledge of basic government structures and responsibilities must be demonstrated, and they must satisfy an interview to ensure they align with Red Zone principles and ideals; (C) ballots shall be cast in paper form only, a valid government-issued photo ID must be presented to receive ballot. In-person registration must be completed a minimum of 3 business days prior to voting.

Amendment 26-R-Addendum: the eligible age for voting shall be 25 years.

Additionally, we seek to enshrine the following guidelines, provisions, and restrictions for considerations not covered in amendments and request modifications to existing Congressional Acts where necessary:

Amendment 28-R: (A) All schools become privately operated and all public schools shall be available to be acquired by private educational organizations. State and local governments shall provide vouchers to cover education costs, and parents shall be entitled to choose the educating body for their child(ren); (B) All schools shall structure tuition to be all-inclusive in order for the voucher system to effectively cover costs without additional individual burdens.

Amendment 29-R: (A) All local and state policies regarding rent control shall be rendered null and void; (B) residential and commercial property taxes shall be restricted and only increased under special consideration by the appropriate governing body.

Amendment 30-R: (A) health insurance shall be entirely privatized; public assistance is provided in the replacement program for social security, and welfare/food stamps; (B) existing HIPPA guidelines shall be extended to prohibit chipping for medical records/medical purposes prohibited.

Amendment 31-R: (A) local governments shall determine the number of new immigrants the zone can absorb each year, thusly, borders are not open; (B) prospective immigrants shall be screened for suitability based on education, work skills, values, and their understanding and embracing of Conservative ideals; (C) the path to citizenship and voting eligibility includes passing of all screening required for immigration, and is extended to assess educational and economic status; provisions shall be available for those who are granted legal residential status, but they shall not become citizens or have the right to vote.

Amendment 32-R: (A) this amendment hereby revokes the Social Security Act of 1935 and a new program shall be instituted to address needs currently covered by social security, health care, food stamps, welfare; (B) all citizens shall receive fixed payment per month in taxable income, citizens currently contributing shall receive monthly payments after retirement based on a percentage of their contribution; (C) those currently receiving SSI shall continue to receive benefits until their death.

In consideration of regulations and provisions not delineated in the Constitution or Bill of Rights, but instituted by Congressional Acts, we propose these guidelines to supersede any and all Acts addressing such concerns:

Addendum R-A: There shall be no changes to the existing currency system. Digital money exchange and crypto currency shall not be considered legal tender.

Addendum R-B: All carbon tax and credit systems shall be eradicated. Clean and renewable energy shall be driven by market demand and only subsidized as is deemed necessary for supporting Zone infrastruc-

ture; there shall be no regulations on appliances, gas taxes shall be reduced, and federal fleet mile per gallon requirements shall be eliminated.

Addendum R-C: Labor Unions shall no longer receive exemption from anti-monopoly laws and members are not protected from termination for participation. All Red Zones shall be right-to-work. Additionally, companies are under no obligation to hire union members and are exempt from prosecution for use of force in protection of properties from union member protests, and any damage resulting from such protests shall be the responsibility of union organizations.

Addendum R-D: When purchasing products and services from manufacturers and suppliers, customers must agree to specific limitations of liability. Transactions are only completed when buyer and seller agree. CEOs, CFOs, members of company boards of directors, and officers of corporations shall be shielded from liability. Specifications for medical practice: physicians and practitioners and their patient agree to cost of procedures. These shall include limitation of liability for compensation in case of physician error. Health insurance providers shall be involved in negotiation and ultimate choice of co-pay/premium and liability cap package. Patients shall have the opportunity for unbundling of services to seek components of care at different rates.

Addendum R-E: Lying to a federal officer shall carry a misdemeanor rather than a felony charge; fines shall be applied in case of conviction. Additionally, federal officers lying to citizens shall also face misdemeanor charges and fines.

Not to be outdone, the Blue Zones presented their own set of adjustments to the laws of the land to ensure they too would be able to live according to their own ideals.

We the people of the Northern Territory, the Left Coast, the New Frontier, Annexico, Appalaciana, First Colonies, and New France, to be col-

lectively known as the Blue Zones of America, do hereby propose the following amendments to the Constitution of the United States for the purpose of securing individual freedoms and protections not previously specified in the founding document:

Amendment 1-B-Addendum: (A) In regard to Campaign Finance, we seek to restrict financial contributions from individuals and unions, determined by the government level and election cycle; however, corporations shall be prohibited from contributing to political campaigns or political action committees; (2) government bodies and agencies, as well as their representatives are strictly prohibited from using references to God, and religiously-affiliated organizations, schools, and churches are strictly prohibited from receiving tax payer funds; (3) the Fairness Doctrine shall be upheld and extended to cover review of all media forms, including but not limited to books in print or electronic format, music, film, television, and various forms of live entertainment.

Amendment 2-B-Addendum: the Second Amendment shall hereby be repealed and replaced with the following guidelines: (A) state and local laws shall prevail; (B) gun ownership permitted on a restricted basis, provided the following requirements are met: a special license shall be issued for semi-automatic guns under highly specialized circumstances; (C) drug/alcohol abuse, use of antidepressants, domestic violence, felonies, poor driving record shall all be cause for complete and permanent revocation of gun ownership privileges; (D) transporting of guns across Zone borders is strictly prohibited; (E) approved hunting and target shooting guns shall be stored in government lockers, only accessible on limited days and times and appropriate ID and authorization forms must be provided for access.

Amendment 24-B-Addendum: (A) 1) In consideration of the eligibility to vote, to cast a ballot and have it counted in local, state, and national elections, voters must present valid government-issued ID prior to or at time of receiving ballot; (B) non-violent felons shall have right to vote restored one year after parole, provided there are no new charges, complaints, outstanding warrants, and a recommendation from the parole officer is presented in writing.

Amendment 26-B-Addendum: the eligible age for voting shall be 16 years.

Additionally, we seek to enshrine the following guidelines, provisions, and restrictions for considerations not covered in amendments and request modifications to existing Congressional Acts where necessary:

Amendment 28-B: (A) health insurance shall be replaced by Medicare for All program, providing no-cost health coverage for all health maintenance examinations and medically-necessary procedures, including subsequent hospitalizations, medications, and follow-up care; (B) existing HIPPA guidelines shall be extended to allow for chipping for medical records/medical purposes.

Amendment 29-B: (A) any individual entering a Blue Zone from another zone, country, province, or territory shall be permitted to seek residency and put on a path toward citizenship where all rights and responsibilities shall be conferred onto them.

In consideration of regulations and provisions not delineated in the Constitution or Bill of Rights, but instituted by Congressional Acts, we propose these guidelines to supersede any and all Acts addressing such concerns:

Addendum B-A: Digital money exchange and crypto currency shall be considered preferred legal tender. All paper money, coinage, gold, silver, and other precious metals shall be prohibited and must be surrendered to government agency. Fair market compensation shall be credited to a government issued account.

Addendum B-B: All carbon tax and credit systems shall be enforced. Gas taxes shall be increased to offset costs of environmental protec-

tion infrastructure; use tax shall be applied to high-mileage per gallon vehicles and federal fleet mile per gallon requirements shall be raised; all electrical appliances shall be regulated for highest energy efficiency.

Addendum B-C: Labor Unions shall be protected from anti-monopoly laws and Blue Zones shall no longer be right-to-work zones.

Addendum B-E: Lying to a federal officer shall remain a felony, and federal officers lying to citizens shall face a felony charge.

The proposed amendments and revisions were born out of decades of discord between Conservative and Liberal factions of the citizenry, and were an attempt for each of the Zones to experience what it would be like to have unfettered control over how they each were governed. The proposed changes would face an arduous process as the Constitution, though intended to evolve with the country and its needs, was not designed to be revised on a whim. However, the first, most important steps had been taken to ensure the divide would continue to widen, and the situation would continue to evolve.

Lydia and her team were dismayed by the developments and felt there was no path forward to furthering their agenda in this political climate. It was time for a radical reevaluation of their goals and how to proceed. Hunter, with growing resentment and frustration over what he'd endured to end up with no options, threw up his hands, and as he walked out the door to get some air, shouted, "I say let 'em rot. I'm gonna hitch the next ride off this planet."

EPILOGUE

Margaret and Winston Marshall opened the ten-foot steel and glass door of their home and welcomed Hunter and Lydia. Behind them Abe, Sarah, their son Zeke, and the Flemming twins, climbed out of a second darkened SUV. The third vehicle in the convoy was transporting Martin Lucas, as well as Charlie and Cady. Several other members of the original crew were in two additional vehicles behind them.

Once the entire group had made their way into the lavish home, they were guided to a ballroom where two dozen arm chairs were assembled in two rows forming semi-circles. In the six months that had passed, Zeke had grown much more independent, so Sarah set him in a corner with a coloring book to entertain himself. Then they all took seats as Margaret and Winston moved to stand before them.

> Hunter sat between Lydia and Lucas on the front row. While the din was still subsiding he leaned over to Lucas and whispered, "Hey, buddy! It's great to see you."
>
> "You too, man. We have a lot to catch up on."
>
> "For sure. After we find out what this shindig is all about, I'll grab us a couple of beers and we can find a quiet corner to talk."
>
> "Sounds good."

Then, in her commanding and still official voice, Margaret spoke over those still muttering.

"Thank you . . . thank you, everyone, for coming. I know you have done so at great risk and without much information, and on the word of a trusted friend that there are remarkable opportunities ahead. So, I do appreciate your being here."

Winston stepped forward, saying, "Yes, we both are grateful for your time and your efforts to come . . . though I do expect the offer for a free trip to a private Caribbean island made it a touch harder to resist."

Laughter and assent rippled through the group. The setting was about as picture-perfect as they come. The warmth of the tropical breeze could not have been more idyllic, and the opulent estate was something to behold—not a bad solution for a world leader in exile. The small island was remote but well developed and was one of the few assets that even the Cabal was not aware of, which made it the safest place for Margaret and Winston to hide in the wake of her ousting and his botched subterfuge with Planet XY.

"I won't drag this out as I know you are road weary and we've been through too much to stand on pretense," the former president assured them. "I'll cut to the chase. As you know by now, Winston and I are the only remaining heirs of one of the twelve Cabal families. We have untold wealth . . . I mean, really, we don't have a clue how much there is. I don't say that to boast. I say that to make it clear that when I say I am putting my money where my mouth is, there is a hell of a lot of it."

The group started to rumble in curiosity.

"Here's the deal . . . we found the schematics of your original ship, and I've had a team of scientists working on modifications for some time now, and we can now reveal that they have built a new ship."

"Margaret, how long has this been going on?" Hunter asked in astonishment with the slightest hint of a sense of betrayal.

"Well, knowing you as I do, you're not going to like my answer . . . since about six months after your return."

"Why . . .,"

"Why didn't I tell you? Hunter, I'm sure you're not the only one wondering that, but the answer is the same for all of you. What good would it do you to know if we couldn't complete our task? It would only stir up a whole lot of feelings and fears and hopes that I didn't want to put on you in such turbulent times."

"I just can't believe this," Lydia said, shaking her head.

"It's pretty incredible. I can barely believe it myself and I've been watching it happen. Now, I'm sure the next big question running through your heads is what is it for? Well, it's exactly what you are imagining."

"Are you serious?" Lucas chimed in.

"I'm quite serious. I'm sure it is not lost on any of you that things have been falling apart here, and I, for one, am quite over it. Winston and I are prepared to fund the production of two additional ships. We want to reassemble the Alpha Centauri crew to lead a new group of people to try again to reach Proxima b. It's still our best option for a compatible environment where we could start over. Scrap all the structures and systems that are so broken they will never be fixed. Let's start over, make a new colony, and get it right this time! Who's with me?"

Stunned silence filled the room as everyone tried to contemplate the possibilities that lay in getting away from the problems they were powerless to solve, of getting to complete what they started so long ago, to begin again. Could this really be their chance for a Utopia? They would soon find out.

ACKNOWLEDGEMENTS

As with the first book, we are amazed at the relevance of the themes we planned to cover and how they are showing up in real life. We hope that reading this story will broaden some perspectives and open doors for conversation about the challenges our world faces.

We would like to thank Angela Moscheo-Benson and Chad Jones for their assistance in research and review of the manuscript as it took shape. Additionally, Angela's sharp eye in the proofing process was essential. And thank you to Mitchell Shea for lending his talent in designing the artwork for this book that elevates it beyond what we imagined. Every contributor to this project has made it really special.

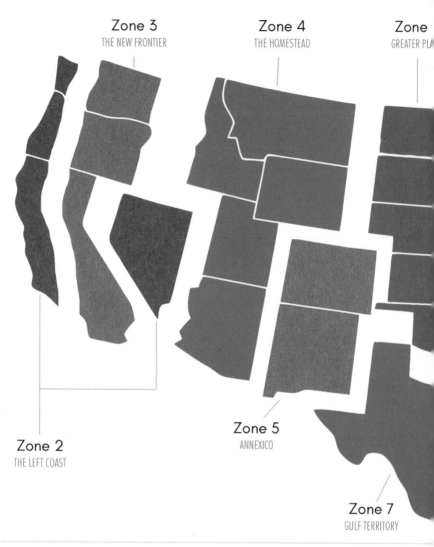

Zone 3
THE NEW FRONTIER

Zone 4
THE HOMESTEAD

Zone
GREATER PL/

Zone 2
THE LEFT COAST

Zone 5
ANNEXICO

Zone 7
GULF TERRITORY

Zone 1
THE NORTHERN TERRITORY

Alaska & Western Canada